ONCE

ONCE

MARY BROOKMAN

Mary Brookman

*For all the family farmers working
tirelessly to feed the world*

ACKNOWLEDGMENTS

I am indebted to family farmers for showing me a way of life that includes hard work, respect for others, and the importance of caring for the land and resources. I must mention the influence provided me by many hours I spent as a child on the family farms belonging to my grandparents, Marion and Clinton Flint and my aunts and uncles, Beulah and Bradford Flint and Barbara and Harry Hoffman. To the family farmer I know best, my husband Don, thanks for encouraging me to pursue any endeavor I chose.

To my first readers: Virginia Fox, Betty Holton, MaryJane Rubinski, Betty Short, Deborah Smith, and Richard Smith (*Something New Every Day*), I extend my utmost gratitude for taking your time to read and respond.

I offer a special thank you to Joan Caska, fellow writer, and the members of our local library's writing group who urged me to continue writing. I recognize Whitney Hubbard and the library staff at the Fort Plain Free Library for their continued encouragement and support.

Thank you to Dylan Garity, my copy/line editor, for helping to bring this book to fruition. His keen eye and expertise ensured my vision was preserved. The final responsibility for any errors is mine alone. Thank you to David Ter-Avanesyan who designed the interior of my novel as well as a cover beyond my expectations.

To my daughters, Kelly and Amy, who inspired me over the many years I spent writing this book, thanks for listening. I value your opinions above all others. Thank you to their husbands, Jamie and Chris, who had to hear about the mother-in-law who was writing a book but never seemed to quite finish it. A special thank you to my grandchildren, Bennett, Riley, and Maya, who have been subjected to hearing about this book all their lives.

CHAPTER 1

A chill drilled through my body at the thought I might have been stuck in Madden the rest of my life. For three years, I'd trudged the streets of LA, one story at a time, until I was viewed as a credible journalist. Now I was headed back to my upstate New York hometown, and only because my brother had guilted me into it. Said it was time I put someone else first for a change. Nate was sure I agreed Annie deserved to have her aunt home for her high school graduation. He even brought out the mother card, pointing out that she wasn't getting any younger. Maybe it had been too long, but it wasn't like I'd been sitting around. Yet he, of all people, had no patience for those who didn't work twelve-hour days.

Unexpected turbulence shoved me against the middle-row passenger and flung me against my seatback as the Southwest 737 lurched toward the runway. Hopefully the rough landing in Albany wasn't a premonition.

Once we landed and I arrived at the baggage area, I spotted my niece. "I've missed you," I said, hugging her. "Where are your mother and father?"

"Mom and Dad couldn't come," Annie said, looking away from me. "Dad will fill you in when we get to the farm. Hope you don't mind riding with me. Dad says I'm a pretty good driver, though I did get a speeding ticket the other day for doing 75 in a 55. Not very smart, huh?" she said.

Annie made me smile. She generally asked multiple questions before allowing time for an answer. Her features were so like her father's—blond hair, strong and straight nose, and blue eyes that sparkled when she was excited. She had her mother's extroverted personality and sensitivity. In contrast, I'd inherited my mother's curly brown hair, a nose a little too big for my face, dull hazel eyes, and my father's nosiness.

Annie and I talked on the drive home, but there were uncomfortable pauses as I tried to discern the problem. She hesitated before answering my questions, drumming her fingers at varying volumes on the steering wheel and staring directly ahead.

When I asked how Mom was, she said, "Grandma isn't quite herself. Dad will explain when we get home."

"Why don't you just tell me now? What's wrong? Is her memory worse?" My stomach turned, remorse setting in as I realized I should have come home sooner.

"It'll be better for you to see for yourself," Annie said.

Dreading the full story, or at least hoping to delay it, I said, "Is your dad making you drive the old clunker as punishment for the speeding ticket?"

"Mom says the other car has to last a long time, so we can't drive it much."

The hour dragged, with Annie and me making small talk. Maybe it was my fault. Although we texted each other once in a while, the conversations were never in depth, and I didn't always reply promptly. After all, I was busy. She was in high school and didn't have my responsibilities. She should have understood, but then again, maybe not.

Annie flipped the turn signal down, its ticking breaking the silence as the old Chevy turned on to Jacobs Road, named for our ancestors. "No one told me the Hardys moved out," I said, cranking my head to get a better look at the deserted place on the corner.

"It was a big deal," Annie replied. "When Tom wouldn't sell to them, the Madden village government took possession using eminent domain. I'm surprised you didn't read about it in the *Review*." Her fingers pulsed on the steering wheel.

The *Review* was Madden's weekly paper. It covered the local news plus who visited whom on Saturday night. My fellow students had made fun of it when I was in college. Of course, I'd brought it on myself. An assignment in my first journalism course was to share a local paper. Most of my classmates were from large cities, but those from rural areas had sense enough not to report on their good old hometown rags. Not me, honest me. I brought a copy of the *Review*. It provided humor for my class when the professor chose to read about Aunt Tillie enjoying a turkey dinner at her sister's house. As it turned out, though, the teacher was suitably impressed and used my small-town newspaper as an example of writing appropriately for one's audience.

"I haven't received the *Review* in months," I said. "Assumed Mom forgot to renew the subscription."

"Not surprised," Annie said in a whisper, not elaborating. "Well, anyway," she continued, her voice returning to normal, "there were protests by the area's farmers and farm organizations, but it didn't do any good."

"What farm organizations?" I said.

"The usual—Farm Agency, all the local milk co-ops, even the Madden Chamber of Commerce, cause they depend on farm business."

"Doesn't sound like they did a very good job of organizing," I said.

"Right," Annie snapped. "Mom and Dad tried to drive over to join a peaceful demonstration, support the Hardys keeping their farm. It was supposed to be a gathering of local farmers, no posters, just citizens showing they were behind them, but people were stopped by the state police and told the road was closed. That night, the news carried a short story about the poor turnout in support. The newscaster concluded the government of Madden had made a wise choice to exercise its right to use eminent domain." Annie's voice had crescendoed over the course of the story until she was almost yelling.

"But why would they want that farm?" I asked. "What's the village going to do with two hundred fifty acres of farmland seven miles out of town?"

"Lots of water. Remember how great the Hardys' spring water tasted?"

"Yeah, when our well went dry, I used to go with Dad to fill the water tank."

"People still go up to the ridge for water, or at least they did. A couple years ago, people in Madden couldn't use their tap water—had Beaver Fever, Giardiasis, in the water supply. Where did they go for fresh water?"

"The Hardys', of course," I said.

"Instead of allowing people to fill their jugs, the village wanted to convert the land to a reservoir."

"Why did they need another reservoir?"

"Because the water in the village reservoir isn't drinkable." Annie shook her head. "The town didn't take proper care of it—too cheap to hire an expert to preserve the water supply. At least that's what I heard. Now they've taken the Hardys' place and will do the same thing all over again. Grandma always said people didn't realize how precious water was. When she was growing up, no one would have believed people would be buying drinking water."

We rounded the next bend. My mouth dropped open. "What happened to Barry and Andrea's place?" Only the rock foundation of the barn remained. Weeds grew up around the Southern plantation-style house across the road from where the barn once stood.

"The Kales owed lots of money," Annie replied. "One night, the barn burned. There was an investigation. We knew Andrea and Barry well enough to know they would never burn their own place down, but because they owed so much money, they were suspect. Although nothing could be proven, the insurance company refused to pay on some technicality, and the Kales had to put the house on the market. There was no money to rebuild. They don't keep in touch, but some say they've gone to stay with her parents out west."

"It's hard for me to believe they couldn't make a go of it. They put every cent back in the farm. Difficult to believe they were that far in debt," I mused.

"That was before," Annie said. "When farmers made enough to live on." Her face turned red, and her grip tightened on the wheel.

I'd never heard my niece sound so angry and bitter.

I was afraid to ask another question, but as we drove by the end of Hank and Colleen Fedder's barn, I said, "What happened here? Where are the cows?"

"Hank sold the herd just after you left. Co-op finally put them on a cash-only basis, making it impossible to afford feed. They paid off their debts with what they got for the cows. Without the income from milk, couldn't pay their taxes. Next thing we knew, they were tearing down the barn and selling the beams, wood, buckets, stanchions, and everything else they could to pay the taxes. Old man Fedder figured it was a way to stay in the house at least a few more years. Mrs. Fedder's not very well, you know. Or, maybe you didn't."

Was it my imagination, or was Annie blaming me for not knowing about Mrs. Fedder's illness? Was I expected to keep up with all the news from home?

"A year from this spring, he's planning to start selling off the land for building lots," Annie said. "Hank said he never wanted to see the land go out of farming, but it's his only choice. Either that or let the government have it, like they took Pete's."

This was hard to believe. Pete James, his father, and his grandfather before him had worked the family's dairy farm for a hundred years. "What do you mean? The government took the Jameses' farm?" I said.

"Couldn't pay his taxes, went too far into debt," Annie replied. "Had to go with GAF. You know, the government lending agency that loans money to farmers who don't qualify for help from the banks."

I'd never paid much attention to farm finance, just spent the money given to me with little regard for the hard work that went into making it.

When I didn't reply, Annie spoke louder. "GAF, Government Aids Farmers. Boy, is that ever a laugh! Pete missed January and February payments this year, and by March, GAF foreclosed. The Jameses had to get off the land by May first."

"I don't think they could do that, Annie. There must have been more to it than that."

"Well, Valerie Jacobs, I guess you don't know everything after all," she said.

A little faster than I thought necessary, she stepped on the gas and maneuvered the car over the next hill, the one we used to urge her mother, Jess, to speed up and over so our stomachs would drop. Beyond the rise and next to the road, a chain-link fence surrounded a quarter acre of land covered in concrete. Enclosed was a white block building and beyond it four enormous white tanks. Wide lights stood on top of forty-foot-high steel poles, encircling the enclosure. It was out of character among the farms and completely spoiled the serenity of the land. I bet you couldn't even see the stars at night when the lights were on. It sent a shiver through me—it didn't belong.

"What's all this?" I said.

"The Jameses sold some of their land to a gas company."

"Why would they do that?"

"Money." Her voice dropped. "They needed the money. They had two choices. They could take the money the gas company offered, or the government would let the firm have it using eminent domain. You know how that goes. They're doing it all over now. I texted you about it a couple times, but you didn't answer. Thought you might have ideas on how we could fight it."

I was ashamed I hadn't always answered Annie's texts or returned her phone calls. Living in the city for a while, I tended to think I knew it all, that the world revolved around me. I had lost touch with reality, with the genuineness of the people who did the work so I could buy cheap food and have money left to enjoy the pleasures of life. Most of my news stories revolved around big businesses and people with money. Unfortunately, no one was interested in hearing about ordinary folks.

On the next rise, there were house trailers, where only a few years ago the land had been in corn. Barns stood across the road from each other, but there was no sign of activity. "What about Blakes and Tubulls?" I asked. "Where is everybody?"

"Sold the cows the same time, about three months ago. Had a big auction, right here, one after the other. They were trying to hang on to the land but had to sell off some acreage to pay taxes," Annie said, taking a drink from the water bottle she'd been sipping.

"Last year," she continued, "the Tubulls fell behind on their social security withholding, federal taxes, and compensation. They managed to get enough together to clear the debt, but a month after they paid, the government slapped them with a huge fine and late fee. That did it."

I didn't know what to say. Annie's voice was growing louder again, more agitated.

"Had to sell their machinery to pay the fine. They were already down to bare bones as it was. Without machinery, they couldn't get the crops in. You know how proud Tubull is. All the neighbors showed up with their machinery to help harvest his crops, but he wasn't the same after that. Felt like a failure, like he was taking charity, I guess. Said he could never go through that again. So he sold the cows."

"But everybody always worked together around here," I said. "Why would he feel that badly?"

"Felt he had nothing to contribute. With no machinery, he couldn't return the favor. The others tried to tell him he'd be able to help them with planting next spring, but everyone knew it would never be the same again.

Blake got tired of working from four in the morning until nine at night while only going further in the hole."

"I can't believe all that's happened here in less than three years. Was there a drought, a big crop failure?" I asked, thinking aloud. "Did all of these farmers mismanage their money?"

"You still aren't listening, Aunt Val," Annie snapped. Slamming on the brakes, stopping in the middle of the road, she turned toward me. "Nobody mismanaged anything, and there were no acts of God, only many acts of government." There was no misgauging the animosity of Annie's utterance, as she emphasized the last words, one at a time.

I was getting more confused and a little more than uneasy. This was impossible. I began to dread what I would encounter at home. "Is our place still there?" I asked Annie with a nervous laugh.

"Not as funny as you think," Annie said. She stepped on the gas, rounding the corner too quickly, and our property came into view, the huge maples along the knoll in front of the house standing out lusher than usual. I knew this spring had been rainier than typical; the different shades of green grass reminded me of the many hues in Ireland. As we turned into the driveway, I saw the huge old evergreen, whose top had blown off more than once during harsh winter storms, rising proudly in front of the smokehouse. Even the smell of freshly spread manure only heightened the vision. Maybe I'd missed this more than I'd thought.

Annie was graduating from high school tonight, and Sunday there would be a party with an abundance of food at the farmhouse. Well over a hundred people were expected, and everyone would have a wonderful time. Or at least I thought they would, until considering what Annie had told me. We Jacobses were known for our hospitality, partly because of my mother and her outstanding cooking and baking abilities.

Stopped in the driveway, sitting in the car with both hands looped over the steering wheel and looking straight ahead, Annie said, "I should get you a little more prepared before you see Grandma."

I sat in silence, dreading what was next.

"She may not know you. She's gotten worse than when you were home last. I guess there's no easy way to tell you. She can't feed herself or walk alone. She's incontinent and needs someone with her all the time. The doctor says she has Alzheimer's."

There were no words. Mom had been a little forgetful for the past few years, confused at times, but I had no idea it had progressed so far. Whenever I'd called in the past few months, I was told she was busy. Occasionally, she'd say hello. Come to think of it, she mostly listened, and no one wanted to FaceTime lately. I should have realized something was wrong. What kind of daughter was I?

Annie jumped out of the car. Hesitating, she looked back and said, "Sorry," then fled into the house.

This was going to be far from the peaceful vacation I'd expected. No stress-free holiday away from big-city burdens. Instead, the pressure of real life, my family's life. The place and the people I'd known growing up had changed in such a short time—or had it been happening before I left, and I was too self-absorbed to see?

I sat for another minute before stepping out of the car, then leaned on its roof, facing the house, steadying myself for what I might find. This was a place I didn't understand anymore. I wanted to run, to not stop until everything was back the way it used to be, back to what I'd expected. I wasn't prepared for this new reality.

CHAPTER 2

My brother walked out the back door and ambled toward the car. My mouth dropped open, startled by his lined face. He looked ten years older than when I'd last seen him. Nate had always had a baby face, but now he looked more than his forty-seven years. His arms wrapped around my back, the stiffness of his embrace conveying that his tension was at its peak. When I pulled back and looked into his face, there were tears—and not of happiness, more like desperation. His eyes sat deep in their sockets, surrounded by dark circles, reminding me, and probably him, how easily we were able to read each other. He quickly lowered his head and turned back toward the trunk to retrieve my suitcase.

We didn't speak, just walked together to what we called the back step. It was more than a step, a back porch, a concrete slab with columns and an end-windowed wall on the east to block the wind. Looking back, I pictured Nate with Don, one of his closest friends, sitting here after milking, enjoying a beer and talking about how much hay they'd put away that day. We sat in the handed-down, well-worn, antique wooden rockers.

"Annie's working two jobs this summer to help with college expenses. She's a real good kid," he said. "Never given us any trouble, a real bright spot in these times, and smart, too. She probably told you she's been offered two scholarships."

I waited. It was a pause I knew Nate would break when he was ready.

"I need to tell you about Ma before you go in the house," he said, his jaw tensing.

Trying to ease his burden, I said, "Annie told me some. It seems impossible she's gotten bad in such a short time."

"Been building gradually. You've been gone a good three years. Before that, you were working in New York and away at college, and you have to admit, you weren't here a whole lot even through high school, kind of in and out to sleep and change clothes."

There was no condemnation in his voice, no judging. I'd been a wild kid; had to be where the fun was. Put my family through some tough moments.

They'd done so much for me. Nate was nineteen years old when I came along, quite a surprise to everyone. Mom and Dad were a little too old to handle my actions, so Nate tried to discipline me as well as he could. He and Jess had also put me through college without much help from me. I did a lot of partying and didn't do very well my first year. Instead of washing their hands of me, which they had a perfect right to do, Jess and Nate helped me get into another college, and things finally clicked. I settled down in my second year and started working. When I took what I thought would be an easy two-credit journalism class, I was hooked, and decided to become an investigative reporter.

Nate's voice brought me back to the present. "When Dad was alive, he watched out for Ma, made sure she put things where they belonged and didn't go where she'd get hurt or lost. Even Jess and I didn't realize how bad Ma was until Dad died, and we were living right here with her. She took care of him physically, which he wasn't able to do with his emphysema, and he took care of her mentally. It was a good combination. It worked.

"After he died, we learned how far her memory loss had progressed. Jess found one of our credit card bills along with a bunch of mail in Mom's pocketbook. After that, I tried to get to the mailbox first every day so important papers didn't wind up in drawers, cupboards, or thrown out. We moved things that would hurt her, like sharp knives, to our side of the house, and started locking the door to our kitchen so she wouldn't hurt herself when she was alone." He let out a sigh as if he'd said it all in one breath.

"It must have been difficult for you with Jess at school and you running in and out of the barn, trying to get your work done and watching out for Ma," I said. No wonder he'd aged.

"It worked for a while," Nate continued, "but pretty soon we had to move the food, too. One day, she ate nine bananas. We suspected she didn't remember eating them and kept eating more."

"Nine bananas! Didn't she get sick?"

"You'd think so, but no, didn't even have a stomachache. She's tough," he laughed.

"Next, she had trouble dressing herself—put most of her clothes on backward. Now, it's pretty easy to turn a T-shirt around once in a while. We all do that, but it got so all her clothes were backward and inside out, shirts and pants. She never realized the difference, or reversals might be common with Alzheimer's. I don't know. Her hygiene went downhill. That was the hardest for Jess. Ma was becoming incontinent, but you know how she is, would never admit to anything, or maybe she didn't know."

"Probably ashamed. I can't imagine how she felt when she didn't have control," I said. I fought to restrain the quiver creeping into my voice.

"Jess couldn't get her to wear any protection, so Ma changed her clothes a lot during the day. Jess would find dirty underwear in dresser drawers and have to rewash her clothes every night."

"How did Jess manage everything?"

"Without complaint," Nate said. "Mom resisted any help, and started getting angrier when we tried to suggest she wash or use some protection so her clothes would stay dry. She tried, but she didn't understand she had to take the pads off and change them. She'd throw them in the wash or put them back in her drawers."

"It sounds like she needed someone with her all the time," I said.

"Jess tried to tell me Mom couldn't be alone, but I wouldn't see it. It was hard for me to think she couldn't take care of her most basic needs when she was the one who'd always taken care of us. You remember, she was always the first one to the barn in the morning. The day she put on eight pairs of underwear, and her shirt on backward, and went out to sweep the back step, I finally had to admit Jess was right."

"Who did you get?"

"We started with people coming in from an agency, couple hours a day. They gave her a bath and helped her dress. That worked pretty well—until she got sick and had to be in the hospital for tests last September. When she came home, she wasn't able to walk or feed herself. From then on, we've hired people to be with her whenever we're not home." He turned to wipe away a tear.

I'd had no idea what Nate and Jess had been through, nor had I been home to check on my mother. "I'm so sorry I haven't been here to help," was all I managed to choke out, laying my hand over his.

"You have your life, Val. It's not necessary for both of us to be here. At your age, you should be doing exactly what you are. Nothing around here for you."

"All this care must be expensive. Good thing Dad left Mom pretty well off."

"He left her well off for a normal life, not to pay expenses for the kind of care she needs. Jess figures the money will last another ten months if we're careful and we have no unforeseen expenses for Ma. After that, I'm not sure what we're going to do. We want Annie to have the opportunity to go to college. She deserves that. She's not only helped on the farm since she was able to push a broom, but she's also helped with Ma the last couple of years, giving her baths, changing her, even giving her insulin injections."

And I'd been selfish enough to think Annie had it easy.

"Can't we get help for Mom's care from her Medicare and insurance? She's paid into it for years and hardly ever went to a doctor. She was never sick, and I don't remember her being much on preventative medicine," I suggested.

"We tried. If she were in a nursing home, we could get help for her supplies, but since we're taking care of her at home, they won't pay anything. Doesn't that make perfect sense? We can take care of her here for about ten or twelve hundred a week. If she were in a nursing home, it would cost at least twenty-five hundred. It seems the 'powers that be' have lost all common sense." I would have expected Nate's voice would have risen. Instead, it became quieter, scary.

"County governments are going broke paying Medicaid costs for nursing home care, and still the government is encouraging institutional care, dumping the elderly. Of course, this is only one of the many ways the government is making it harder and harder for the working person to survive," Nate added in a bitter tone.

Dreading what I would find, I took a deep breath and stood to go into the house. "Why didn't you tell me how bad she was?"

"What would you have done? Fly home? Given up your dream to become a reporter? It's not like you could accomplish your goals in Madden. Jess and I wanted you to have a chance to do what you wanted. I've always wanted to farm and have been fortunate to do what I loved for the last forty years, no matter what happens now."

I understood what he meant. During vacations from high school and college, I looked forward to the times I spent dragging, disking, mowing, and baling hay. What a peaceful feeling it was. Probably as close to God as anyone could get—that is, if one truly believed in God. Of course, there were the machinery breakdowns, sick cows, broken fences, and all the other things that made me want to leave the farm.

Nate's voice interrupted my thoughts. "It's hard work and can be discouraging at times, but to me, farming's a way of life, not a job, at least until the last couple years. I'm pretty sure it's the same way you view reporting. Not a job, but something you can't wait to get to each day."

I wanted to explore Nate's comments about farming, but I was more concerned about Mom. As much as I didn't want to see her like Nate described, I had to. "Where's Jess, by the way?" I asked.

Nate held the door. "Gone for an interview for a summer job," he replied.

"I thought she always used the summers to catch up around here," I said, walking into the backroom. After Dad died, Jess took over the bookwork for the farm. She was usually too busy teaching during the school year to do anything but the necessary bills and required reports. She caught up over the summer and helped Nate with the fieldwork.

"This year's different," Nate replied. I walked in the door. There was a smell—antiseptic mixed with bowel movement. I wrinkled my nose. From the kitchen, I could see Mom sitting in front of the TV, her tiny feet crossed on the footrest of the recliner. She was laughing, and between giggles talking to the people on the screen as if they were in the room with her. I heard Nate continue talking, but I didn't take in the words at first.

"I just changed her, sprayed with deodorizer, but it doesn't always work. She may not recognize you," Nate said.

I walked hesitatingly to her and knelt by the chair. She turned toward me only after I said, "Hi, Mom. How're you doing?" I couldn't believe how small she looked. She turned to me, eyes wide, a look of fear on her face. "It's me, Mom. Valerie."

Mom turned to Nate, scrunched her face into a disgusted look, then back at me, and again at Nate. She repeated her movements twice before she turned back to the television and resumed giggling.

"Mom, you remember me, don't you?" I continued hopefully, sure that if I kept talking, she would certainly know her own daughter. She was laughing at the TV as if I weren't there. Tears stung my eyes. It wasn't personal, I told myself. It was the disease. Still, I felt like someone had punched me in the gut, and the guilt I felt because I hadn't been home in so long nauseated me. Or was it the smell gagging me?

I turned to Nate. "How do you live with this? How can you stand seeing her like this, day after day?" He said nothing, just stood there, his shoulders slumped and his eyes moist as tears slipped down my cheeks.

"Come out in the kitchen," he said. "I think she understands sometimes. We don't talk in front of her."

CHAPTER 3

F riends began arriving for Annie's party. I couldn't help but think about past neighborhood parties our family had held. There were always well over a hundred people, and for some reason beyond my comprehension, the sun always shone in a blue sky, and there was just enough breeze to take the edge off the heat. Perfect days. The kids played volleyball or basketball, or just goofed around while the adults enjoyed a break and caught up on the news.

There was talk about how much hay was down, the number of bales mowed away, how many acres of corn were planted, or who was building on, adding cows, or constructing a milking parlor to make the process less physically strenuous. New equipment and how much who paid for an apparatus at what auction were also at the top of discussions. Farmers were so open.

In Los Angeles, people pretended they owned more than they did or tried to hide their assets, fearing someone might take their prized material possessions. Not farmers. They'd tell you exactly the way things were and how much things cost—not to brag, usually, but to inform. Of course, it was always easier to tell about the good deal you made than about the piece of equipment for which you paid too much.

The guests brought their favorite dishes to pass, and Jess made lasagna, garlic bread, rolls, and tossed salad. We put the big walnut table in the mudroom. The table's thirteen leaves stretched twenty feet from the back door to the enclosed porch. Food covered the table, which had been in the family longer than anyone alive could remember, and spilled out onto a row of card tables in the screened porch. No one needed to ask where to find the food. The scent of the lasagna with sausage and homemade sauce seemed to overpower the other dishes. Large metal pans held ice under the salads, and Jess rented chafing dishes from a local restaurant to keep the hot dishes steaming. She was a little neurotic about having everything preserved properly so no one contracted food poisoning.

All the guests helped themselves, coming in the side door, picking up whatever they wanted and exiting through the back to the picnic tables nestled among the hickory and black walnut trees.

The picnic tables were borrowed from the neighbors, and they would likely be moved to whoever was having the next gathering of the summer until they were returned to the true owners in late fall. Jess put old cotton tablecloths on the picnic tables, all with different designs, sometimes even having unlike patterns on a single table. The cloths had been saved from her grandmothers and ours. She said anyone could buy plastic, paper, or cloth that matched. These had character and reminded her of the people who'd originally used them.

"That's part of what all this is about, Val," Jess said, smiling and practically running to welcome guests and lead them to the drink stations. I was beginning to understand what she meant. Looking at the varying designs and colors, it crossed my mind what some of my city acquaintances would think of this scene. If one of them had a picnic or party, the tables would have to be covered with matching tablecloths, neat and perfect. None of them would get this. What a narrow life they led, while thinking they had it all together. I saw why Nate loved it here. It was real. Was that where the expression "down to earth" had come from?

Between trying to help Jess replenish food and ice supplies, I was able to talk with almost everyone attending the party. It was small talk, with most people asking me how things were in the big city and if I was happy. Some of the women asked if there were any prospects.

"I haven't had time to look," was my honest answer. "I was too busy working." It was hard to get established in the business, although I hadn't done badly, getting a few bylines with which I was pretty pleased. I'd had a couple of other offers, too.

One was from a small paper in Washington, DC, specializing in digging into government issues, getting the inner facts not always known by the public. I hadn't considered it seriously. I didn't think it was well-known enough, considered a little on the fringes, maybe even too antagonistic to government. Another offer had come from a fairly well-established Midwestern paper, but I had decided to stay in LA, where there were always plenty of news opportunities. If I wanted to get ahead, that's where I needed to be. And, if I was honest with myself, it was my safe spot.

Most people finished eating, and my duties lessened. I was replacing some ice in the large beer tubs when I heard some comments that got my attention and turned to look.

Bob Tate rubbed his arthritic knee. "I don't know how much longer we can hang on. If we keep bleeding money like we are, we'll end up losing the whole place. The farm's been in the family for sixty years. We've never had this bad a time. Had ups and downs, but don't see any way out this time. Couldn't pay the county taxes in January, and know I won't be able to come up with school taxes in September. They've gone up fourteen percent this year. Not much point in borrowing more money." His voice lowered. "Can't make enough to pay it back."

"Hate to be more pessimistic," said Joe Chakarski, "but the price of milk is supposed to drop two more dollars a hundred over the next three months. I've been trying to reckon what we can do to last 'til fall. Decided to sell out then. I put the farm on the market yesterday. Took me a while to find a real estate agent who would even take me on. One agent told me he'd been getting an average of five calls a day from farmers wanting to sell within a three-county area. He said he was only taking on the ones who agreed to subdivide. Said no one wants to buy a whole farm."

"Why would they?" Norm Skeeter added. "Most of the guys I know have already sold their cows and taken jobs off the farm so they can pay their back taxes, at least keep their land, although I don't know what for. Who's left to rent or sell the crops to if no one's farming?"

I moved to the soda tub with another bag of ice.

"Did you hear that the village government over near Capeson took fifty acres of land from Dexter Jansen?" Norm said. "Took it using eminent domain. Said the village needed the land for a water treatment plant. Amazes me these people don't understand what's gonna happen when all the farms go out. The storekeepers in Madden are already feeling the pinch—can't understand why we're not coming in anymore. They think we're going to the malls in the city or ordering online. They don't get it. Can't afford to buy *anywhere*. Most of us are doing without."

"Well, how many farm-related businesses have gone out in the last two years around here?" Sally Pritchard said. "You'd think somebody would make the connection and understand the impact on the whole economy."

My mind jumped back to Annie's comments, or lack of them, on the way home from the airport, then to some of Nate's remarks. What was going on? If all these farmers were having trouble, some of the best farmers in the county, what was happening to others? Were farmers all over the state or country having trouble? What would happen if most of the farms went out? Where would we get our food? My mind was swimming with questions.

Nan Sands pulled in. I hadn't seen her since the summer before our second year of college. We'd been close friends through high school, but had lost touch in the years since. She grew up on a family farm across the river, and her parents were good friends with our family. Throughout our high school years, Nan and I confided in each other and managed to skirt getting into trouble on occasion.

"Hey, Jake!" she yelled, crossing the driveway. She threw her arms around me and gave me a bear hug. Nan tended to be demonstrative.

Seeing the similarities between my father and me and watching me follow him around, the neighbors had started calling me Little Jake when I was a toddler. "Don't you think it's about time you stopped calling me Jake?"

"Why? You'll always be Jake to our high school crowd." Nan knew the name annoyed me, but she couldn't help herself, or maybe she wanted to aggravate me.

"How's law school?" I asked.

"I graduated in May, finally!"

"So, what's up for the future? Any job offers?"

"My parents think I'm crazy, but I've accepted a position with a small firm in DC."

"Why're they upset? DC's a great place for a young attorney to learn and get ahead," I countered.

"They were disappointed because I didn't take a position that offered more money. Cramer and Kodtz in New York offered me a position at their firm, but I couldn't face handling corporate cases. I'm still not sure why they were so upset. Money was never their number-one priority when I was growing up. They wanted me to be happy. Always said it wasn't important how much money you made, but whether you liked what you did. At least, that's what they used to say. Now they've taken an about-face, telling me how important it is to make a good income. Go figure," Nan raised her arms, palms upward, and let them drop.

"They seem to be pinching every penny. When I suggested ordering pizza from Joe's—you know how I love their pizza—they said, 'Oh, why not make some instead. It's just as good and a lot cheaper.' I almost laughed, but realized Mom was serious. I think they're getting a little funny in their old age." She twirled her finger in a circle at the side of her head. Nan had always used her hands and arms to accentuate her conversation.

"They're not that old. When did you get home?"

"I flew in last night, arrived about nine o'clock."

"Then you haven't had time to talk to anyone. Walk around and listen to people. Something strange is going on. Every farmer here seems to be in some sort of financial trouble. Maybe it's hit your parents. Loads of our friends have either gone out of business or are talking about it. I haven't had time to talk with Nate or Jess about it in detail, but Nate looks worried. He's aged since I was home last."

"Who's gone out?" Nan inquired.

"Did you drive up our road today?"

"No," she said. "Came in across Beaker's."

"You wouldn't have noticed, then. No cows left on this road until you get to our place. I heard Bob Tate say they're having trouble, and the Chakarskis have already put their farm on the market. Someone else mentioned the Capeson village government took someone's land by eminent domain."

"Eminent domain?" Nan's interest was piqued. "They must have had a powerful reason. You can't use eminent domain unless it's proven the land is to be used for a specified purpose for public use. Although, come to think of it, I have seen quite a few strange rulings using eminent domain lately. I didn't think too much of them at the time, but in my last property law class, we discussed a few precedent-setting rulings that differed from past practice. The government has taken land from one entity and passed ownership to another individual or company. I believe there was protest, but the Supreme Court has upheld the decisions in most cases."

"I don't know the legal technicalities like you do, but I have to admit I was more than a little confused, wondering why a village would have to take farmland. It seems water is the main reason. Maybe it's time we asked some questions.

"Sorry, Nan, I didn't mean to hit you with all this. We should be getting personal updates. I won't monopolize your time. I'll let you visit with every-one, and we'll get together tonight to talk. Do you have plans?"

"No, let's meet at Freddy's about nine. That good with you?"

"See you there," I said.

As Nan moved toward a group of old friends, I spied Jay—blond hair, thick as ever, and a little too long, making me want to run my hands through it. Wow, where did that come from? I walked over to him. "How are you?" I asked.

His blue eyes sparkled as he put his arms around me in a too-short, greeting-type hug. "I'm great." He pulled back and looked down at me. "You look fantastic."

Jay lived on the next farm up the road, and after his stint in the ser-vice, he'd returned to his family's property. He could have done anything he wanted, graduating first in our class of a hundred. He'd always loved farm-ing, though, and couldn't understand why anyone would want to leave here to go to college or for any other reason, except to serve his country. He read incessantly, seeing no need to sit in a classroom to learn. He said he could learn everything he needed to know from his parents and grandparents, by reading, or by doing.

"I guess city life agrees with you," Jay said. I thought I detected heaviness in his tone.

"I'm almost afraid to ask you how things are with you after the conversa-tions I've overheard today. What's going on around here? Why are so many people going out of farming, and why are so many of our friends having financial problems?"

"You haven't changed, Val," Jay laughed. "Still one question after the oth-er without waiting for an answer. And your niece is the same way. Have you noticed?"

"I guess it's my way of thinking aloud." I laughed. His smile was even more contagious than I remembered.

"I'll be glad to tell you all about it, as well as my opinion of why these things are happening. I have a feeling what you've heard has only touched the surface. But today is Annie's day. What are you doing tonight?"

"I just made plans to meet Nan at Freddy's around nine. Want to join?"

"Sure. You can pick me up."

"About eight thirty," I responded.

I watched as Jay crossed the yard and pulled Nate aside. They talked seriously for a short time, Nate shaking his head back and forth and pointing his finger close to Jay's face. Nate continued moving his head, side to side, lips pursed tightly, chin wrinkled and tense. His shoulders sagged. The two friends split, Nate heading to the house and Jay to chat with others.

My eyes followed Jay, pulling my thoughts to some of the great times we'd had when we were growing up. We probably could have been more than friends. I'd always felt something special for him, sensed the same back, but I'd been determined to leave town and do something with my life that couldn't be accomplished if I stayed here. I knew Jay would never leave the farm, so neither of us did anything about our deeper feelings—if, in fact, he had any hidden affection for me. We were friends, and I could talk to him about everything. Everything except that.

I helped Jess, replenishing dishes, refilling pitchers of iced tea and lemonade, and restocking beer tubs. Although conversations were limited because I was busy, I found time to catch up with neighbors and friends.

In spite of the rumors I'd heard, people smiled as they visited. Frowns and serious faces appeared intermittently. Friends were putting forth effort to enjoy the day. It was evident Annie was well thought of by the genuine smiles on those who congratulated her. When people were not talking to each other, heads drooped or eyes looked into the distance.

We were pretty well cleaned up by 8:30. Only a few of Nate's and Jess's closest friends lingered. Jess told me to take off, so I left with Nate's pickup to find Jay. He was racing out of the barn when I arrived at his place.

"Sorry," he said, "had a milk fever. Give me five minutes to shower." I remembered all the times we were either late for or missed an event because a cow had freshened and developed milk fever. I had to hold the bag above the cow while Dad punctured the vein and allowed calcium to run through the IV tube, hoping the cow would stand and survive. My father never understood why I was disappointed.

"You helped save a life," he'd said with a smile while I stomped away, only thinking about the event we'd missed. "There'll be other parties," he'd added. I'd wondered if he felt the same way when he was younger.

"Mom's in the kitchen," Jay said. "I know she can't wait to see you." Marion hadn't made it to the party today.

I found her sitting at the table, a wet compress on her head. When she saw me, she jumped up, let the cloth fall to the table, and gave me a hug. "It sure is good to see you. Jay was right. You look great. He's really happy you're home, you know, not that he'd tell you how much he's missed you. You're his best friend. Too bad you two seem to be going in opposite directions." Marion had tried to push Jay my way or me his when we were younger. "Sit down and tell me how you are. You know Jay will be longer than he said. Want a soda?"

"Sure—diet coke, if you have it. You look tired," I said, realizing after that it probably wasn't what she wanted to hear.

"Oh, it's just the leftovers from one of those hellish migraines," Marion said, handing me the diet. "I don't get them as badly as I used to, and damned if I didn't get one the day of Annie's party. She's a great girl, you know. We're going to miss her. So are Nate and Jess. She's such a pleasure for them to have around, a bright spot in our otherwise dreary and hectic lives."

"Say, Marion, what's going on around here? Everyone seems to be in financial trouble. Did the crops fail last year? Everybody seems tense, even when they're trying to relax."

"There's plenty going on, and it's not just here." Marion's voice had changed from her delicate, loving tone to hostility, foreign to her usually calm nature. I wanted Marion's take on the situation. She was the most truthful person I knew, and she saw things others didn't.

Jay walked in, interrupting my chance of pursuing what Marion had said. "All set," he said, grabbing my arm. "Let's go."

CHAPTER 4

Jay didn't say much on the twenty-minute ride to Freddy's. He asked questions about LA, if I was happy there and if I'd met anyone. I did my best to give an honest picture of my life since I'd last seen him, and told him there was no man in my life.

He had a way of getting information from others without giving back, exhibiting a genuine interest in people and their opinions. While he was set in his view of the way things should be, he always showed respect for others' outlooks.

Nan was waiting outside the bar for me. When she saw Jay, she raised her eyebrows and grinned. Nan believed Jay and I belonged together and always thought I'd end up on the farm with him. I could tell what was going through her mind, but I also knew there was no way her prediction would be realized.

"Hey, Jay! Good to see you," Nan said as we entered our old haunt. There weren't too many places to socialize in our area, but we were about the only ones in the bar. The smell of fresh-roasted peanuts and alcohol permeated the building, taking me back to my post-high-school days. A couple sat in one corner talking intently, eyes sparkling at each other, hands touching lightly. It occurred to me that I was missing the company of a partner for the sake of my work, but that was the way I wanted it, at least for now.

Nan and I slid into the vintage red vinyl booth, while Jay went to the horseshoe bar and ordered some beers for us. He grabbed a bowl of peanuts as well before joining.

"Tell us what's going on here," Nan said, reaching for a handful of peanuts. "After I talked to Val at the party, I walked around visiting with neighbors. Couldn't find anybody who had a positive thing to say, unless they were talking about Annie."

Jay took a deep breath. "I'm surprised at you two. The nosiest people I know, having no inkling what's going on. I'm not sure where to start. I was sure word would have spread to the cities by now."

"Obviously it hasn't," I said. "Spill." I waved away his offer of peanuts.

"Dairy farming is in big trouble, and I suspect most other farmers, including vegetable and crop producers, aren't far behind. Even in cities, consumers should start seeing the effects by this fall. Everything government has done to farming in the last ten years is catching up. Farmers can no longer pay the taxes governments and schools are expecting. If you tell me what you heard at the party, I might be able to explain specifics, or at least start to acquaint you with them."

Turning to Jay, I said, "In the past couple of years, for one reason or another, just about everyone on our road, except your family and mine, has gone out of business."

"That's true," Jay confirmed, "but it's not only here. I've been talking to people across the country. The picture is bleak, maybe even more so elsewhere."

"But why is it happening?" Nan said. "Everyone needs food. There's got to be a market."

"Sure there is," Jay replied, "and there always will be, but there's nothing mandating who'll provide the products?"

"What're you saying?" I asked, growing more curious.

Jay leaned forward, both hands planted firmly on the edge of the table. "You're probably going to think I've gone off the deep end, but I have a theory, and there're more who've drawn the same conclusions. If I share this with you, I don't want to see it in the next edition of any paper, not yet anyway. Understand, Val?" Jay never called me Jake like our other friends.

"Of course," I replied, mildly insulted, as if he had to tell me not to print our private conversations.

"Let me give you some facts and see what conclusions you draw. Okay?"

"Shoot, just let me get my notebook," I said, reaching in my bag.

Jay didn't laugh. He never did get my sense of humor.

"Starting in the 1970s, banks encouraged farmers to expand, loaning massive amounts of money to buy bigger machinery, add on cows, build bigger barns, and clear additional land to grow more crops. The government partially subsidized and encouraged improving the land, making it more productive. You might remember when we were kids and Salty was around digging up the fields and laying tile, allowing the fields to drain so crops had the best chance. That was all part of the program."

We all remembered Salty—Gerry Salter. He was a character in his own right: tall, beard to his waist, laughing eyes, and always ready with a story about his younger days. He ran a backhoe, digging and laying tile lines. He and his wife, Lea, worked side by side and were as hard of workers as you'd ever find. Salty knew exactly what he was doing, ensuring the tile was laid correctly, never leaked, and always did the job for which it was intended.

I was brought back to the present as Jay continued, "In the late seventies and early eighties, the government set the milk price higher, sometimes up to seventeen and eighteen dollars a hundred-weight. It even hit over twenty dollars in the early two thousands. After all, everyone's income in the country was going up and never went down. Why should the farmer think he would be any different? "In the mid-eighties, the government started dropping the price the farmer received until it was down to ten dollars per hundred-weight. Everyone else's wages stayed up. The price farmers paid for supplies and equipment still climbed steadily. The expenses farmers paid to run a dairy farm kept increasing. The farmers' incomes dropped by almost a third. This is how the government kept relatively cheap food in stores. The farmer's experience has continued this way ever since, income up and down, but expenses always up."

"The food doesn't seem particularly cheap in the Casa Market downtown," I replied. "I had to get some last-minute supplies for Jess and thought it was a bit overpriced."

"People in the United States still pay a smaller percentage of their income for food compared to those in most other countries," Jay said. "This country has had it good for a long time."

He sighed, then continued. "Jess started teaching in Caldwell twenty years ago. When she started, she was making $12,500. Now she's making $62,000. She'll be the first one to point this out. Who contributes the majority of the school taxes to pay for the increased teachers' salaries? In this area, it's the farmers. So on one-third less money, we pay two-thirds more in school taxes, to say nothing of other expenses.

"I'm not condemning teachers. I know quite a few, like Jess, who spend a great deal of their time doing extra for the kids. They have a hell of a hard job, what with the lack of motivation promoted by our 'get something for doing nothing' society. But that doesn't change the fact that school taxes are only one of many expenses going up for the farmer, while the price of the product they sell is decreasing.

"Farm wives work outside the home now. This is putting more stress on the farmer, because his wife, his right-hand man, is gone most of the day. She used to be able to run for parts, fix meals for the help, do some of the barn chores, and provide the needed mental support when the weather or other events of the day didn't go quite right."

"That's a chauvinistic attitude," Nan interjected. She was sensitive about women's rights, and never missed a chance to assert her equality.

"I hope you haven't fallen into the trap of being biased against women who chose to stay home and work with their husbands in the family business, instead of choosing a different career. Farming is a business. Coming from a family farm, you shouldn't lose sight of what your mother's done to help your farm prosper. Most of the women working in farming serve as accountants, time management consultants, and much-needed sounding boards and decision makers for ideas concerning the future of the business—as well as hired hands, ones you can trust. Many women now own farms on their own."

"Of course, you're right, when you look at it that way," Nan said. "Guess I took my mother's contribution to the farm for granted."

"Most people have," Jay said. "When women are taken away from the home for ten to fourteen hours a day, the power of the other partner to run the business is affected. I see a difference since Mom is working out. She's physically and mentally drained. Torn between doing her best at her outside job, which requires work beyond her time in the office, and trying to keep up with all she does for the business. I realize I'm getting a little off topic, but it's important you understand all that's happening."

"Go on, Jay," I coaxed, impressed he didn't take the role of women on farms for granted. Many did, belittling and misunderstanding that farming was not only a business, but a twenty-four-hour-a-day way of life—a way of life that, if not chosen by so many, would result in a scarcity of food. No chance of that happening in our country, I thought. I couldn't help think about Jess, teaching, helping on the farm, and now, taking care of my mother.

"The GAF loaned thousands to farmers who couldn't get money from any other venue, millions of dollars in the 1980s to keep them in business and making their loan payments. The government-run agency lent them money based on seventeen- and eighteen-dollar milk. How were these farmers to pay back the money they owed when their income was cut by a third and their expenses had risen?

"In the nineties and now in the twenty-first century, banks and the GAF abruptly began cutting farmers off and foreclosing. GAF, which as of last week owns one-third of the farms in the United States, has foreclosed and taken over half the farmland acreage in the country. Of the farms the banks have taken over, none have been resold to individuals. Of the farms taken over by GAF, none have been resold by the government, not to private industry for development, or for any other reason. Remember, that means they are off the tax rolls and just sitting there. For what?"

Neither Nan nor I replied.

Our silence encouraged Jay to go on. "I've been corresponding with farmers across the country for about nine months, and I can tell you this is not turning around, and it's not isolated to this area. There's a definite, alarming upswing of foreclosures in the last three months. Farmers who have been holding on, using their savings from good years to stay afloat, while their equity has shrunk, have had enough. They're ready to sell before they lose everything. They've used money they'd set aside for retirement, thinking the situation would turn around.

"Many of the farms being sold now aren't being bought by individuals, but by conglomerates. It's been difficult to trace all the purchasers. Whoever's buying is acquiring at the lowest farm real estate prices in years. If farmers can get out from under what they owe and break even, they're taking it and running. Most aren't so lucky, losing everything or close to it.

"I haven't even gotten into the psychological effects this whole change has had, and I don't mean only on farmers. The whole economy is affected as more and more farms go out.

"Well, what do you think, investigative reporter?" Jay asked, looking at me. He took a long draw on his beer. "What do you think is going on?"

I didn't dare look at Nan. I could imagine her expression. She had to be thinking the same thing I was. Jay was always such a firmly based person. It seemed incredible he could think there was some grand government conspiracy to buy or take all the farmland in the country. He'd become paranoid. What was I going to say to him without hurting his feelings?

"You're not usually at a loss for words," Jay commented. "What about you, Nan?" I knew Jay understood exactly what we were thinking.

Suddenly, Jay guffawed, almost hysterically. Was this a big joke, just to get us going? Nan and I joined in the laughter, but hesitantly.

Jay gained control and said, still with a smile on his face, "I hadn't thought it'd be so hard to convince you there was a problem. Both of you are always so ready for a good mystery. It probably does sound ludicrous. That's what I thought at first, too. It looks like I'll have to work to convince you. When're you heading back to your respective cities? How long do I have to prove to you that this country has a serious problem?"

"I have a couple weeks," I answered.

Nan cut in, "I'm out of here tomorrow. There's a case they want me working on by Tuesday. Of course, I'll have to start at the bottom, but I was happy to get a position with a firm with a reputation for honesty. Jay, as for what you told us, I don't know how I feel. At first I thought you were crazy, but you seem so serious, I suppose something could be going on."

She continued, "I think you need to get a grip if you think this's some type of big conspiracy, though. Possibly there's an entrepreneur buying up the land or obtaining it for taxes. While it's not kind or ethical to take advantage of others' misfortunes, it's not illegal per se. As for this taking place across the country, I'm sure there's someone waiting at every turn to take advantage of those with money problems, whether in agriculture or any other business."

"I understand your reluctance. At first, I was skeptical. It goes much deeper. The more research I do, the more tributaries I find leading to who knows where," Jay said, his voice falling off in an exasperated sigh.

"I'll keep my ears open," Nan said, "but I think you'll find a logical explanation that'll lead you to a wealthy tycoon trying to get wealthier, buying up land while it's cheap. I have to run. It's after ten, and I have a 7 a.m. flight. You know that means a 4 a.m. wake-up call."

"I'll take you home," I said.

"No, stay. My brother's picking me up. I didn't want to put a dampener on the party. Thought there'd be more people around," Nan said, scanning the bar. "Remember when we couldn't walk through the place?" I said.

"Seems like ages ago. It was great to see you again," Nan said, leaning over to give me a hug. Turning back to Jay, she said, "Let me know how you make out. I really will keep my eyes open. Call if you dig where you shouldn't and need a good lawyer." She winked as she walked away.

Jay paid for the beers, and we walked, without talking, to Nate's blue Silverado. "I know you think I'm crazy. I don't have a college degree like you, but while you've been off studying journalism, I've been studying what's happening in agriculture across the country. Not what's in the textbooks or journals, where ideas aren't practiced for years after they're printed. The real world, right now—and the more I learn, the more frightened I become, not just for me, but for our country and way of life."

We rode the rest of the way home in silence. I drove in the driveway and turned to Jay. "I want to hear more," I said.

"Thanks for having enough faith to listen. Free for dinner tomorrow night?"

"Sure," I replied. "I don't know what there is to this, but I know how hard farmers work and what they get for their efforts. Just because I don't want to live the farmer's life doesn't mean I don't have respect for it."

"See you tomorrow night," Jay said as he leaned closer, tipped my chin slightly, and kissed me. Then he turned and went into his house.

I was stunned. We had kissed before as friends. This was different. He lingered a little too long for a "just friends" kiss, and I didn't fight it. He's just caught up in the moment, I thought, grateful I'd listened without judging. I had to admit he'd awakened a few feelings I hadn't had in a while. I'd been working too hard, I assured myself. He was one of my best friends. That was all it was going to be.

CHAPTER 5

The back door was unbolted, as it always was. We'd felt safe—no need for locks. Jess was at the kitchen sink, sprigs of blond hair hiding her face, ponytail loosely held by a hair tie. She was thinner than I remembered.

"Still washing today's dishes?" I asked, grabbing a dishcloth.

"Couldn't sleep," she replied. "Thought I might as well accomplish something." Weariness permeated her voice. Getting ready for these big parties was no easy task. It involved planning and work. When I thought about it, Jess must have been exhausted. She'd worked at school until Friday, then had the party two days later, all the while taking care of Mom. The barn work always had to be done, so Nate wouldn't have been much help.

"How do you do this, Jess?" I asked. "Taking care of Mom, teaching, and helping Nate?"

"Oh, it's not so much. We knew we could give your mom better care at home. I visited my grandmother in a home when I was younger. Saw a lady sitting in wet clothes with a huge puddle under her wheelchair. Judging from the odor, she'd been there for some time. If that wasn't enough, when I visited my grandfather in a different home years later, I found him in a line of wheelchairs, eight people deep, one behind the other, all reeking of urine, unshaven. I guess he was waiting his turn to be washed. Not surprisingly, all of them had their heads down. No one deserves that kind of degrading treatment, least of all your mother.

"It was really harder when she was up and around, hiding things and falling downstairs. Now, it's just physical care and trying to guess what's wrong when she's unhappy. That gets frustrating."

"I'm sorry I haven't been here for you," I said. "It should be me taking care of her."

"I feel badly when she cries and we can't help her feel better. Most of it, I think, is reminiscing, remembering times when her mother and grandmother were alive. She went through a time when she relived their deaths. That was the worst. She screamed in despair, as if she'd just learned of her mother's passing. If it had happened only once, it would've been easier to deal with, but it went on for a few weeks. Each time, she acted as though it was the first time she'd heard the news. What a helpless feeling, not being able to comfort her. Can you imagine reliving the most painful experience of your life over and over?" Jess wiped away tears.

I walked into the living room, where Mom was asleep in her hospital bed. She looked peaceful, but so tiny. It didn't seem fair that a woman as good as she, one who'd worked all her life for everyone else, had to endure this terrible disease. My eyes wandered to the compressor beside her bed.

Jess's eyes followed mine. "It's for her breathing treatments—four a day to help open her airways and ease her breathing. She's developed chronic lung disease; goes along with Alzheimer's. I suppose it's because she's so sedentary."

Disposable underwear was stacked in a crate by the bed, and a wheeled cart in the corner was covered with medicine bottles and boxes, soap, shampoo, and lotions. "Wouldn't it be easier for you to move Mom into the other room, especially when company comes? Then you'd have a living room here."

"This is your mother's living room. It has been for years, ever since Nate and I were married and your parents moved to this side of the house. It's familiar to her. When I wheel her to our side of the house to give her a change of scenery, she's content for a short time, but then wants to 'go home.' It'd be too confusing for her. If that's a little inconvenient for us, it's okay. People take the easy way out and stick their parents in nursing homes. If they kept them home, it might be bothersome or change their lifestyle." Jess's voice took on an edge, and her face turned red, like it always did when she was upset.

"Maybe we can't go out all the time," she continued, "but what's a little disruption compared to the dignity of our parents? Think what they've done for us. This is the way it should be. Our parents brought us into this world and gave us a good life. We should be able to take care of them when they need it. You're familiar with the circle of life? We may make a little less money and have a pretty limited social life, but we'll be able to look back with no regrets.

"Sorry, Val. I sound like I'm on a soapbox. I know not everyone can handle taking care of family members. Who am I to tell others what they should do? I know some need constant nursing care provided by nursing homes. Your brother reminds me I'm judgmental. I'm working on that. But let's hear what's going on in your life. With the party, we haven't had a chance to talk. How's the job? Everything you thought it would be?"

"It's been great. I've learned more about reporting than I ever dreamed I could. As soon as he found out I was willing to extend myself and my hours, my boss in LA was happy to give me extra assignments and additional guidance. I even became friends with his family. His wife asked me over to dinner several times and helped me settle in my apartment."

I glanced down. "I was offered a job in DC, but haven't considered it until the last two days. With Mom like this, I could get home more often, help you and Nate, give you a weekend off occasionally."

"We've missed you, but we'll take care of your mom. You should be taking some time for yourself, too, Val. You shouldn't be working all the time."

"Look who's talking," I said. "You and Nate work twenty-four seven."

"Well," Jess responded, "maybe we shouldn't have. Maybe we should have learned to relax. How about your social life? I imagine there're many opportunities in LA."

"I haven't had time. Men tend not to understand when I'm called away from dinner or an evening at the opera to cover a story. They'd rather invest in someone who will be with them for the whole evening."

"I suppose so," Jess said. "You know how sensitive men's egos are—don't want to think your job might be more important than spending time with them. Are you seriously considering the DC job? If the only reason is your mom, we really can handle things here."

"I'm not sure," I responded honestly. "With Mom as she is, I'd like to see her more often. I wish I'd spent more time with her when she was herself. I don't want to be saying this again next year. Wouldn't you like me closer?"

"Only you can make that decision. I don't want you leaving your dream job to be closer to home. By the way, how'd things go with Jay tonight?" she added with a smirk on her face.

My face felt hot, and I was pretty sure I didn't turn fast enough to hide my reaction. I debated whether to tell her about the kiss but decided against it. It was probably my imagination, nothing more than a friendly kiss. "It was good to see Nan and him," I replied. "I'm having dinner with Jay tomorrow night. By the way, do you know about his conspiracy theory?"

"Just forget about that," Jess said firmly. "Don't get involved."

"Why not?" My interest immediately was piqued.

"If he keeps going, there's going to be more trouble, and we don't need it. Most of us can't handle it." Jess's whole demeanor changed. Her body stiffened, and I thought she might cry. "Don't ever mention it again, especially to Nate."

Not wanting to upset Jess any more, I changed the subject. "Is Annie ready for college?" I asked, choosing a safe subject.

"She's getting ready," Jess said. "She was fortunate enough to get local scholarships that will cover her books, and she's been given a break on her tuition at Georgetown. She'll borrow some and we'll have to come up with the money for an apartment and food. That could be expensive, but it's month to month, so I think we'll be all right."

"Maybe I can help," I said. "I'm making pretty good money, and after I pay my student loans, I have enough left over to swing at least her food and maybe some cash. I can't think of anything more worthwhile."

"That won't be necessary," replied Jess proudly. "Your brother wouldn't hear of it. We can handle it."

"You're taking care of Mom, and I haven't contributed a thing, not financially or by being here. I know you and Nate could have had more if you hadn't sent me to college. I want to help. If I take the job in DC, maybe Annie could live with me. That would eliminate the rent expense."

"We'll see. Don't consider us when you make up your mind. Nate would be furious."

After we finished cleaning up, I turned in, comfortable in my old room. Although Jess could have turned my room into an office to make her life easier, she said this would always be my home. I'd have a room whenever I wanted it.

I settled in for the night, questions running through my mind. Why did Jess get so upset when I mentioned Jay's theory? Was Jay interested in more than a friendship? Did Nate look so stressed because our farm was in trouble, too?

CHAPTER 6

I spent the next day sleeping, talking to Mom, and following Nate around the farm. He didn't want to talk. When I asked a question, he ignored me. When I asked what the problem was, he said he was just busy and trying to think of a million things at once. I gave up after a while and decided to get up early the next day and try to pin him down, find out what was going on with him.

I was ready when Jay drove in the upper end of the semicircular driveway that night. He stopped in front of the barn and talked to Nate. I headed toward his car, but hesitated when I saw that Jay and Nate were having yet another disagreement. What was it with these two? Their voices were raised, but I wasn't able to make out the words. Nate threw his arms in the air toward Jay in a gesture for him to leave. As Nate turned toward the barn, his shoulders drooped, and he walked into the milk house, not acknowledging me.

"What was all that about?" I asked, opening the passenger door as soon as Jay pulled up beside me.

"Nothing," Jay replied, "just a difference of opinion. You look great."

"Thanks. I hope we're not going anywhere fancy. I didn't bring any dress clothes with me."

"No," Jay said. Laughing, he continued, "Where would I find an extravagant place without driving sixty miles? I hope you don't mind, but I need to make a stop before dinner. You might find it interesting."

"Mmm," I said, a little intrigued.

After five minutes of small talk, I couldn't keep my curiosity in check. "Where are we going, Jay?"

"Oh, I thought we'd go to Addie's. It's not elegant, but the food is beyond reproach."

"I don't mean for dinner," I said impatiently, knowing he knew exactly what I'd meant.

"Here we are," he said, driving into a forested area. Unless a person knew it was there, he wouldn't have seen the path. About a half mile in, he pulled his Jeep Wrangler to a stop.

"We're parking?" I joked.

"Would you like that?"

We dropped that subject. As we stepped out into the fresh night air, I couldn't help feeling apprehensive. This whole thing seemed strange at the least, and a little eerie. I shivered. "Now, you might be surprised at what you see here," Jay said.

We rounded a corner. A barn-type structure with natural, vertical wood siding stood among the trees and brush. Large wooden doors hung on iron rails at the front of the building.

"Did you buy a new toy?" I asked, recalling some of Jay's motorcycles, snow machines, and miscellaneous four-wheelers.

"You'll see," he said.

The door opened with a groan as Jay pulled it back along the barn. It took a few seconds for my eyes to adjust to the brightness. Fluorescent lights lined the high ceiling beams. I was speechless. I'm not sure why I thought it would be dimly lit, except that barns usually are.

People leaned over tabletops, studying stacks of papers or state-of-the-art computers. The tables themselves were hardly visible, a conglomeration of castoffs, old and out of fashion, probably gathered from area farmers.

Older farmers had a penchant for not replacing anything that hadn't completely worn out, unlike the younger generation who threw out perfectly good furniture and equipment because they wanted new.

Dad shook his head when people from cities moved to rural areas. They'd bulldoze old farmhouses and build new, modern homes, ready to erect new schools, tear down old structures, thinking fresh construction would improve education. Jess laughed at that. People moved here because they didn't like what had become of their previous cities. Then they proceeded to make their new locality exactly the same as what they'd come from.

I scanned the room. I knew many of the neighbors, husbands, wives, and high school and college students who manned the computers. None looked directly at us as we threaded our way between the tables, but they nodded their heads, touched the brims of their caps, or gave high fives acknowledging us—or, I should say, Jay.

Neither of us had spoken. Jay turned to the left and we entered another small office-type room with a desk. He led me to an old, overstuffed, living-room-style chair in front of the desk, closed the door, and made his way around to an office chair. Seeing Jay move behind the desk gave me an uneasy feeling, as if I were the employee and he my supervisor. I'd always considered us equals and didn't like him relegating me to this subservient position, if that was his intention. Maybe it was my imagination. There I go again, reading something into nothing. I mentally scolded myself, but the uneasy feeling didn't subside.

I waited for Jay to speak. He looked at me with what my father would have called a "shit-eating" grin.

"What *is* this?" I finally asked.

"Not quite what you expected?" Jay said with a quasi-serious tone. "Did you anticipate a survivalist group in army uniforms with weapons, training to take over the government?"

I felt my face grow red, and he laughed. I couldn't help but join him.

"Want a drink? Coffee?" he asked, pointing to the pot in the corner. "Thanks."

He poured the coffee and added cream to mine. "We subscribe to on-line services, correspond, and get information to and from the rest of the country and the world—the same reason everyone else is on the internet. We need information. We're trying to save agriculture and our world, as we know it. Sound crazy?"

"Why all the secrecy? Why have all of these computers here? What's wrong with people working in their homes?" I asked.

"This makes more sense than everyone learning the same information at home and getting together to discuss it. This is more organized. Each computer has its own assignment. When manning a computer, the person is looking for specific information. If farmers were at home, they'd be working their farms, not manning computers in their houses."

"You're right there," I agreed.

"You need to use your imagination. Think ahead. Are you familiar with the success rate of government-run programs? What do you think our lives and those of everyone in this country, and possibly the world, are going to be like if the United States government owns or controls all the land? How efficient do you think the operations will be compared to a farm owned and operated by people who love the land?"

"I remember Dad's complaints about government-run programs like the buy-out plan to encourage farmers to stop producing. He said it benefited big farms not run by individuals, or some operations sold their cows then re-purchased in their partners' names, not accomplishing the planned outcome. And the program was paid for by other farmers," I said.

"Exactly. Think about Nate and Jess. Your ancestors have been on that land since the 1700s. Do you think the government will care about pre-serving the land, the smokehouse, and slate roofs for the next generation and for history? The government pretty much controls the price of food now, but what do you think will happen when the politicians feel they must make a profit, unlike the way it is now, government making sure farmers don't break even.

"Look at how much it costs the government to run its business. How much do you think we'll pay for food if government officials, whose friends provide materials at exorbitant prices, run farms? Remember the $1,000 toilets and $500 hammers the government bought in the past?"

Jay was rambling and getting agitated, but I caught the general idea.

"None of us will be able to pay our bills or taxes as the price of everything we need to operate escalates and the price of milk continues to decline," Jay continued. "What do you think will happen after the government has taken over all the land? What's to stop them from concentrating on the other areas of agriculture? From success comes confidence. More will be their goal. Power is an aphrodisiac. Remember reading about Nixon and his arrogance?"

He pointed to the coffee pot in the corner. "More coffee?"

"No," I responded. "I'd like to understand what you're talking about. I'm not sure what you're trying to accomplish."

"Our goal," Jay replied, "is to talk to farmers all over the country, to help them understand what's going on in other parts of the United States and to let them know they're not alone. We pass the word of current affairs in farming."

"Do you pass on the facts, or your interpretation of the facts?" I asked.

"Ah, skepticism?" Jay asked.

"With everyone so busy, how do you manage to get these farmers here to spend time?"

"It's simple," said Jay. "They love what they do, or did before it became so hard to make a living and hang on to what they had. They sleep less. You'll notice these are not only farmers. They're people from the community who want to purchase and eat high-quality food and pass that legacy to their children and grandchildren.

"They don't want to have to tell stories to their grandchildren of green fields, wheat and corn growing against clear blue skies. They want them to experience it. They don't want to have to say, '*Once,* there was food that was fresh and tasted good and wasn't manufactured in a lab,' or '*Once,* we had neighbors who worked together, talked to each other, and came to each other's aid whenever the need arose.'"

His voice had been rising as he talked. "We think these are values worth fighting for." He paused, waiting for me to speak.

I chose my words carefully, not wanting to sound unsympathetic. "I understand how you feel, Jay. You chose to stay in farming, and it's not going well. Times change in every profession, and if we aren't willing to change with the times, we get pushed aside."

"I don't think you get it yet, Val. We're not talking here about a change in technology. As you can see," Jay said, pointing to the room filled with computers, "we're not still farming as our ancestors did a hundred years ago. We've changed with the times. What we're talking here is a change in the basic fabric of our whole country. We're talking about the government not only controlling, but also owning the farmland in this country. How long do you think it will be before the government owns other industries as well? Our country is very young compared to many, and we've had it good for so long the citizens have become apathetic.

"You probably know that only 40 percent of our nation voted in the last presidential election. Look at the caliber of the people willing to run for government office. Have you ever watched congressmen and senators on TV when they're conducting a hearing? It's quite a sight. With few exceptions, the people being interrogated by the officials are more intelligent than the interviewers. Don't you realize what is going to happen if something isn't done? If farming is taken over by the government, the rest of industry will follow and soon we won't have any freedoms."

I was trying my best to listen to Jay's tirade. It was hard to sit there and not react with my true thoughts. We've had freedom forever. I couldn't see any chance we'd lose it.

"Think of all the freedoms we've lost in just the last few years. There's been a push to socialize medicine and take away our choice. Where are the education programs to help people learn a trade? Do you think there is a move to help poor people because the government politicians are compassionate? The more people who are dependent for their food and health care from the government, the more control the government has. Forty percent or more of your money goes to pay for government programs now. How much do you think will have to go to these giveaway programs if the trend continues? As more of your money and the money of the people who work for a living go to the government, you also become more dependent on government. Sooner or later, you must start buying into taking advantage of government giveaway programs in order to survive. Why not provide free education and training programs to help people out of poverty, give them the support they need to become productive?

"How can you *not* want to do anything about this, Val?"

"What is it you want me to do?" I asked. I didn't agree with all that he'd said but could hear his frustration at what I perceived was his reaction to not being able to make a living doing what he loved.

CHAPTER 7

Jay moved from behind the desk and sat on the arm of the chair. "I want you to do what you've always done well and what you've developed expertise in. I've kept up with you, seen your articles. I want you to investigate and find out who's actually behind the land takeover. Is it just the government, certain government officials, or are others involved?"

"I thought you were sure it was the government," I replied.

"The government is taking over the land. But, as I said before, look at the caliber of our public officials. I can't believe these people are capable of coming up with a long-range plan like this. And it is a plan. I can show you a timeline of the events to date. And the timeframe is escalating, especially in the last month."

Jay's eyes penetrated mine, but he hesitated before he continued. "If you accept the position you've been offered with *Washington In Depth* in DC, you'd be in the perfect place to look into certain aspects of this situation. The editor of the paper would be willing to let you run with this, give you the time and help you'd need. He believes there's something to our theory."

"What?" I asked incredulously. I jumped out of my chair. "What are you talking about? What do you have to do with *Washington In Depth*? You know the editor?" I couldn't believe what he'd said. I must have misunderstood.

"It's really all a crazy coincidence. I've been reading *Washington In Depth* and about Ken Bentz, the editor, for some time. He prints information the mainstream presses won't touch, follows up on leads. Although he runs a small paper, he knows how to get the word out, and he has connections. He welcomes comments and leads from anyone and anywhere, even a hayseed like me."

"You've got to be kidding," I said, moving away from the chair.

"Just listen a minute," he said. "After reading Ken's paper for several months, I contacted him. We've kept in touch for the last year, either by internet, texts, or visits. I traveled to Washington a few months ago, and last month Ken stopped here on a trip upstate."

"So, you're telling me that I got this job offer because of you? You got me the job?" I was furious with him. "And all the time I thought I was doing well, that someone recognized my talent. Was I a fool, or what?" By this time I was so irate I was pacing in the small office, my head down and my arms flailing.

"No!" Jay said. "This really is an amazing coincidence. I never mentioned you to Ken. As a matter of fact, I didn't know anything about the offer until you told Nan and she mentioned it to me. I couldn't believe it myself.

"Nan was hoping maybe you'd take the DC job and share her apartment. This might be the biggest story you'll ever write. I know you haven't really given any serious consideration to the job, but will you please think about it? Think about what's at stake here—our whole way of life, the life of our country."

I couldn't believe how dramatic Jay was being. It wasn't the old Jay I'd grown up with, the carefree boy who liked to party, always a hard worker but never interested in outside influences. He'd always made up his own mind, often reading and researching so he could argue issues.

He didn't know I'd been contemplating the job because of Mom. No matter how crazy his whole theory sounded, I had to admit explanations for some events I'd recently learned about were pretty weak. And, even if there was nothing to his belief, DC was closer to home and family, so I could help with Mom.

"I assure you, Val, I never mentioned your name to Ken. I couldn't believe it when Nan told me you'd been offered the job. I should tell you, though, Nate is against your involvement in this. He's upset with me because he knew I'd try to influence you to take the DC job so you could devote your time to it."

"Why is Nate concerned? I'd think he'd be happy I'd be closer to home."

"You have to realize, with the amount of land and money we're talking about, we're looking at big power here. Where there's that much power, there's arrogance. Whoever's behind it has purchased a great deal of land. They're not going to stop. Questioning is bound to be dangerous. Nate doesn't want you hurt, but then again, neither do I," Jay said. He reached for my hand as I continued to pace, trying to digest all the information he was throwing at me. After looking at my face, he pulled his hand back. He knew when to give me time.

"Show me what you've got. I mean black-and-white figures and facts."

We spent about two hours going over details of just how much land had been seized by the local, state, and federal governments. Jay showed me statistics, how many small family farms had gone out of business in the past five years and how many farms were feeding the people of our country today compared to five years ago. I cringed at the number of farmers declaring bankruptcy.

"Let's go to dinner," I said, not able to deal with any more. I needed time to think. Jay didn't argue, and he didn't mention anything about farming or the job while we ate.

CHAPTER 8

The sun shone through my window, dust particles dancing on the rays. I glanced at the clock—6:30—dressed quickly, and ran out to the barn, hoping to talk to Nate. He'd still be milking and wouldn't be able to walk away from me.

"I've decided to take the job in Washington," I raced to say. I wanted to get what I'd imagined would be an unpleasant confrontation out of the way. It was selfish on my part, giving the worry to him to lessen my burden. And I couldn't say I wasn't worried. I'd tossed and turned last night, thinking about what could happen if I delved into places I wasn't welcome, especially if this was as big as Jay believed. But with my curiosity, a little danger never stopped me before. I wasn't only thinking of the impact on my family and the country. If there was anything to this, breaking the story could be huge for my career.

Putting a milker on a cow, Nate looked up from a kneeling position. He had chosen not to grow the farm bigger as many farmers had, so he didn't have a parlor. He still had a stanchion barn and had no intention of adding more cows. "I'm not surprised," he said in a defeated tone. "Nothing else has been going right. I knew Jay would get to you." Seeing his drawn face, I was sorry I'd hurt him further.

"Don't worry, Nate. I'll be okay. I've worked on some touchy stories before, and I've learned to be careful."

"You have no idea what you could be getting yourself into, Val. Jay thinks this may involve our government and business, a widespread conspiracy to take over the farmland in our country. It may even extend outside the country. He's probably told you that."

"Yes, and I admit it sounded pretty far-fetched until he showed me statistics. At the very least, there's room for thought. I have to say I'm even getting anxious to start investigating."

"Getting excited, huh?" Nate said. "Just make sure you're careful who you talk to. Don't trust anyone. Anyone!" he repeated. "I think this may go even farther than Jay realizes."

"It can't be much deeper than the government. Do you mean you think it goes to the top?"

"I don't think it stops there. How could it? Our illustrious leaders sure as hell don't have the intelligence, the imagination, or the balls to carry out this kind of undertaking. I work fifteen hours a day and make less money all the time. People are still paying the same or more for milk in stores while farmers don't earn enough to pay expenses. We keep going deeper in debt. Makes you wonder why we do it, doesn't it? I hope someone can make people wake up before there's no food in this country.

"You check in with us at least every other day. No, every day. Be really careful what you say in emails, texts, and on the phone."

"You're getting awfully protective, big brother," I retorted, trying to lighten his mood. "It's not like I'm going into battle. And you admit this has to be done."

"You're going into something a whole lot more dangerous than battle. You need to realize that. When you go into battle, you know the enemy. You can plan on that basis. Here, you're not sure who you're up against, so it's hard to know how to play," Nate said.

Annie saved me from further advice as she catapulted through the barn door. "The heifers are out over at Casey's," she shouted. "Mr. Casey just called."

"Let them be out!" Nate said. "They won't hurt anything. I don't suppose they could get off their lazy asses and put them back themselves. I'll be done in half an hour, then I'll go over."

"We'll put them in," I volunteered. Annie's eyes rolled. I laughed. "Still love the cows, huh, Annie? Come on. It'll be like old times."

"Yeah, just like old times," she groaned. "I can't wait."

We jumped in the rusty old Dodge. I hadn't driven standard in a while, so when I shifted into first, Annie lunged forward as I released the clutch.

"Sorry. I'll do better," I promised, jerking the vehicle out the driveway.

"You never really could drive stick."

"Come on," I reminded Annie, "we learned to drive on this truck, picking up bales of hay from the fields."

"Yeah, and I remember being thrown off the back a few times when you were doing what I'd loosely term driving!" Annie laughed.

"Complain, complain," I quipped as we drove into Casey's upper driveway. "Where are they, Annie?"

"They're way up in the back field, probably into the corn by now. I hope they didn't do too much damage. That's all we need."

We bumped through the field over the tractor-made trail, sometimes hitting the ruts so hard our rears popped off the seat and thumped back down. There they were. Not bad. It looked as though someone had left the gate open. "At least they didn't knock it down or go through it and get all cut up," Annie said.

"Why don't we go around the other field? Maybe we can do this the easy way, without getting out of the truck."

"Let's," said Annie. "I don't feel like chasing the dumb creatures."

We had the heifers back in the field, gate locked, and were back to the barn before Nate was done milking. It wasn't usually that easy. We'd been lucky.

"What will I do when you two go?" Nate said when we got back to the barn and told him how simple it'd been. "I won't be able to run the place."

"Are you coming in for breakfast, Nate?" I asked.

"He never does," Annie answered for him.

"Come on," I pushed, "you can take a few minutes off."

"If I could, I would!" he snapped.

I looked at Annie as we walked toward the house. "This is how it is, now," she said. "We have to be careful what we say. Anything seems to set him off. I'm glad I'll be going to college in a couple months. I feel a little guilty even going. I know Mom and Dad don't have the money, but I don't think I could stand to stay here. Mom's not much better. She gets bent out of shape just about as fast as Dad. Neither of them have any patience anymore, especially with each other."

"They have a lot to handle, Annie," I said.

"So does everyone else. That's no excuse to snap at everybody. It's not my fault the price of milk is low and they can't pay bills because the taxes and expenses are so high."

"I thought the price of milk was up the last couple of months. Maybe there'll be a turnaround."

"Not likely," Annie replied. "It's an election year. The president wants everyone happy. As soon as he's reelected, you'll see the price drop again."

"Where'd you get that idea?" I asked.

"I watch the news, read, and listen, and I suppose I'm becoming cynical living around farmers. Remember how it used to be? Everyone worked hard, but there were fun, relaxing times, too. People were more positive. Maybe times are just changing and it's time for farming to end, too."

"What will we eat, then? How do you expect people to live, Annie? You're not serious."

"I mean, maybe it's time farming ends as it's done now. You know, small farms, individually owned farms. I hate to see the way I grew up disappear, but none of my friends are staying on their families' farms. Wow, I'm getting serious and maudlin. How do you like that word, maudlin? You can tell I've been reading, huh? I guess it's time to change the subject."

"I can do that," I said. "Have you decided for sure on Georgetown? Jess said you had another possibility. Don't you have to make up your mind pretty quick? Do you have a place at both?"

"I thought I'd go to the local community college, but a couple weeks ago, I heard from Georgetown. They offered me a great package, a big portion of my tuition. Evidently, somebody who'd previously accepted a package opted to go elsewhere, and I was next on the list. I have enough money saved for the first year of room and board, but I won't be able to come up with the following year's. I hate to start there for a year and then have to quit. The tuition is over $50,000 a year, so it's quite a deal they're offering. I don't want Mom and Dad to have to pay much, and it would get me away from here."

"The way Jess talked, you were definitely going to DC. You'll appreciate Jess and Nate a lot more when you're not here," I answered. "I've decided to take the job I was offered in Washington. You can stay with me. Then you could use what you've saved for tuition, borrow less."

"Woah! I bet Dad was happy about the job!" Annie exclaimed.

"Not so much," I answered, "but telling him wasn't as bad as I thought it'd be. I'm not sure it's the right decision, but I've made it now. Hopefully, it'll work out for the best."

"Are you trying to convince me or yourself?

I didn't answer.

"I guess we could talk about rooming together, but I don't know how much I could contribute."

"You don't have to worry about that. I'll be getting an apartment there anyway. Your mother and father helped me through college, and I'd like to help you."

The rest of the day I spent time with Mom, although I wasn't sure she knew who I was. She talked to people who weren't there, yelled at me for not making them leave, and whimpered intermittently for no apparent reason. Jess said Mom experienced what were called "sundowners" about four o'clock every day. What a helpless feeling it was to watch her. I couldn't figure out what was wrong, and there was no convincing her that everything was all right. I just frustrated her and me.

I called my boss in LA and gave my notice. He wasn't surprised I was leaving but expressed his concern I wasn't making an upward move. He said he respected Ken Bentz and thought of him as a fair and honest journalist, of which there were few. I was surprised he'd even heard of him. After making reservations on an 8:30 flight out of Albany for Wednesday night, I called Jay to tell him I'd be leaving for LA in two days.

"How long will it take you to clean things up out there?" he asked.

"About a week. I phoned Ken today. Told him I'd be in Washington by the middle of July. I'd like to get settled as soon as possible."

"How much do you have to move?" Jay asked.

"Just some clothes. I've been living in a furnished apartment, and I'm not sure where I'll be living in Washington. I was hoping to find a small furnished flat, but I might have Annie rooming with me, so I'll have to rethink location, make it convenient to the university."

"Do you have a car in LA?"

"Yes. I'll drive it back and leave it with Jess and Nate. They might be able to use it. I don't think I'll need a vehicle in DC, at least not for a while. I'm used to public transportation. I'll be staying with Nan until I get a place for Annie and me—that is, if she decides to live with her aunt."

"I'll come out and help you drive back," Jay said. "I don't want you driving it all alone, and I have some people along the way I'd like you to meet, if you don't mind."

"That really isn't necessary, Jay. I'm capable of driving myself across the country."

"I've talked you into this. I wouldn't feel right if I let you make that long drive alone."

"You know, Jay, I've lived alone and driven and flown all over for the last five years without your help," I snapped at him.

"All right, it's not just keeping you safe I'm concerned about. I want you to meet some people who are in the middle of everything that's going on. It will help your investigation."

"The magic words. I have to admit, since I've made up my mind, I'm anxious to get started. It would be good to have company for the long ride. When are you able to be on the West Coast?"

"If you can be ready by a week from Thursday, I'll fly out the night before. We'll leave bright and early Thursday. I'll set up a route so you can meet the key people. How many days do you think we should take? I don't want to rush you."

"As long as I get six hours of sleep a night, I'll be fine," I replied.

The next couple of days passed quickly. I spent my days with Mom, Jess, Nate, and Annie, and my evenings with Jay. He continued to fill me in on his research and cautioned me to be careful. There were no further close moments with Jay. I'd probably exaggerated the meaning of his kiss the night of Annie's party. Jess, on the other hand, thought there was more to it.

CHAPTER 9

'd packed my clothes, cleaned out my office, and donated the odds and
ends from my apartment to the local hospice store. And it was only
Monday. The only people I knew in California were coworkers who were
far too busy to meet for lunch or dinner, so I spent time on my laptop
researching everything I could about agriculture across the country. I also
researched in libraries and on websites, gathering USDA statistics.

Time went rather fast. On Wednesday night, I met Jay at the airport.
After returning to my apartment, we walked the two blocks to my favorite
restaurant, The Turn Around, for dinner. We started with a merlot. I ordered
my usual—filet mignon, garlic mashed potatoes, and a Caesar salad. Jay
had prime rib and a salad. Nothing vegetarian about these two farm-raised
people. In the last few years, I'd tried to be more careful with what I ate, but
when I ate at a restaurant where I loved the food, there was no way I wasn't
having steak.

We talked about everything but the farm situation, and ordered a second
bottle of wine—probably not the wisest thing to do, especially when I knew
what wine did to me, but it was so comfortable. We laughed together, probably exacerbated by the alcohol, and found we had more in common than
we had when we were younger. We thought alike.

By the time we walked to the apartment, we were both feeling good—
really good. I stumbled on a crack in the sidewalk. Jay caught me. One of

his muscular arms scooped me up. I looked up at his face. His eyes were half open, and he pulled me closer to him and kissed me. I melted into him. It must have been the wine, but I knew I wanted him and I had no trouble understanding he wanted me. We struggled back to the apartment, trying to keep our hands off each other until we shut the door. He unzipped my dress as I tried to unbutton his shirt with wine fingers. We made it to my bed, and neither of us said a word. We woke partway through the night and enjoyed each other again. No regrets.

Jay was holding me when I awoke in the morning. The wine had worn off, and I wasn't sure how I felt or how I hoped he felt.

"Val, I've loved you since we were kids. I want us to be like this forever. I hope you feel the same way about me."

"You know I have feelings for you. I've thought about us being together, but to be honest, I'm not sure how I feel. I'm not ready to commit for a lifetime.

And you know we want different things out of life." I did care, more than I was ready to admit to him yet. I knew he'd never leave farming and I'd never live in Madden again. I wanted more out of life. I hadn't come anywhere near completing what I'd planned to accomplish. I had to keep a distance.

"I'm not asking you to commit now, but there are ways to work out our different goals. Let's enjoy the time we have now and not worry about the future. It's enough that we care about each other. I don't have to be back home for a week and a half. We can take our time. You can learn more about what's happening, and we can enjoy our evenings together. Let's not leave until tomorrow."

"Sounds good to me," I said, pulling him closer to me. We didn't get out of bed until mid-afternoon, and I was more than a little exhausted. We showered, packed the car, and went to dinner. We decided against wine, wanting to get an early start in the morning. When we climbed into bed together, we lay in each other's arms and fell asleep. We awoke at about five in the morning but decided we didn't have to leave that early after all.

We finally got on the road around eight and headed for Olene, Utah, our first stop on Jay's list. We started on route 80 out of San Francisco for the 770-mile drive. It promised to take at least twelve or thirteen hours, even with only brief stops. We didn't plan to travel this many miles every day, but we wanted to make our first day out count. We made good time and arrived in Salt Lake City, south of Olene, around 8:30 p.m. We stayed at a Best Western off the highway. Jay placed an order from one of the takeout restaurants he said he'd eaten at before, and we had time to shower and change before it arrived. I had my doubts, but it was delicious—penne pasta Arrabbiata with a Caesar salad. We were both tired, and we had to be up and checked out by seven in order to meet with the Fisher family in Olene at nine.

I didn't wake up until my phone alarm rang. Jay wasn't there.

After packing, I was concerned that he hadn't returned, but my worries were unfounded. I closed my suitcase just as Jay knocked on the door. "Come on in, the chain's off."

"I see you're ready. You look fantastic." He took me in his arms and kissed me, a kiss that I didn't want to end. I cared about him but wouldn't let even myself admit that I loved him. That would mess up everything. When he released me, he said, "I guess we'd better leave if we're going to make our meeting with Kate and David."

"You're right, but I wish we had more time." I moved against him.

"You're not helping," he said, pushing me away with his hands on my shoulders. "I've scouted out the breakfast. It looks great. Come on." He took my suitcase. "I'll put this in the car and meet you in the dining room. Go ahead and help yourself."

After breakfast, we drove twenty miles north to Olene. Jay turned right onto a long dirt road with no house in sight. The dust smell filtered up through the rust spots under my old Subaru. Corn and wheat were planted on both sides of the road.

"The crops look good," I said.

"The Fishers are known for their yields. They're hard workers who care deeply about land use. I don't know how much you know about farming in the western states, but it's different than in the East."

"I didn't travel by car out of California while I was in San Francisco, so this is my first trip in the West, other than by plane. From the shape of this dirt road, I assume one of the major differences is the availability of water."

"That's right. If Olene gets twenty inches of rain a year, the farmers consider themselves lucky. Even the water flowing in the rivers is controlled by a commission that is under the purview of . . . guess who."

"The government."

"Right. I'll tell you more later, but first I want you to hear the story from the people who are living it."

When we turned the next corner, a house and barns came into view. "The house is tiny," I said. "Do Kate and David have children?"

"They're expecting their first in December. That means David loses his main hired hand. Don't get me wrong. She'll still be his equal partner. They have equal input on all decisions, but until now, Kate's been beside him in the barn and fields."

I didn't say a word. What I was thinking, Jay wouldn't want to hear. I saw how hard my mother had worked on the farm. It was expected she'd have meals on the table, clean the house, do the bookkeeping, run for parts, and still go to the barn or fields when she was needed. She never had a chance to do much of anything else. And no one helped her in the house. When the men came in, they sat. She fell asleep as soon as she hit her chair at night. That was never going to happen to me. Never.

We hadn't made it to the door before a woman in her mid-twenties with long, blond hair arranged in a high ponytail came out to meet us. "Jay, how are you?" She gave him a hug. "And this must be Valerie. Welcome, come in.

I have coffee and scones ready. I hope you're hungry."

"This is Kate," Jay said.

She turned, and I noticed her sparkling green eyes.

"We ate at the hotel," Jay said, "but I'm sure we can make room for your homemade scones, huh Val?"

"It's good to meet you, Kate," I said, reaching for the woman's hand.

"Sit here. We don't hold with formalities. Most of our friends sit in the kitchen."

"Same as home," I said.

Kate poured the coffee while Jay asked, "Where's Dave? Still milking?"

"No, he's changing, be right down." Kate turned to me. "I hear you're coming on board."

"I agreed to take the job in Washington, but I'll be honest with you, what Jay tells me seems a little fantastical. But after limited research, I found there are questions to be answered."

"I'm sure it does sound strange at first," Kate laughed. "You listen to Jay and the other people you'll be talking to on this trip across the country, though, and it may not sound like fantasy. At any rate, I'm glad you'll be looking into it. Jay says you're quite a reporter as well as a special person." She smiled at Jay. "He certainly talks about you lots."

My face warmed. I wondered what he'd told them.

Dave walked into the room. I wasn't sure what I'd expected, but this guy was gorgeous. Six feet tall, blond, blue eyes, and shoulders and arm muscles like a body builder. Jay was built well, too, but I took him for granted.

"You must be Valerie," he said. He shook my hand and sat next to his wife, with whom he was obviously enamored. His arm immediately encircled her shoulders, and his gaze into her eyes was riveting.

"Glad to meet you, Dave," I said. "I like your place. It must be nice to be this secluded. Our farm is next to a road—no privacy at all."

"I do like that about this place," Dave said. "Though I think Kate would prefer to live around more people. It took me a while to get used to it, coming from Manhattan. However, I've grown to love it in the five years I've lived here. I don't think I could go back to living in a city again. Where shall we start, Jay?"

"Val needs to hear about the water situation in Utah. Since you and Kate are living it, would you start?"

"Sure. Val, do you know how we get our water here?"

"If it's at all like home, you dig a pond and/or drill wells."

"We could dig and dig, but we wouldn't be able to make much of a pond. The water table here is too low. And even if it weren't, the water is controlled. We're not allowed to dig a well or a pond. There are separate water conservancies throughout the state that control the water for the distinct districts. Ours is the Stamp Water Conservancy. There are eight dams and reservoirs under this conservancy. There are also seventeen deep, large-capacity wells for backup, some up to twelve hundred feet deep, capable of producing three thousand gallons per minute. The conservancy is allowed to sell water to other districts, too, unless there's a moratorium on water diversions."

"It sounds as if you have plenty of water," I said.

"It seems like a lot, but one reason for the conservancies is because the southwestern states don't have enough water for their needs," David continued. "And not all the water is drinkable, or for culinary use, as the conservancy calls it."

"So, do you have enough water for your needs, for the cows and your personal use?" I asked.

"Our supply is sufficient most of the time, but we, as with other farmers in the area, are having a time deciding what to do. We want to add more cows in order to make ends meet, but we're not allowed any more water. Therefore, we can't add stock. We're at the mercy of the conservancy, and if there's a moratorium on water diversions, we can't obtain a contract for more water. The price we pay to use the water has been increasing over the past ten years while what we receive for our products decreases. No business can survive expenses increasing and income decreasing."

"Who controls the conservancies?" I asked.

"Our conservancy was originally set up under the Bureau of Reclamation, and the United States government was paid back by property taxes charged to the landowners," Dave said.

"Who's in control now?" I asked.

"That's a good question. There's a person in control who is appointed by the legislature of the State of Utah. That person has pretty much been given carte blanche, and although the original dams and reservoirs were paid for years ago, our taxes continue to climb to support the upkeep and salaries of employees needed to run the water conservancy. And we still have to pay for our water in addition to the taxes."

"I'm beginning to understand your conundrum. But it seems you must have these conservancies in order to preserve water so you can farm," I responded.

"You're probably right, and in 1949, when the Bureau of Reclamation started these conservancies, they did a great thing, probably begun by people with forethought. However, I want you to think about what power an agency has over you if they control your water and disperse it as they see fit. What's to stop people in power from charging people more than they can afford? What happens if the water supply is stopped or slowed to a trickle? If the people in charge are responsible and ethical, no problem. But if they're not honest? Greed is a powerful motivator."

"I need to think this through," I said. "Has there been a move to lessen the water you're getting?"

"Not to us, but we have a few neighbors who've been driven out of business because they weren't able to obtain water they needed," Kate said.

"Do these people still live on their farms?" I asked.

"No," Kate replied, "and surprisingly, business associates of the current head of the conservancy purchased the farms that were lost to the banks."

"Now you're giving me something to look at," I replied. "Do the people who lost their farms still live in the area?"

"Two families live here still. The Dawsons moved in with their daughter and son-in-law in Danver, and the Pauls live in an apartment in Benchwith. They're both willing to talk to you if you and Jay can stay for the day," Dave said.

I looked at Jay. "Sure," he said.

Kate called the Dawsons and Pauls and set up appointments later in the afternoon. She drove me to the meetings while Jay stayed with Dave to help on the farm for the day.

We met with the Dawsons first. Carrie welcomed Kate, literally with open arms. "You look wonderful," Carrie said to her. "I think it's a girl. And you must be Jay's friend, Valerie," she said, turning and giving me a hug, too.

"Good to meet you," I greeted her.

"Come on in the kitchen. I have tea and cookies. Let me call Steve. He's out back doing some yard work."

Carrie and Steve Dawson were happy to talk openly and at length about their troubles. They'd paid off most of the mortgage on their farm, but in a matter of two years had been forced to borrow more money against it due to the price of their water and property taxes. It seemed there'd been a mistake on the previous ten years of water bills, and they were required to pay a total of $50,000 to the conservancy for that error. At the same time, all the property in the county was reevaluated, and wouldn't you know, the Dawsons' property taxes doubled. They had grieved the increase and contrasted it with three comparable properties whose taxes did not increase.

"And what do you think the government did?" Steve asked.

"They wouldn't have a choice but to decrease your taxes to a similar level," I said.

"You'd think, but no, they increased the other three properties instead.

You can imagine how popular *we* were. We had lifelong friends who wouldn't talk to us anymore. Couldn't blame them. Everyone's so distraught they have to blame somebody. Work hard, get rewarded, right? I wish we knew exactly who to blame. Maybe you can find out."

"That's terrible," I said, meaning it. "You had no other alternatives? You couldn't appeal higher?"

"There is no one higher in the county," he said. "Coincidentally, the grievance committee chairman for the county is the brother of the head of the Conservancy."

"Talk about nepotism," I said. "Can you give me their names? I'd like to speak to them." I wrote the information in my notes as Carrie read names, numbers, and addresses.

"We've already lost our farm," Carrie said, "but believe me, if something isn't done pretty soon, our whole food supply is going to be controlled by very few people, just as our water is now. I hope you can help us, Valerie."

"So do I," I said, becoming somewhat alarmed by the gravity of the situation as I began to see it. These people were putting so much hope in what they thought I could do. What had they been led to believe? Had Jay spoken to them, or had the Fishers alluded that I could solve their problems? "You know I'm only a reporter, right? I don't want you to think I can fix this. I can only investigate, try to find what's going on, and report on it."

"We know," Steve said. "But we have a great deal of respect for Jay and what he's trying to do, bringing the information to the public about what's happening in agriculture, and he has faith in your abilities. That's good enough to give us hope."

"Thanks for your time. We'll see you soon," Kate said. She gave Carrie an affectionate hug.

"The Dawsons seem reconciled to the loss of their farm," I said to Kate on the ride to the Pauls'.

"They had no choice. They're in their early sixties and wouldn't consider starting a new business. It's too bad they couldn't have sold the place at a profit for their retirement. Carrie's working nights at McDonald's, and Steve's mowing lawns and doing yard work. After all their years of hard work, they should've been able to retire and enjoy life. Thank goodness their daughter and son-in-law welcomed them into their home."

I thought about Jess and Nate. They were only in their forties. What would happen to them if they lost the farm? That was all Nate had ever done. He wouldn't be happy working for anyone else. I hadn't talked to them about taxes or their expenses. It was obvious they were in financial trouble, but looking back, that happened from time to time on a farm. How deep were they in debt? Had I offered to help them out financially with Mom? Not until now. I'd have a serious conversation with Nate when I returned east.

We arrived at the Pauls' and heard a similar story from Edna and Gary. Not enough water to survive, and rising property taxes. Having enough water where I'd lived in the East, it was hard to believe water was at such a premium here. Without water, there wasn't life, and certainly not a farming life.

"Do you see there's more than high taxes involved?" Jay asked in our hotel room that night. We'd planned to leave in the afternoon to continue our trip, but because I'd spent so much time with the Dawsons and Pauls, we returned to the hotel in Salt Lake City after having dinner with Kate and David.

"I do. I wasn't successful setting up meetings to speak to the County Grievance Committee Chairman or the head of the water conservancy," I said. "After telling the secretary I was only in town another day, she said no one was available until next week. Fat chance they're both out of town."

I'd always taken water for granted. If the government controlled the water at home, it would mean Nate, and anyone else for that matter, wouldn't be able to increase his herd in an attempt to keep up with expenses. Depending on the weather, with a cow drinking fifty to seventy gallons of water a day, it would be impossible.

"Do you think there's any chance of the government controlling the water in the East?" I said.

"Probably not yet. When we have high precipitation years, we can dig ponds and put in filtering systems. It would be too hard to control individual farms right now. But I wouldn't take anything off the table. You know the creameries picking up milk from the farms test the water in the barns and check the sources, right?"

"Sure, the inspectors for the co-op used to come when I was a kid. You're opening my eyes to much more, though" I said. "I'm exhausted. Shall we get some sleep?"

"We should be on the road by five if we want to make it to our next stop by tomorrow night," he said.

"You'll probably have to wake me up."

"I'd enjoy that," he said, winking at me.

CHAPTER 10

We were on the road by 5 a.m., breakfast from the hotel in takeout containers so we could make it to Shutter City in eastern Nebraska by nightfall. It was about nine hundred miles and would take us about fourteen hours with stops.

We took route 80, leading us straight east, until we'd almost reached Shutter City, where we switched onto 81 North. I'd been to Yellowstone Park in northern Wyoming, one of the most beautiful places I'd ever seen, but southern Wyoming was desolate, pretty much all flat, rocky land. I was glad Jay was driving. I fell asleep halfway between Rock Springs and Cheyenne, and when I woke up I thought we hadn't moved. Good thing we didn't have car trouble. It would be forever before we found help. It made me appreciate the hills and trees and green of upstate New York.

The terrain remained flat through southern Nebraska, but there were small cities along the way breaking up the monotony. It didn't seem nearly as barren, and I enjoyed the ride. Jay and I continued sharing where we were in our lives, and I thought again how it was astonishing what we still had in common. Even though we'd changed in the last six years, we seemed to have grown in the same directions.

In the silent spaces on the ride, I couldn't help wonder about him. Even though what I'd heard so far on the trip made me speculate about a conspiracy by the government or who knows whom, I pondered if he was paranoid.

Jay seemed just a little off the edge. I looked at him and realized I'd been away from home for what seemed a much longer time than the actual years. Could he be wrong about everything? How radical had he become? The people we'd visited so far had seemed like decent, sane folks, but what if that was an act just for me? One minute, it seemed Jay and I thought alike. The next moment, I'd look at him and feel I didn't know him at all. I shivered.

Now *I* sounded insane. I needed to accept things as they were told to me, investigate what was true and what was exaggerated as always. I had to be a reporter, I told myself, and stop the imagination. Maybe someday I'd write fiction. I actually planned on it, but right now, I was investigating facts.

When we reached Shutter City, I commented that I hadn't seen any hotels in the city that boasted 285 residents on its welcome sign.

"We'll be staying at the Evanses' Farm," he said. "Mitchell has plenty of room and will make you feel comfortable. His place reminds me of yours. Your mom and dad always made visitors feel they'd come home, just as Mitchell does."

"You haven't told me anything about Mitchell. How'd you meet?"

"He was my commanding officer. Mitch signed up after he finished Cornell Veterinary School. Wanted to serve his country. When his father died in an accident, Mitch came back to run the farm. He's in his late thirties, never married, but has a girlfriend, Amy Perkins, who's living on the farm. I haven't met her yet. Again, I'd like you to hear his story firsthand, but his issues have nothing to do with taxes, although they remain a problem for everyone. And his issue has nothing to do with water."

"I'm intrigued," I said. "After all his education, didn't Mitch work as a vet?"

"He practiced in Michigan until his father died. He's a good man, does a lot of gratis work for his neighbors. He does his own work, of course. Vet bills can get high, and he knows some can't afford it, so he trades services."

"Why did he come back to run the farm when he could be a vet full time?" When Jay didn't answer, I glanced at him.

Jay was looking in his rearview mirror, slowing the car. He kept his eye on the mirror, stepped on the gas until we were twenty miles over the speed limit, then braked again, continuing his gaze on the mirror. I said nothing, but looked at the passenger side-view mirror. The same black SUV was behind us. We hadn't gained any ground, even after Jay's acceleration. I was silent.

"We're going to make a stop at the sheriff's office up here. I want to talk to a friend of mine. Okay with you?"

"Sure," I said.

Nate's words came back to me: *You don't know what you're dealing with. Be careful.*

"Who's following us?"

"Not sure." He continued to check the mirror.

"Is this the first we've been followed or just the first time I've noticed?"

"I don't think we were followed before, but I've been tailed in this area on past trips."

I wasn't sure I believed him. We pulled into the sheriff's office complex, drove to the closest parking spot near the door, and watched the black SUV drive past. The windows were darkened, making it impossible to determine how many were in the vehicle. We walked into the station, where Jay asked for Deputy Pete Latimer.

"Sure thing, I'll get him right away, Jay," said a tall officer with curly black hair.

How did Jay know all these people? I kept my mouth shut for a change and listened.

"Hey, Jay, we didn't expect you back this soon. This must be Miss Jacobs, the reporter," Pete said, reaching for my right hand. "You were right, Jay. We weren't sure he could get you to help us, but Jay was sure he could talk you into it."

"He was, huh?" I said, looking at Jay. What was this? Jay was pretty sure

I would say yes, or that he could talk me into doing whatever he wanted. Was what Jay and I had over the past few days real, or was it his attempt to convince me to join his group? My mouth tightened, hiding my lips. I was sure Jay knew exactly what I was thinking.

"I'll explain later," he said. "Do you have the license number?"

I told Deputy Latimer the number without looking at Jay. "Wait here," Latimer said. "I'll be right back."

I turned away from Jay and headed for the door. I needed some fresh air to clear my head so I could think. Jay followed me, but I waved him away. He didn't press it when Latimer called him back to the desk. Taking deep breaths, I continued outside and down the steps. I thought back to Jay's comments about knowing my new boss in Washington, DC, before I was offered the job. Had I made the most gigantic mistake of my life? I should have thought more about it before I took the position. I'd been sucked in. Had Jay felt anything for me except his desire to draw me into his mission? I didn't know. I was halfway across the country with someone I no longer knew.

Jay walked out and put his arm around my shoulder. I pulled away. "I'm sorry about that, Val. It's not like it sounds. I told Latimer that I knew you would want to help when you understood the situation, and I still think you will once we've visited other farmers across the country who have been unwittingly marked to lose everything they've worked for their whole lives. If you aren't convinced by the time we get back east, no hard feelings, but I hope you won't give up what we have. We do have something special, right? I know you're not committing, but please don't say there's nothing."

I didn't want to speak to him. I couldn't. I said, "We'll talk later. I can't do this now. Anything from the license number?"

"The SUV belongs to a waste company."

"That doesn't sound good," I laughed. Couldn't help it. "Get it? Waste company, waste us?"

Jay looked at me, a question on his face, like I was a little off.

"Forget it," I said. "What's the name of the company?" I took my notebook out of my pants pocket.

"It's Waste Magnet. The company's been known to strong-arm others in the area. Two other locally owned waste companies were forced out of business, and although nothing could be proven, it was thought there were threats made against the owners' families. The company had a reputation in other locations, and when the locals heard what happened to owners who tried to fight, they backed down. No one would testify against them."

"I've been followed before, but nothing I couldn't handle. Do they know where we're headed?"

"Maybe, maybe not. We'll take Latimer's car out the back lot and pick your car up tomorrow. Hopefully, the Waste Magnet people will figure they'd missed us by then."

"Sounds like a plan," I said. "Pete Latimer and you set this all up in the few minutes you were in there?"

"Not exactly."

"You've done this before," I stated.

Jay shrugged. "No sense letting them know who we talk to. We'll take the car around to the back lot and meet Pete."

We met in the enclosed garage and switched the luggage we needed into his car, a late-model red Mustang with tinted windows—nice ride. Pete drove out the gate with my car. We waited in the garage for his call. Within five minutes, Jay's phone sounded.

"The SUV's on my tail," Pete said. "I'll drive south until you have a good start north, then I'll turn around and lead them back to the station. I live for pissing off the bad guys. Good luck, Jay, Val."

We drove north, then east on route 81 past Shutter City about twenty miles. We turned right onto Evans Road and drove a few more miles. Nearing the end of the road, I saw a large, well-maintained white house on the left side. A red mailbox sat atop a fence post at the beginning of the driveway. "Mitchell Evans" was written on a metal strip along the top of the box. There were several long barns ahead to the right of the road.

"How many cows does this guy milk?" I asked Jay.

"Seven thousand," he said.

"Oh my God!" I said. This was nothing like home. The biggest farm in our area had about a thousand. "How in hell does he manage help and keep track of so many cows?"

"He's an effective manager, and all things being equal, would be doing a fantastic job. He *is* doing an incredible job. Most people would have given up with all the obstacles."

"What's his particular problem?" I asked.

"Again, it's better coming from Mitch."

This was getting old. I was still pissed, although I'd decided I'd give him the benefit of the doubt until we were able to talk, probably when we left the Evanses'. We'd have at least three more days of travel, probably four or five. There'd be plenty of time to hash it out. I needed to concentrate on work. I made sure my notebook was in my bag. Jay pulled into the driveway alongside the house.

A tall, thin woman with a killer shape and wide smile glided out on the front step. She must have been about my age or a little older. "Welcome, welcome. We're so glad you're here. Jay and Val, right?"

"Yes," I said, "and you must be Amy."

"Right. Mitch's at barn seven. There's a problem with the water line. If you want to go out, Jay, he might be able to use your help. There're some coveralls in the office, and the four-wheeler's around the corner."

"I'll do that. Okay, Val? Won't be long, I'm sure."

"Of course," I said. I had no problem being with people I didn't know. I could probably get some information from Amy, if she knew what was going on, but I'd work into it, let her show me around first. I wasn't sure how long she'd been involved with Mitch Evans, so maybe she didn't know the whole story yet. She really didn't look like the typical farm wife—more like a model.

"Come in, Val. I'll show you around. The guys will bring the luggage in later."

Amy turned out to be extremely amicable. She took me through the house, and I laughed easily. She had a contagious sense of humor. Jay had been right. I felt right at home. Amy showed me to Jay's and my room and asked if I'd like to rest or come down for a drink. I chose the drink. I even forgot to ask questions. Our talk was purely social, and I told Amy my personal history. She seemed to have a way of garnering information. If I didn't know better, I would have thought she was the reporter.

Amy was a school counselor. She wasn't working at present, having recently moved to Shutter City from Washington, DC. She gave me some pointers about places to go, restaurants, and people to see if I needed something. When Mitch and Jay came in with our bags, we were sitting at the kitchen table, deep in conversation.

Mitch was a good-looking man, but not what I'd call handsome, more rugged, with chiseled features. His dark hair was almost to his shoulders, and like Amy, his smile was wide.

"Val," Jay said, "this is Mitch."

"Hello," he said. "I've been looking forward to meeting you for a long time."

"A long time?" I asked, shaking his hand. I couldn't help smile at him.

"I've known Jay since we were in the service together. I can't remember the first time he talked about you, but I knew if Jay and I remained friends, I'd meet you someday."

Why did my face feel hot?

"I see you and Amy have become fast friends," Mitch continued. "Jay, I'd like to formally introduce you to Amy, who will be my wife in a few months."

"Congratulations! You didn't mention marriage when I talked to you on the phone," Jay said.

"Proposed last night," Mitch said. "We haven't even picked out the ring yet."

"I told you, I don't need a ring," Amy said, smiling.

"Best wishes to both of you," I said.

"Thanks." She nodded. "Would you like to freshen up before dinner? You look like you'll want to, Jay." He was wet from his knees down.

"Thanks. After our drive, a shower would feel wonderful," I said.

"If you need anything, help yourselves."

"Thanks."

"See you at eight for dinner?" Mitch asked.

"Sounds good," Jay said. He picked up our bags and walked upstairs behind me.

After a refreshing shower, we napped for an hour before dressing for the meal. Falling asleep, I thought Jay and I had a great deal to talk about, what with the unresolved issue of why he roped me into this investigation. Was I the only investigative reporter he knew, or just the one he could talk into getting into this mess? I drifted off, wondering what additional information Mitch and Amy would provide.

When I awoke, Jay was already dressed and sitting on the end of the bed, looking at me. I jumped. "What time is it? Why didn't you call me?"

"I was going to in a minute. You looked so peaceful, so unlike your real self. Don't worry, we have fifteen minutes, plenty of time."

I told Jay to go on down and I'd follow. He took me up on it, giving me a quick kiss on the cheek before leaving. I washed my face and applied some moisturizer, the only thing I ever put on my face, and thought about living in this isolated area. I shuddered, thinking our farm was in the boonies, but this was probably twenty miles from the nearest town, and I didn't see any stores on our drive in. After living in the city, I could never go back to living in a rural area. What was I doing with Jay, assuming he really had any feelings for me? He would never leave the farm to live in a city, and I wasn't about to move back where there was nothing going on.

I put on a yellow sundress and sandals and walked downstairs. When I neared the kitchen, I overheard Jay. "I think I've made a terrible mistake. She may not be with us, and she's not the type of person you want against you. She'll keep digging until she gets the truth."

"And what is the truth?" I said with a smile on my face.

"We'll talk all about it at dinner," Mitch said. "Would you like a cocktail?"

"No, thank you," I said. "I think I'd better have a clear head."

"Let's sit down," Amy said. "Dinner's ready. I hope you like ribs."

"Who wouldn't?" I replied. As we ate, Mitch talked about the problems farms in his area were having. The biggest problem was the milk-processing plants going out of business. Because Mitch produced such a large volume, he hadn't had a problem finding a plant to pick up his milk, but the biggest plant in the area was closing in a matter of weeks, and Mitch was still looking for a new processer to take his product. He said the smaller farms around him would probably be run out of business as a result of the last closing.

Mitch would find a new processor to come to his farm, but he'd have to pay more for transportation, given the longer distance. The smaller farmers, however, didn't even have that option. They weren't going to be able to afford the added transportation charges. Many of them had already put their farms on the market. If they weren't able to sell the properties by the time the processing plant closed, they'd sell their cows and stop farming.

"Unfortunately," Mitch continued, "many of them are advertising their farms worldwide. Pretty soon, we're afraid other countries will own a great deal of our country's land. Repercussions of foreign ownership are numerous."

"So," I said, "the reasons for farms in this area going out of business are the processing plants closing and transportation costs being too high for farmers to send their milk farther from home, and an effect of this is that foreign interests are buying up US agricultural land."

"That's simplifying it. The processing plants closing and transportation costs are the current reasons, but numerous reasons came before," Mitch said. "Government kept the price we receive low so there'd be cheap food. You may not think the price we pay for food in the United States is low, but if you go to other countries, there'd be a big difference. We're headed for high prices, though, because of less food grown in this country. Have you noticed you can't find many juices made from products grown exclusively in the United States? There are other whole areas of the agricultural processing industry that are purchasing vegetables and fruits from other countries.

"You know, living on a family farm, the stringent regulations farmers in the United States must follow in order to ensure quality products. Farmers in other countries don't always follow similar controls. Have you noticed the large number of recalls in recent months?"

"I'm aware, but the recalls I've heard of have been products produced here—some on organic farms," I replied.

"Problems happen in any industry," Mitch said. "I'm just saying we don't have control over the quality of farms producing foreign milk, cheeses, fruits, and vegetables. You should check to see the types of inspections the farms in foreign countries, that are producing products for this country, need to undergo before shipping products into the United States. Also check the level of corruption in those governments and draw your own conclusions."

"Mind if I take a few notes?" I asked no one in particular.

"I'd expect it," Mitch said.

I reached in my dress pocket for a small notebook and pen. I wrote: *foreign supplies of food – quality, inspections required for importing to U.S., food recalls (organic vs. regular, foreign vs. domestic), how imports effect U.S. sales, what came first—lower U.S. production or more imported food, what caused more imports?*

"Why do I have the feeling you have all of these answers, Mitch?"

"We'd like you to be on board because you know there's a problem, not because we say there's a problem," Jay said.

"Okay," I said. "Do you know how many farms have gone out in your area in the past five years?"

"Over half," Mitch said.

My head popped up.

"I'm talking farm numbers—many family farms especially, small farms, not acres. It's either get bigger or get out," Mitch said.

I told them about my recent trip home and discovering most family farms on our road had gone out over the past two years. I noted that in many cases, the land was lying fallow.

"How much does the land cost in your area?" Mitch asked.

"A few years ago, it was a few hundred an acre. In the last few years, I think some were getting two to three thousand. Now the bottom has dropped out again."

"The foreign investors and our government wait until it hits rock bottom. Then they swoop in and pick it up. You remember those forms Nate and Jess and your mother and father before them are mandated to fill out at the end of each year, supposedly so the government will have all the farm statistical information? What do you think they did with that statistical information?" Jay asked.

"Haven't a clue," I said. "I'm afraid I didn't pay much attention."

"I hope you'll check," Mitch said. "The government knows exactly what every farmer planted, what type of soil he planted it in, and every other detail of the farmer's life. Do you know any other industry that has to report such in-depth information to the government?

I didn't answer, but took a few more notes.

"Well, I think that's quite enough for tonight," Mitch said. "We need to unwind. Jay tells us you can shoot baskets with the best of us, Val."

"I haven't played since high school."

"Let's get changed and give it a try," Mitch added.

"I'm game," I said. If I was honest with myself, I was overwhelmed, and sorry I'd agreed to the trip. I could have been back in LA doing my thing with a story that had nothing to do with me personally, then moving on to the next. I'd be on this story for the rest of my life. That sounded dramatic, but it felt like when you agree to do something, then dread the hell out of it. And my trepidation was not all about working the story. It was my personal life, too.

Playing basketball turned out to be cathartic. We played Jay and Amy against Mitch and me. I was probably too aggressive, at least toward Jay. Physically exhausted when we finished playing, I slept without dreaming. Jay hadn't approached me. He knew we had some talking to do before we were intimate again, if ever. Why did I feel so deflated?

We slept late the next morning, our travels catching up with us. After thanking Amy and Mitch and promising to attend their wedding in the fall, we set out to return Deputy Latimer's car and retrieve mine. After a short chat with Pete and well-wishes on both Jay's and his part, we left the police garage and started south on route 81 to pick up 80. I was hoping the trip from here on would be a little more scenic.

It was definitely more interesting. When we pulled out onto route 81 South, I looked in the right side-view mirror and saw a black SUV pull in behind us. I turned toward Jay and saw he already had an eye on it. "Hang on," he said.

He stepped on the gas and pulled away from the SUV, but only momentarily. It glided behind us with no problem. I was jerked forward when the SUV rammed the back of my car. Jay maintained control and turned the wheel sharply left, spinning us around as the SUV sped ahead. Then Jay immediately spun the wheel to the right again, so we were behind the SUV.

"Watch out!" I yelled. "He's slamming on the brakes!"

"Time to confront," Jay said. I looked at him and saw his face was contorted in anger. "Wait here," he growled.

"Jay, stop! Don't provoke them. What if they're armed?"

No one had exited the SUV, and the road was deserted. I reached for my phone and called 911. By the time the dispatcher answered, Jay was next to the driver's door. He yelled at them, flailing his hands around. This was not the Jay I knew. I told the dispatcher what had happened. She said she'd notify the sheriff's office immediately.

Jay returned to the car. When he opened the door, I told him I'd called 911.

"Why'd you do that?" he said.

"Are you kidding me?"

"It's under control," he said. The SUV continued down the road. Jay called his deputy friend and told him to ignore the call. He'd taken care of it—all a misunderstanding, he said.

When he hung up, I said, "A misunderstanding? Are you kidding? That guy tried to kill us."

"Brakes failed," he said. He put our car in drive and continued down the road, saying nothing more to me. I was fuming. I was with someone I didn't know, someone who couldn't have cared a rat's ass about me. So condescending.

"Who was it?" I asked Jay. "Tell me now, or I'm done with this."

"Calm down, Val. I'm not trying to minimize the situation. It was a mistake. The guy thought I was someone else."

"Who, for God's sake?"

"The guy was a federal agent. He thought we had something to do with a militia organization they've been staking out."

"How could they get us mixed up with that group?"

"The FBI thought one of the sheriff's deputies, Garth Jenkins, was involved in a local militia group on the terrorist watch list. The feds had been staking out the sheriff's office and following anyone who looked suspicious. Since we were relative strangers, we were considered suspects. When the feds figured we'd switched cars in the garage, they were pretty sure we must be involved.

"So, you can see how this was a big misunderstanding. Yes, they could have caused us to have an accident, but they didn't."

"And they told you all of that confidential information out of the goodness of their hearts. Are you kidding me, Jay? Do you think I'm stupid or something? Feds don't share information with civilians, unless—you're not a civilian, are you?"

"I can't say much now, Val."

"Well, you'd better start saying something. There's no way I'm going into this with only partial information. Either you tell me everything, or you can take me home."

"Don't you want to talk about our personal situation?" Jay said with a smile.

I felt like hitting him, and might have had it not been for what happened next. A car pulled out of a side road ahead of us, traveled east, then suddenly veered off the road to the right, did a 180, and faced us in our lane.

Jay slammed on the brakes. Before he pushed me down on the seat and threw open the driver's door, I saw a man step out of the other car's passenger-side door and raise a rifle. I heard gunfire, but not a rifle shot. Having been brought up on a farm, where target practice was a given, I knew the difference between a rifle and a handgun. Three shots later, Jay jumped back in the car. I rose in time to see him swerve around the other vehicle, which sported two flat tires. I waited until we'd traveled route 81 a few miles and Jay had turned off onto a side road, paved, but narrow. I didn't remember seeing a road sign.

"We can get back to route 80 from here, but I think it might be a good idea to skip the rest of the road trip and fly home."

"I want to know who that was and what's going on. I'm not flying anywhere if you don't start telling the truth."

"I'll tell you everything on the way to New York. Mitch expected we might have some trouble when we left his house, but I thought he was overreacting. Evidently not."

"What about my stuff?" I said.

"We can ship it home, or to DC if you want. We can put it in storage until you're settled."

"And the car?"

"Are you serious?" Jay said.

"Well, it's not much, but I thought Annie might be able to use it for a while."

"I have a friend with a flatbed who transports cars. He'd bring your car, probably within a week, and your other stuff, too. Just bring what you need for the next week."

"Is there an airport near here?"

"I have a friend who'll fly us. You haven't developed claustrophobia, have you?"

"Why?"

"It's a small plane, but he's the best pilot I've ever flown with."

"Marine, I suppose? This is moving very fast, and I still don't have all the facts. Sounds like you have a lot of friends standing by. Tell me what's going on, Jay."

"I will. It's about an hour to Ned's. Mitch contacted him and told him to be available in case we had trouble."

"If it's an hour to the plane, that should be plenty of time to fill me in."

We kept to the back roads while Jay explained he knew people in the government who were also concerned, not only with agriculture but other areas over which the government had control. I asked why they'd share confidential information with him. He admitted he had more than a passing acquaintance with certain people in government service. He'd been with the Special Operations Command when he was in the Marines. Most of the people he had contact with now had been in Special Ops, the FBI, Homeland Security, or local police departments.

"So, does this mean you're working with a covert group?"

"Of course not," he said. "When I left the Marines, I left it, but I kept in touch with my friends. Don't worry, we're not an underground group, just concerned citizens who don't like what's going on. And the fact we have a few special skills is just a plus."

We pulled onto a dirt road, and before long I saw what could pass for a runway. Down the road a short distance was the hangar, a tin shed that housed one small airplane. I'd never been on one. I didn't tell Jay, but the smallest airplane I'd flown on, up until now, was a 737. I did have claustrophobia and was starting to sweat just thinking about getting into that little space. I'd have to talk myself through it. No one was going to find out I had a problem with spaces, a flaw. There was no room for weakness if I was going to be successful.

When I climbed into the plane, I was cramped and started to hyperventilate. I breathed deeply, but as inconspicuously as possible. Jay didn't notice, or at least hadn't acknowledged it. He was busy talking to the pilot. I thought of everything but being in the confined space. I didn't think about my movements being restricted and that I couldn't escape—well, not much, anyway. Then, as Jay talked, I was able to actually relax and stop the negative thoughts. I was thankful Jay talked for much of the flight home.

He filled me in on what had happened in the North Central states, since I wouldn't be able to see for myself. It took my mind off the closeness in the plane.

Independent companies had developed programs to entice farmers from other countries to farm in the United States. Universities tried to turn around the trend of family farms disappearing and being replaced by large farms by collaborating with those companies. Many of the programs backfired. People came here from Europe, invested their savings, and were initially encouraged, but found reality to be much different than promised. The farmers were required to invest their own money in order to obtain residency status. The price of feed was high, and milk prices dropped to 1970s levels. Some were unable to make a go of it, went bankrupt, and returned to their home countries, defeated.

"That's terrible," I said. "Why on earth would we try to get people from other countries to come to the United States to farm? I know young people who want to farm but can't get started."

"One reason, as far as I can tell," Jay said. "Money. The young people in our country who want to farm come from small family farms that don't have the money to support multiple generations. The people from other countries had to guarantee an investment. You can be sure someone made money from the program."

We landed at Albany Airport at 6 p.m. Jay's mom was waiting for us. "I'm hungry," she said. "Your dad's milking. Stan's still helping him for the week, so there's no hurry getting home, and I want to go out to dinner. Any particular restaurant?"

"Wherever you want as far as I'm concerned," Jay said. "What about you, Val?"

"I'm good with anywhere," I said, wishing we could go directly home.

"Then it's The Vegetarian Café," she said.

Jay wrinkled his nose.

"Just kidding. We'll go to The Steak House." Marion laughed. Jay always fell for her jokes.

CHAPTER 11

At home, the week passed quickly. Time to start my new job. As the plane began its descent into Reagan National Airport, I wondered if everyone felt the same surge of patriotism on seeing, from the air, the Washington Monument, the Lincoln Memorial, and the White House for the first time. It was a clear night, and the lights shone on the major landmarks. I could see the entire city. What a sight!

Nan met me outside the luggage area, and we were off to her apartment via her new BMW.

"You didn't waste any time getting into the rich lawyer mode," I teased her.

"Don't be so sarcastic," she responded. "You know me better than that. This certainly wouldn't be the car I would choose if I had the money. My law firm provided it. I guess it's important to them to have their lawyers appear to be of stable financial means. I have numerous student loans to deal with, so when they offered me a lease car as part of my salary, I jumped at it. You know I certainly wouldn't spend $100,000 on a car, at least not now."

Nan pulled into a modest apartment complex and waited as a security guard approached the car. He checked her picture ID and plate number, then motioned her into the chain-link-fenced parking area. Nan helped me with my luggage, and from there led me to a side door and then to an elevator that took us to the fourth floor. Nan's apartment was more than comfortable, with new, modern furniture. There was a kitchen, a combination living room/dining room, three bedrooms, and three bathrooms. It was bigger than I'd expected. I stepped out onto the tiny balcony that overlooked a courtyard in the complex.

"Pretty impressive, Nan. I could get used to this."

"I hope you will. I told you you're welcome to stay as long as you want. I wouldn't mind someone to help with the expenses. With the hours I'll be working, I won't be here much, so you'd be pretty much on your own."

"I'll think about it," I responded. "Why did you choose a three-bedroom?"

"Actually, I didn't. My law firm did. They would ordinarily have put me in a one-bedroom, but there were none available. The firm puts all their new people in this building or the one next door. My boss said I could pay the one-bedroom rate and the firm would pay the rest until I could find some roommates."

"I'll definitely consider it, but I have to find something so Annie can live with me beginning the end of August. She'll be starting at Georgetown."

"I'd like nothing better than to have you and Annie live here. Like I said, I won't be here much. Work, work, work—twelve to fourteen hours a day, I'm told. I'll have to say no late-night parties, though. My days will start early."

"Annie wants to finish her undergraduate work in three years, so I doubt she'll be doing much late-night partying. She's pretty determined."

"I was talking about you," Nan laughed. "Haven't had much time to cook, so I ordered in. It should be here anytime. I thought you might want to relax tonight."

"Perfect," I answered. "I have to check in at the paper in the morning, and I probably should get some rest. What's the best way to Cambridge Place from here?"

"The Metro, then the bus. I'll write it down for you."

"I'm not looking forward to riding a subway every day."

"You won't mind it. The Metro is clean and safe. No eating or drinking allowed. It's a pretty good method of transportation, and you don't have to worry about parking."

"We'll see," I laughed. "You sound like you've settled in and found your way around already."

"It doesn't take long," Nan said. "When L'Enfant laid out this city, he knew what he was doing. I think I'm going to like it here. The first thing I did when I arrived was to go to the Supreme Court Building. I stood across the street on the capital lawn and stared for a long time. When I finally walked up the steps and moved slowly through the pristine, marble-walled halls, I was overwhelmed. It sounds a little corny, but I feel like I belong here."

"Not corny at all. I had a similar feeling flying in tonight. My breath caught for a minute, and I felt an excitement, an impatience, to be involved in our country's future."

A voice over an intercom said, "Your order is on its way up." A short time later, there was a knock on the door, a security person delivering takeout from a local Thai restaurant.

"I'm surprised the delivery person doesn't come to the apartment," I said.

"Not here—secure building. No one gets past the security personnel without clearance," Nan said.

CHAPTER 12

I was a little groggy when the alarm sounded. Looking forward to my first day at *Washington In Depth*, I hadn't slept well. After jumping in the shower and dressing, I found Nan had already gone to work. She'd poured me some juice, made coffee, and left fresh bagels on the table. What a friend.

A note on the table instructed me where to catch the Metro and gave directions to the paper. Nan noted I should stop in the building security office on the first floor and pick up a picture ID, required of all visitors.

After savoring the bagel, I introduced myself to David Nare in security, who, according to his nametag, was the assistant head of security. He entered my stats into his Mac, including the names of my closest relatives. Within thirty seconds, he brought up a text dossier complete with my picture.

"So, you're a reporter?" he asked. "I see you're starting at *Washington In Depth* today."

"Yes," I replied. "You must have quite a database."

"The biggest," he said flatly. "We're careful about who comes in and out of this complex. How long do you plan to visit your lifelong friend?" he continued.

Did he always enjoy shocking visitors with the information he could find in such a short time? "I'm not sure. I may move in with her. At any rate, I'm sure I'll be in and out. I'm planning to stay in Washington."

"Would you like to put in a request for residency? It takes a while for approval."

"No, thank you, not yet. If we decide that's what we want, Nan should be the one to initiate the paperwork. It's her apartment," I replied.

"I think I have everything I need for now," he said, handing me my picture ID. "Good luck on your first day!" he called after me.

"Thanks," I replied. I didn't like someone knowing so damned much about me. I was sure I hadn't mentioned I was starting a new job that day. Maybe Nan had left word with him.

Her directions were accurate. I caught the Metro. What a difference from the subways in New York. I didn't think it could have been brighter inside—not that New York was bad. The subways there had improved dramatically over the years.

Georgetown was not exactly as I'd expected. The paper was in an old building, more a house than a business, probably built in the early 1900s. The smell of ink was prevalent when I walked in the door.

A little woman with flyaway red hair jumped from behind an old oak desk. "Here she is!" she yelled over her shoulder in a high-pitched, almost squeaky voice. We're so glad you're here." Turning, she grabbed me and gave me a hug.

"How do you do?" I said cautiously, not knowing what to expect next.

A man about my height, five and a half feet, with disheveled sandy hair, stepped from an office behind the redhead's desk. He smiled and held out his hand.

"Hi, I'm Ken Bentz. Welcome, Valerie. I see you've met Rosemary. I hope you had a good trip." His smile remained, and his eyes didn't waver from mine. I liked him immediately, a man who looked me in the eye.

"It was a great trip," I replied. "You have a very . . . quaint office."

"Yes, you might say that."

"I see you have an old printing press. Do you do demonstrations for tourists?"

"You might say that, too," he replied. "I hope you won't be disappointed you came. When we talked, you understood this was a small operation, right?" His eyebrows rose in question.

"Sure, and I can't wait to meet the rest of your staff and tour the facilities. I'm excited to get started."

"Well," he said, "you've met the staff, and you've seen the facilities, except your office, so we can get right down to work." He looked at me hesitantly and waited for my shock.

Had I heard him correctly? This couldn't be all. Sure, I knew this was a small operation, but—I must have been crazy to do this. What had I done? Maybe it wasn't too late to call Joe and get my old position back. I started to panic, and it must have shown.

Moving closer to me, Ken tried to be reassuring. "I know this is very different than what you're used to, but I guarantee you'll acquire additional skills, and I think you'll be happy here with what we're doing. After following your work for some time before I contacted you, I was sure we'd work well together. Remember, you've read *Washington in Depth*, and hopefully, the coverage was a determining factor in your decision to join us."

I had to admit, if only to myself, that he was right. I breathed deeply so I could speak. "I guess I was just expecting something different," I managed to get out.

"Let me show you your office. Then we'll go out for breakfast. Give us a chance to get acquainted." He led me into an office and said he would return shortly. He needed to speak to Rosemary about the morning schedule.

The office was much more than I expected, a complete contrast to the initial impression. It was huge for a reporter who was used to one cubicle among forty in a huge room. A large, dark oak desk with two filing cabinets next to it stood in the middle of the room. Filled oak bookcases lined the back wall. There was a large, black, well-worn, but totally comfortable leather swivel chair. When I sat in it, my initial shock disappeared, and I relaxed.

I hadn't expected an office of my own. Maybe this would be all right.

At breakfast, I learned Ken was not your typical boss. He was easy to talk with, and I learned we had a great deal in common. He was raised on a farm in upstate New York. His dad sold the farm when Ken decided to go into journalism. Although he never had an interest in pursuing farming as a career, he had an avid interest in the well-being of the farming industry and a genuine concern for the people involved in farming. "They're the thread that holds our country together," he said. "Farmers work the hardest of anyone in our country and receive the least in return, at least in money. Most farmers I know are among the most intelligent people I've met and definitely have more common sense than other elements of our society.

"I hope you're not too tired to get started right away," Ken continued. "There are some people I'd like you to meet and talk to tonight. We don't have a lot of time to waste. Events are moving at a rapid pace. We need to alert the country to what's happening before it's too late."

He sounded worse than Jay. "You and Jay have been talking," I said.

"Almost daily, by text, email, or phone," he said. "Jay's been here a few times, and I've also visited his farm. And, by tonight, you'll see the urgency."

We finished our breakfast, and instead of returning to the office, he took me on a tour of Washington. We took the trolley to the Capitol building and walked down Pennsylvania Avenue to the Lincoln Monument. Until I saw it in person, the size of it, I didn't know how awe-inspiring it could be. We walked back past the Holocaust Museum, the Mint, the Department of Agriculture, and the Smithsonian Museums. I was amazed at the number of white buildings, wondering how I could possibly ever visit anywhere as stirring as this.

The day sped by. Around 6 p.m., Ken said we'd be meeting some friends for dinner. "We'll be going to a hotel room and ordering in. It's not a good idea for these high-profile people to be seen with us. Although the paper is only being viewed as a bothersome nit right now, there's no point in tickling the monster, so to speak."

"I'm not dressed for dinner," I said, "especially if we're meeting with high-ranking officials."

"Don't worry about your dress. That's the last thing we need to think about. You're fine."

Spoken like a man, I thought. We entered the Metro and headed toward Alexandria. I expected we'd be going to a four-star hotel if these mystery people were as important as Ken had insinuated.

I was wrong. When we left the Metro, Ken hailed a cab and we traveled to a country road and modest bed and breakfast set on a side hill. We were shown to a small lobby and registered as Mr. and Mrs. John Smith. Ken put his arm around my shoulder and looked at me tenderly as he filled out the registration card. To the clerk, I'm sure we looked like a loving pair meeting for an affair. If he hadn't explained the necessity of his action on our ride, I most likely would've twisted his arm behind his back. I'd had self-defense training and had used it.

"We would like to sample several of the specialties from your dining room. Please be generous with your portions. Send several dinners and we'll sample them all. We'd also appreciate the suite facing the back of the house. Once our food is delivered, we'd like not to be disturbed." He again looked at me with a smile and handed the desk clerk several large bills.

What an actor, I thought. No one would've suspected anything beyond a tryst.

My new boss led me out the door, and we walked around behind the building. We entered through a double glass sliding door from outside. Pretty insecure room for high-ranking officials. Ken switched on the light.

"When are they coming?" I asked, hoping I could trust this man. I thought of Jay, and knew he wouldn't have set me up with anyone I couldn't trust. At least, I didn't think he would.

Holding his right hand up with this left index finger on his lips, Ken checked behind curtains, running his hand down the seams and along the hems. "The food will be here soon." He winked at me. Next, he took a small screwdriver from his pocket and loosened screws on the louvered, metal duct cover next to the bed. He looked and felt inside the duct, then replaced the cover. Next, he searched the two rooms and bathroom, running his hands over the walls. When he was convinced there was no bug, he relaxed and filled me in.

"I've used this place a lot. Because of the stories I've covered and the digging I've done, I'm watched. That means you'll be watched, too, as soon as they know who you are and that you work for me."

"Who are *they*?" I asked.

"To be honest, we don't know everyone who's involved. In time," he continued in a low voice. "They usually give up and leave me alone if they think my rendezvous is purely social, which is what they think about you, at least today. By tomorrow, that'll change."

I told him about the security guard at Nan's building, about my fear I was in some huge database.

"Don't worry," Ken said. "I know David Nare. Your information will be safe with him. He knows you're working with me. Do you think your friend would have room for you to stay at her place, at least for the time being? You'll be safe there."

"Yes, she's asked me to stay with her. If you think that's best, I don't have a problem with it." A hundred questions swirled in my mind. What did David Nare have to do with this? Why was Nan's building more secure than other buildings? How was this involved in what was going on with farms?

A light knock sounded at the sliding glass door—two taps, pause, three taps, pause, two taps. Ken slid the door open. Two men in dark suits with earpieces entered. They swept the room and reopened the sliding door. I had to sit down. I was not prepared for who stepped into the room.

It was Dan Daly, the vice president of the United States. Next through the door was a slight woman who looked like someone's grandmother, Beverly Leach, Deputy Secretary of Agriculture. I recognized John Banyon, the president's press secretary. Talk about high power! I was speechless. Ken invited them in, locked the doors, and closed the drapes. After introducing me, Ken noted I was *in* and could be trusted. Nothing would be seen in print until the right time. I wasn't sure exactly what he meant.

Looking directly at me and then at my boss with concern, the vice president began. "The timetable has been moved up. Within three months, the Department of Agriculture, other governmental agencies, and banks plan to own or be in control of two-thirds of the farmland in this country. The president has discouraged states from passing any legislation allowing dairy farmers additional time to meet loan payments. They're worried because of an upswing in grassroots efforts to support dairy farmers. People are beginning to wonder why the legislators won't help farmers.

"Those behind the takeover can't take a chance the state legislators will be pressured into voting for anything giving farmers more money. It's becoming public knowledge that the government is allowing and even encouraging imports of tremendous amounts of butter and other dairy products, vegetables, and fruits that don't have to meet the quality standards to which US farmers must adhere. The general public is suspicious of why, when our dairy farmers are in trouble, we would import products and undercut them more."

John Banyon broke in. "Tomorrow, the president is announcing the success of experimental state-run farms, having shown a profit for the second quarter this year. It's the beginning of a push to persuade the public to believe state farms can outperform independently owned farms. The theory is to convince people cheaper food will be available if farms are state run."

"Of course," Beverly Leach added, "they're not giving details of how the profits are being made."

"That's where you come in, Ken and Valarie," the vice president said.

"You'll have a pass for the press conference."

A knock sounded at the interior door of the suite. Everyone was silent and moved into the bedroom. Ken shut the door behind them. "Thanks. Please leave the cart. I'll put it in the hall after I set the table. Did you bring a tablecloth?"

"Yes, sir," the waiter replied. "It's on the cart. If you don't mind me asking, how are you going to eat all this?"

"My wife and I like to sample different meals," Ken laughed. "Maybe you won't mind if I ask *you* something."

"Sir?" he said.

"How much do you make an hour?"

"Fifteen dollars plus tips," he replied.

"Well, how about three hours' wages for a tip?" Ken said. "You didn't see us here, right?"

"Thank you, sir," he said, opening the door, obviously grateful for Ken's generosity.

As soon as the waiter left, Ken opened the door to the hall, making sure no one was there. Then he opened the bedroom door and said, "Soup's on." He set the table and took paper plates, napkins, and silver from his luggage. Everyone fixed his plate and ate a little before the conversation continued.

"I imagine you have questions," Ken said, looking at me.

"Who, exactly, is behind all of this?"

"That's a difficult question to answer," the vice president said. "There are so many people involved in this deception against the American people, I'm not even sure it can be stopped. But if I don't try, I wouldn't be able to live with myself. I have children and grandchildren. I want them to be able to grow up with freedom. There are so many greedy people entangled in the conspiracy, it may be too late to stop the progression. We aren't sure of all the people involved, but we know there are government officials, bankers, industrialists, and other countries involved."

"What exactly is their end goal?" I asked.

"As near as we can tell," Ken said, "the idea is to get all or most of the farmland in this country under one umbrella, out of the hands of individual ownership."

"What is the object of that?" I asked.

Leach answered this time. "Think about what can be charged for food if it's being sold by one entity, no competition. Our food prices will double or triple in order for a few to fatten their pockets. Everyone out for themselves."

"Is there any way all the small farms going out of business and the farmland being scooped up by investors is the result of a natural progression of change that would happen no matter what we did?" I asked.

"No," most said in unison. Nervous laughter ensued. The vice president continued. "We are all in different positions in the government. We have either overheard"—he looked at Leach—"or have been privy to meetings in which discussions have gone on about bringing the country's food under one umbrella so they can help the American people. The people in government involved are not led by their intelligence. They're being used. Ken can help you out with a list of the government officials who are definitely involved either directly or indirectly."

"Tomorrow, you'll meet people in the industry who have more information from their side," Banyon said. "I think it's time to call it a night. See you all tomorrow. Want to try the second location, Ken?"

"That's good, but we'd better make it 10 p.m. Val will be more visible tomorrow. We'll have to be more careful," Ken said.

Everyone agreed, and the security guards slipped out the glass door. They returned in a few minutes, and the one I thought must be the lead gave a small forward shake of his head. The vice president followed, then the press secretary and Leach. Ken turned to me and said, "Well, what did you think of your first day? Exciting enough for you?"

"You might have warned me," I said, but knew there was no way I could have prepared myself to meet the vice president of the United States.

"Better that it be a surprise," he laughed. "Let's get you back to your condo. Ready to playact again?"

"Sure," I said.

When we got to the desk, Ken said, "I'm afraid something has come up, and we need to get back to the city."

"Yes, Mr. Smith," the clerk said like he didn't believe a word of it. Ken put his arm around my shoulder and we walked out.

"You weren't very convincing," I said.

"The more he thinks this is a tryst, the less he'll think it could be anything else."

"I get it. So where's the second meeting place?"

"Tomorrow night," he answered without telling me. "You don't need to come in until noon tomorrow. It will be another late night."

"What time will you be in?"

"Probably around nine."

"I'll see you then," I said.

When Ken dropped me at the apartment, Nan had just gotten in.

"You keep late hours," I said.

"You too," she answered. "Been out to dinner?"

"A working dinner."

"How was your first day?"

"Interesting."

"Come on, tell me more."

"Can't talk about a story when I'm working it—a rule of mine and most other reputable journalists."

"But I already know what you're working on."

"I wasn't *working* it when I was home. How was your day? Want to tell me about the case you're working on?"

"You know I can't do that," Nan said.

"Of course I do. That's why we have to agree not to discuss work."

"Got it. I'm beat anyway. How about you?"

"Yeah, I'm going to turn in. I'll see you for breakfast in the morning?" I said.

"Yes, I don't have to be in until nine tomorrow."

CHAPTER 13

The next day, Ken and I attended the press conference at which John Banyon announced the success of government-run farms. While other reporters asked fairly inane questions, Ken asked where he might get a copy of the books that showed in which specific ways they were successful, including where the government farms obtained their corn, hay, and other supplies, how much they paid for them, what the wages were, etc. He also asked if comparing the government farms with independently run farms was like comparing apples to oranges, since the government farms were given help beyond what independent farms were supplied.

The press secretary said he'd check on those facts and see that Ken received the information as it was available, but Ken had managed to get some thoughts out there. Now, hopefully, others would begin questioning.

I spent the rest of the day in the office, researching everything I could find about the government-run farms and filling out right-to-know forms to obtain more detail about them. The location of each farm was on the government website, and there were a number of them within driving distance.

Ken and I ended up working in the same office. He had been willing to give me his office for my exclusive use, but I insisted we could work in the office together. By moving a few files into the outer office with Rosemary, we easily fit in a smaller wooden table that was more than adequate for me. I put a half-sized file cabinet under one end of the table, which served as drawers for supplies, so Ken was able to maintain his own desk.

He provided me with a MacBook, although I told him I'd be happy using my personal one. He said that business should be separate and he should provide me with my working materials. Under no circumstances was I to use my personal computer for business. My old paper, the much larger city paper, had no problem with me paying for my supplies and using my own computer.

I looked at Ken, and realized after less than two full days on the job, I had a great deal of respect for my new boss. "Ken, I'd like to visit some of these government farms tomorrow. Want to go?"

"Good luck," he said. "I've tried, but was told they don't allow visitors for fear of people bringing disease to the cows."

"That's ridiculous. People visit farms all the time. If I can get us in, will you come with me?"

"Knock yourself out," he said. "Do you know where to call?"

"I know where I'm going to start," I said. I checked online—I wasn't sure Pete Engle was still a representative from New York, but if he was, I was certain I could talk him into getting me onto some of the government farms. Pete was the father of one of my fellow basketball friends from college. I'd spent quite a bit of time at their house and even went to the Assembly in Albany when he was an assemblyman. Since his daughter Becky and I went to school in Albany, he'd occasionally take us to dinner. After that, he was elected to the United States House of Representatives.

"Hello, my name is Valarie Jacobs. May I speak to Representative Engle, please?"

"To what does this pertain?" the assistant said.

"This is Val—I'm a friend of his daughter's."

It was only a minute until I heard, "Val, how are you?"

"Well, I'm in Washington, and I was hoping we could get together for lunch."

"Of course. Are you busy right now, or have you already eaten? I didn't realize it was so late."

"As a matter of fact, I've been working and haven't had lunch yet. How's that little Irish pub near the Capitol? I don't remember the name."

"The Dubliner," he said. "In an hour?"

"Perfect. Mind if I bring my new boss?" I asked, looking at Ken with my eyebrows raised to confirm his consent.

"I'd love to meet him—or is it her?"

"Ken Bentz of *Washington In Depth*," I said.

"I would love to meet Mr. Bentz. I've heard about him and read his paper. I also heard the questions he asked Banyon today. I may have some questions myself for Mr. Bentz."

When we met at the pub, I ordered my usual shepherd's pie, and we all ate while making small talk. I filled Mr. Engle in on what I'd been up to, and he let me know how Becky was doing. When we finished with the chitchat, I brought up the subject of the government-run farms. Engle looked up quickly when I mentioned them.

"Are you investigating that?" he asked, looking at Ken and me.

I had already told Ken I knew Engle to be an honest person whose main concern was the country, and that I was sure he could be trusted. Ken bowed his head toward me, indicating I should fill him in. I started at the beginning and told him pretty much everything I knew, except the attendees at last night's meeting. I didn't think it was my place to give up the vice president of the United States.

Engle lowered his head and shook it from side to side.

I misread his nod. "You don't think this is possible?"

"Oh, quite the opposite. I've been suspicious of those farms. Serving on the Budget Committee, I've seen discrepancies that no one seems able or willing to explain. Having spent much of my political career trying to help farmers get a fair price for their products, I have some knowledge of how hard it is to remain in the black running a farm. The government-run farms consistently make money, no matter what the price of milk being paid to the farmer—or in this case, the government. Something is wrong. It's not possible."

"Do you have any idea how they're doing it and who's pushing the government farms on your end?" Ken asked.

"Not yet. I know the books we're getting can't be accurate. I'm guessing there are two sets. Whoever is behind this will have to be able to explain the actual cost of everything to their bosses. When they have control of the majority of the farms in the country, they need to know what they have to charge people for the goods in order to make a profit. They're in this for the money. There's no doubt in my mind—money and power. Think of the power they'll have when they control the food of 310 million people in the United States. Since we export so many products, there'll be worldwide effects."

"I think we should consider meeting in private next time, Representative Engle," Ken said. "Don't look over your shoulder, and Val, don't look up, but we're being watched. A woman at the counter, second from the end by the door. Notice her when we leave so you can spot her if she's tailing you in the future. Let's make this look like a real light social lunch. Follow my lead on the way out."

Ken waved to the waitress for the check. We laughed as we left. When we were behind the woman who'd been observing us, Ken said, "We'd love to do that interview with you, Representative Engle. Our readers would like to learn what's involved in your duties as Chairman of the Budget Committee. We plan to do an interview with all committee chairmen as part of our educational component."

"I'd be glad to give you that interview. If you'd submit your specific questions to my assistant a few days prior to the interview, I can make sure I'm totally prepared to answer them fully," Engle said.

When we walked outside, I said, "That should convince those watching that we're doing a routine article."

"Hopefully," Ken said. "You might keep an eye out, though, Representative Engle. Let me know if you see anything suspicious. If I were you, I'd keep your questions about the farms to a minimum."

"Who can get me onto the farms?" I asked Engle.

"I can do that, no problem. As a past resident of my district, I can give you a pass. Visits are discouraged, but representatives and senators have passes to 'show off' the facilities. The powers that be would like people to think the government farms are the answer to lower food prices and good-quality food. Because they're supposed to be using only organic feeds and no antibiotics or growth hormones, they have the support of those interested in organic. However, because I've seen the high production figures, I question the claims. Would you both like to visit the farms?"

"I don't think I should go," Ken said. "Valarie knows more what to look for. Do you have an aide who could take her? I don't want her out there alone. We might be able to get her in and out before anyone knows who she is."

"Sure. Jason Kennedy is an assistant of mine who is aware of my concerns. He can be trusted. He's the son of a friend of mine, and I've known him all his life, so you can be free to ask him anything, Val," he said, turning to me.

"Thanks, Mr. Engle," I said. "Would it be possible to go tomorrow?" I was anxious.

"What about an hour from now?" he replied. "Jason will meet you, let's say at the train station entrance near the Capitol, in one hour?"

"I'll make sure she's not followed," Ken said.

"You'll have to sign in at the farm and show ID, so you'll have to use your own name. But you should be fine. By the time your name flows through the computer system and someone checks it, you'll have whatever information you need. By going late afternoon and evening, you might find employees more willing to talk to you, not so many bosses around."

"Okay, let's get you to the train station, and I'll distract our tails," Ken said.

He didn't say how he'd distract them, but Mr. Engle hurried me into his Acura, then jumped in himself, and his driver took off before I could think what was happening. In the rearview mirror, I could see a car pull out and follow us until Ken's Prius pulled into the side of it.

"Woah!" I said. "Ken doesn't monkey around. I wonder if he's always been a newspaper man."

"If you check his background, he was off the grid for a few years. Might have been CIA, but that's just a guess," Engle said. "He can definitely handle himself."

I was sure my mouth gaped open, but I didn't respond. Did everyone know everybody's business in Washington?

"As long as we can keep a tail from us, we'll meet Jason at the train station parking lot. He'll drive you to a farm. The visit should give you an idea of what's going on. Be careful what you ask. Most of the workers probably don't know a whole lot of what's going on. Jason knows who the bosses are, so he might be able to get you a little time with those he thinks will talk."

"Thanks so much for this," I said. "You'll be okay, right?"

"You're welcome, Val. You be careful. I'll be fine. I don't want you hurt, and if this goes as far as I think it does, they'll stop at nothing. There's a lot of money and power at stake."

"I won't be foolish," I assured him.

We met Jason in the north parking lot at the train station. After Engle's driver made sure we weren't being followed, Jason drove us out of Georgetown toward Virginia. He wasn't very talkative, but by that point I was happy for a little respite. It was comfortable to feel like I didn't have to speak. When we were about five miles from the farm, Jason told me to act like a tourist, not a reporter. He said he had a small recorder in his pocket so it wouldn't be necessary to take notes.

"Shouldn't I ask any questions?" I said.

"The staff knows me. They also know how they're supposed to answer questions. I'll follow my usual routine, telling you information as we go through and letting them add facts as they usually do. There'll be one difference. As I finish with each person, I'll tell him that you're a silent investor and he should answer as if he were talking to the attorney general. We think he's one of the major participants, so you should get some honest answers. We've done it before, and for some reason, these people don't talk to each other much. This has been one of our major sources of information. No one seems to catch on."

"Got it," I said.

We drove up to what looked like a prison. Barbed-wire fence curled around the top of a high wall as far as I could see. There was even a tower with guards in a parapet. Jason drove to a guardhouse outside the fence. A uniformed woman walked out with a clipboard. Jason and I were asked for our IDs, which we handed over. She told us we could retrieve them when we left. We were handed high rubber boots that we were to put on before we left the car and turn in when we went through the gate to retrieve our IDs. Then we were directed to a parking lot to our left.

Beyond the large lot was a white cement block building. Outside, there were two wide white pails filled with liquid. Jason told me we had to wash our boots with the liquid. "It's a disinfectant so we don't bring any disease into the barn with us," he said.

After washing the boots with a long brush, we went through a house-type door next to an approximately fifteen-foot-tall, twenty-foot-wide overhead door. Two huge milk tanks took up most of the space in the room. I learned they were each capable of holding 180,000 gallons of milk. We walked through the first room into another with two state-of-the-art rotary milking parlors. At home, our whole barn, cows and all, couldn't house the parlors. My brother still milked in a stanchion barn with hoses that carried the milk from the milking machines attached directly to the cows into the milk house. The milk dropped into a thousand-gallon tank. What a difference from this modern equipment.

The cows practically led themselves into the rotary, which constantly moved at a slow rate. Two workers at different positions behind the cows on the rotary washed the cows' udders with a spray wand of disinfectant and wiped them with a blue paper towel. The worker then put the claw on the cows' teats. After the cows were milked, the machines dropped off automatically, but not to the floor. They were suctioned into stainless steel, box-like containers to the left of each cow. Looking up, I saw small monitors above each cow that registered the number of pounds produced during that milking. At the floor level was a laser light that recorded the cows' numbers from the ankle bracelets attached above their hooves.

I was told the information was forwarded to a central computer in the office behind glass windows overlooking the parlor. "I'd love to get a look at that computer," I whispered to Jason. After the cows were milked, the worker sprayed the udders with the wand connected to disinfectant, and the cows moved out on their own when released. An antiseptic smell filled the air. It reminded me of the iodine-smelling dip my brother used to use on the cows at home.

"Before we go to the cow barns to see what they do after being milked, let's go up to the office," Jason said to our tour guide.

"Certainly, Mr. Kennedy. Go ahead. I'll join you when I can."

"Sounds good," I said. As we walked away from the guide, I continued talking to Jason. "I can't imagine how much all these apparatuses cost. Do you know how long it takes to break even?"

"No one that I can find has actually seen those figures. Representative Engle has been asking those questions for quite some time. He's been stonewalled. That's what we need you and Ken to find out. Common sense tells us this machinery can't pay for itself if purchased by the ordinary farmer. We're not sure where the money came from to buy this. We suspect some of the companies that manufactured the equipment provided it free or at least at discounted prices with the provision that they'll receive the government contracts when there are more government farms across the country. Then the companies' owners will also get rich. They know the average farmer can't afford to purchase this and make money from producing milk."

He continued, "Jay probably told you about the program to bring European farmers who had cash to invest into the country. They couldn't even make a profit."

"You know Jay?"

"Sure. He's been in touch with us for quite some time."

This was unreal. How did Jay have time to be in contact with all these people in Washington and across the country? Jay, from a little town in upstate New York. I'd think about that later.

"Those farmers were encouraged to purchase machines that were much more than they could afford," Jason continued. "That's one reason they went out of business so fast. They were led to believe they'd be able to make their payments with the money they made from the milk produced. Then the price was set so low they couldn't pay back their loans."

"I know my brother certainly couldn't afford to buy this sophisticated equipment."

"The people trying to control the farmland underestimated the stamina and intelligence of the farm family community," Jason said. "They thought almost all the small farms would be out of business by the middle of last year. As hard as the powers that be have tried to drive the farmers out of business, however, the agrarians have hung on. Most didn't rush into buying new equipment and getting bigger when they didn't want to. To be honest, it was mostly those who left the farm and went to colleges that were deemed excellent for their cutting-edge agricultural practices who overextended themselves and lost their families' farms. They forgot to incorporate what their parents taught them about not going too far into debt. The old-time farmers knew they had to sock away the money in good times to help them float through the low-milk-price times.

"Anyway, many of the small farmers have hung on, so we think the plan is to do something drastic to drive out the ones still in business. Let me show you more."

We stepped out of the milking parlor structure. Cows were housed in long, free-stall buildings with open sides as far as I could see. Sun shone on the silver tin roofs, requiring me to shade my eyes from the reflection.

"Carmen will take us," Jason said, pointing to a golf cart next to the first building. Carmen held out his hand to Jason, then to me. His smile was wide. Could this be a person who actually enjoyed his job? The grin never left his face as he drove up and down between the barns, pointing out how the cows were fed and the bedding was blown in to soften the concrete pads. Then he drove us to what he called the hospital building, where his face became even more animated.

Carmen explained this was his real passion. He told us he was taking classes at a nearby college, where he was studying to become a vet tech. The hospital was amazing. It was a huge, circular building, the outer walls all glass with steel supports at approximately eight-foot intervals.

First, the future vet tech drove us around the entire building. Then we entered. It was unbelievable. It looked like a real hospital, with what must have been the latest equipment. Carmen showed us through, eager to point out the ultrasound and other radiological devices. I'd have been happy to have this equipment in my own physician's office.

The more I saw, the more I knew this operation couldn't possibly make money while purchasing all this equipment. I made a mental note to re-search the cost of the ultrasound and other medical devices. When Carmen left us momentarily to check a cow in an isolated, glassed-in stall, I spoke the model numbers to make sure they were recorded on Jason's phone.

Carmen returned us to the parking lot, where we started our trip to another farm. We toured three farms, and I saw more of the same: expensive equipment, topnotch dairy cows, all-new buildings, and the best technology money could buy.

Before we arrived at the third farm, night had fully descended. After that visit, Jason drove me to Nan's apartment and I entered through the front. There was a different doorman on, so I had to show identification and answer several questions to assure him who I was. Nan hadn't arrived home yet. I was exhausted to the point of not even wanting to think.

CHAPTER 14

When I arrived at the office the next morning, Rose greeted me with her usual jovial welcome. "Ken had to go out, but he'd like you to meet him at noon on the Capitol steps if you don't have appointments. I'm to let him know."

"Of course, I'll meet him," I said. "What's up?"

"He didn't say. Just asked that you meet him."

"Of course. I'll be doing some research if you need me," I said, walking into my office.

"Do you need any help?" she asked.

"I'm trying to find how much was paid for equipment on government-owned farms and where the money came from."

"I can help you, then. I've been tracing the funds. So far, everything I've found points to the Department of Agriculture. I have its budget on my desk." She pawed through the stack of papers until she found the correct folder and handed it to me. "You'll notice this department is loaded with 'discretionary' funds—not that the other departments aren't, but the Ag Department could justify these expenses easier than the others. Look at the amount."

"Holy . . ." I didn't finish my thought. I couldn't believe undesignated funds could be allotted to a governmental department in such an extraordinary amount. I would have thought the oversight committees would approve only necessary expenditures. After all, the money did belong to the American people.

Poring over the material Rosemary had researched, I realized what an asset she was to Ken. I was so engrossed in the material, she had to remind me to leave for my appointment.

Walking up the steps of the Capitol, I took a deep breath as a surge of patriotism ran through me. Then my face felt hot and my arms stiffened. Everyone in this building should have been working for the people of the United States, not against them. How did they get turned around once they were elected? Money? Power? Greed?

Ken stood near the top step talking with Representative Engle. He signaled me forward. After a greeting to Engle and Ken, I waited for them to continue, looking around to see if there was anyone watching.

"It's fine," Engle said. "There'll be an article in the paper written by Ken about me and my fight for an unrelated bill that's coming up in the House. No one will know our relationship is anything but publicity. Everyone is after it, even if it comes from Ken," he said.

"Thanks a lot," Ken said.

"What's up?" I asked, not able to wait while they joked around. My feet were practically dancing waiting for them to tell me what was going on.

"I need you to go to the House during the session this afternoon," Ken said. "Make yourself visible, and take notes. Be especially aggressive with your note-taking when Representatives Smith from Nebraska, Clark from South Carolina, and Tallman from Washington are speaking. I want them to know you're onto them."

"Am I?" I said. "Since when?"

"They're big players involved in the demise of the individually owned farms and the establishment of national farms. They're probably closest to the president. They'll be watching you. They probably think we have no idea they're involved. It's time we want them to know. We'll have some people watching them today after session, and by their actions, we hope they'll draw out some others."

"Maybe we should sit down later. You can tell me just who's involved so I don't say the wrong thing to the wrong person." My words were curter than I meant, but Ken didn't seem to mind.

"See what I meant?" said Engle, smiling at Ken. "I told you she'd stand up for herself if necessary."

A young man approached. "The session will be opening soon, Representative Engle," he said.

"Thanks, Ethan. Valerie, this is one of my aides, Ethan Scott. Ethan, Valerie Jacobs, a new reporter with *Washington In Depth*. She'll be working with Ken."

"Good to meet you, Ms. Jacobs. I hope you'll enjoy Washington. Perhaps I can show you around town, help you learn your way."

Before I could answer, Engle said, "That's an excellent idea, Ethan. It'd be a good idea for you to meet Valerie after the session and return her to her apartment in Georgetown. Keep an eye out for anyone who might try to follow you."

"Be glad to, sir," Ethan said.

"I'm perfectly capable of getting myself back to my apartment without help from anyone." Who did they think I was, a little kid? I'd worked in Los Angeles for two years without a babysitter. I certainly didn't need one now. Before anyone could answer, I thought about what Nate had said, about how dangerous this could be, but I wasn't giving in.

"Sorry, Val," Engle said. "Just trying to keep you safe. Perhaps you'd accept Ethan's lift home just this once, and he'll bring the list of people we know are involved."

"I'm sorry, too, Mr. Engle. I'm just used to doing things on my own."

"Then just this once, it's alright?"

"Yes," I said. Turning to Scott, I said, "And please, call me Valerie. Where shall I meet you?"

"Representative Engle arranged for your seat in the gallery. I'll be there by the end of the session."

"Okay, then. I guess we'd better go in. Ethan will show you to your seat," Engle said.

"Please, call me before you come to work in the morning," Ken said. "Depending on what happens after your show this afternoon, we may want to meet somewhere other than the office."

"Will do," I said. I followed Scott into the chamber and took my seat.

All in all, it was a pretty boring afternoon. Smith, Clark, and Tallman all appeared to be pompous asses, who just wanted to pat themselves on their backs and boast about what they were doing for the people. What else was new? Putting Congress on TV might have been the worst offender in slowing down the legislators' accomplishments. Instead of encouraging them to get something done, it provided a forum to tell the people how great they were. I did as I'd been told, taking notes furiously when they spoke, sometimes looking up and feigning interest, determining who was watching me.

I didn't know every face by name. I'd have to study the legislators that night. It was important I learned them all. If I was going to work in DC, I needed to know the actors. There'd been no presentations about the agricultural industry or the national farms. I guessed most of that was done behind the cameras so citizens didn't become curious.

After the session, I waited about twenty minutes for Ethan to show. Representatives and spectators continued to file out. My right heel bobbed up and down, and my thumbnail moved to the left side of my teeth. When only a few remained talking to each other, I'd had enough. I saw no reason to wait any longer. Nothing bad had happened to me since I'd been in Washington, other than being followed when I was with Mr. Engle. I found it difficult to remember to call him Representative Engle after knowing him for so many years before.

It was already after five, and Ken hadn't expected me to return to the office. I paused to look out over the lawns. No one suspicious in sight. There weren't many cool July days like this in Washington—probably around seventy degrees, nice breeze. I decided to walk until I got tired, then I'd take the Metro toward Nan's apartment.

I was enjoying the evening, walking down Pennsylvania Avenue. Before I knew it, I was at Freedom Plaza, only a short distance from the White House. Glancing at my phone, I noticed it was already six o'clock. I pulled up the Metro schedule. I'd have to turn around on Pennsylvania and go down to the right past the Old Post Office toward Constitution Avenue. The Federal Triangle Station was located in the Ariel Rios Building.

I turned abruptly and noticed there was a man fairly close behind me. He put his head down. Too late. I'd seen his face and he knew it. Maybe I was imagining that he'd been following me, but he looked shocked that I'd turned. I took out a compact that I kept in my purse for such occasions. I wasn't one to primp. I was a wash-and-go type, no makeup. I brushed my hair once in the morning. That was usually it for the day. Worrying about what I looked like all the time wouldn't get me anywhere in the journalism field. Hard work would.

He turned and followed me. My intuition had been correct. I slowed down and pretended to read the mall map indicating the stores located in the buildings.

When I stopped, he pretended to look in windows. I decided I might as well walk into the station and make a break for home. The station was filling with commuters, and I knew he wouldn't be able to keep up with me. I was used to losing tails. I rounded a corner and was able to skirt into a ladies' room before he could get around the same corner. I used the facilities. Who knew when I'd have another opportunity?

Exiting the restroom, I was surprised to see him across the hall waiting. His eyes met mine, but he didn't look away this time, just had a hint of a smirk on his face. He'd outsmarted me. Even with his red cap with the white W on the front pulled down slightly, I could see his clear blue eyes. He wore a plain blue T-shirt, worn blue jeans, and what looked like brand-new trail running shoes. I was pretty sure the W on the hat was a team logo. I went for the shock value, raised my phone, and shot before he could look away. In hindsight, taking his picture was probably not the most brilliant move. He'd have to catch me.

I should've called Representative Engle when Scott didn't show. Oh, well, too late. I had to lose him in the crowd. I decided to head for a restaurant in my neighborhood, just in case I couldn't lose him. I didn't need to lead him to Nan's apartment and get her involved. Although, by then, I supposed whoever was having me followed probably knew where I was staying.

Trying to lose myself in the growing commuter crowd, I picked up speed, descended the lighted steps, and walked onto the platform. There was a magenta engine heading into the station. I determined to take it if I could get through the crowd ahead of my tail. At that point I didn't particularly care if he got on the train, too. I was disappointed in myself. I should have lost him when I'd gone into the ladies' room. I squeezed between two people into the door of a car as it was closing. I turned, looked out the side window, and smiled when I saw him still on the platform. He looked thoroughly pissed.

Tired and not feeling like taking any more chances, I got off at the next stop, where I grabbed a bus and took the DC Circulator down M Street to Wisconsin Avenue to Q Street. I stopped at Costello's Restaurant and picked up a penne pasta dish with marinara and hot sausage. I'd share with Nan.

Turning my back toward the door at Nan's apartment building, I pushed, but a doorman I didn't recognize stepped out and stopped me. "I'm sorry, Miss, but I need your ID. I'm new, so I need to check everyone. Please understand. I'll lose my job if I don't."

"Of course," I said. Juggling my backpack and the dinner, I took out my

ID card. The chucklehead didn't even offer to hold some of my load while I struggled to balance everything. He wouldn't last long here.

"I'm sorry—I don't have you on the list, Miss Jacobs."

"I'm there," I replied, not at all concerned. I knew he'd find it. New guy, a little slow.

"I'm sorry, ma'am. Your name's not here, and this ID number's been reported stolen. I'll have to detain you until the head of security gets here."

It didn't take me long to realize either this guy didn't work here or he'd been given erroneous information. I wasn't successful at convincing him there'd been a mistake; he insisted on calling the head of security, or that was what he said. I couldn't take the chance on being turned over to the bad guys, whoever they actually were, so I said, "Forget it. I'll come back later, when my friend returns and can vouch for me." I started moving away, but he grabbed my arm and twisted.

I turned into him and stomped on his foot. I surprised him and he dropped his arm. I threw the food at him, turned, and ran as fast as I could. Glancing back, I saw him half limping, half running after me. I ducked into the park across the street and lost him. After running through the trees, I came out on the north end. I caught a cab and gave the driver the address of the newspaper. Maybe Ken was still in the office. If not, I planned to bother him at his apartment upstairs.

With commuter traffic, the cab ride took over half an hour. Instead of taking the turn that would land us on 30th Street, which eventually ran onto Cambridge Place, putting us in front of the paper, the driver turned in the opposite direction. She probably thought I was a tourist and was trying to run up the fare.

"You were supposed to turn right. Are you new?" I said, letting her know she couldn't mess with me.

"No, ma'am. My dispatcher signaled me. There's a fire on Cambridge I need to avoid. We'll come in at the other end, off 31st."

I had a bad feeling. Cambridge Place wasn't that long. "Do you know where the fire is?"

"Dispatcher didn't say."

"Please, hurry."

"Yes, ma'am."

It seemed to take forever. I knew for sure when we turned onto Cambridge. Smoke poured from the windows above the paper, and the acrid smell of wood burning penetrated the cab. "Let me out here," I said. Handing the driver a twenty, I sprinted the length of the street toward the paper. I could see Ken standing outside talking to a policeman. He saw me coming and waved me toward the café across the street.

I crossed, took a seat at the counter in front of the window, and waited. Before long, Ken came in, went to the counter, and ordered two coffees. He didn't look at me but came close to my table as he walked out, pausing only momentarily. "Meet me in the research room at the Georgetown Public Library in an hour," he said, still looking ahead but leaving one of the coffees on the counter in front of me.

I waited a few minutes, then made my way to the street to hail a cab.

In the research room, I opened my laptop and searched for any news on the fire. The local stations had already picked it up and were touting it as a possible arson at the controversial paper site. No duh, I thought.

Ken arrived about eight. "Over here," he said, opening a door with a sign that read "Private."

I followed him into a small conference room. "I use this occasionally when meeting with a source. The librarian is a friend of mine and never sees me or whomever I'm meeting."

"Convenient," I said.

"Anyway, the fire didn't do much damage, other than a little water. I've already called the insurance company. They're contacting a restoration crew and they'll be there first thing in the morning. We won't miss an issue. Don't come in the office tomorrow, though, until after 3 p.m. I'm told it'll be fine by then. We've canceled the meeting for tonight."

"I was actually hoping to spend the night in the office. There was a problem at my building."

"What?" Ken asked.

"A different doorman was there. At first the replacement wouldn't let me in, said I wasn't on the tenant list. When I tried to leave, he grabbed me."

"How did you escape?" Ken asked, his face showing concern.

"I stomped on his foot, threw food in his face, and ran into the park. I caught a cab, and here I am. There was also someone following me from the House to the Metro this afternoon."

"How did that happen? Wasn't Scott with you?"

"He never showed," I said. "I told you and Mr. Engle I could take care of myself. By the way, where will you stay? I'm sure there's extensive damage to your apartment, the obvious target of the arson."

"How do you know it was arson?"

"Cab driver told me," I laughed. "Kidding." I pointed to my computer. "Speculation because of the 'controversial nature of the paper.'"

"Figures," he said. "I'll take you back to your building. I'm sure your assaulter is long gone, but we need to make sure the actual doorman at your building isn't lying wounded somewhere. As the timetable heats up, I'm pretty sure these people will do whatever it takes to accomplish their goals. To date, we haven't had any physical assaults. Obviously, that's changed."

"Where will you stay?" I asked.

"Dory, the librarian, will put me up," he said. "I think we'd better check on Scott before we do anything else." He pulled out his iPhone.

"This is Ken Bentz. Representative Engle, please." He didn't form the request as a question, sure that his call would be taken.

Ken spoke with Engle, but I couldn't tell what information he was getting until he signed off. "Scott was detained by the police—supposedly a case of mistaken identity that was cleared up shortly after you left the House. Engle's been worried. He's had people out looking for you."

"Sorry," I said. "I probably should have called him when Scott didn't show up."

"Obviously, these people know you well enough to know you wouldn't do that, that you'd take it in stride and go off by yourself. Please, don't do that again. If you want to venture out by yourself, at least let one of us know where you're heading."

"No problem," I said, not meaning a word of it.

Ken shook his head. He knew I didn't mean it. Then again, he wouldn't have hired me if I'd been a wuss.

Ken flagged a cab and rode with me to Nan's apartment. The regular night doorman was on. It turned out he'd been relieved by another doorman and called to the manager's office downtown. When he'd arrived, he'd been told he wasn't summoned. The manager proceeded to write him up for leaving his post without permission. He wasn't happy. Ken left me at the apartment and presumably took the cab on to Dory's.

Nan was home by the time I returned. Having thrown my dinner away, I was happy to see she had fixed a kale and apple salad for us. I hadn't realized how hungry I was.

CHAPTER 15

The next day, I worked from Nan's apartment until two, then grabbed a cab to the office. I didn't have the patience for dealing with people on the Metro or ducking in and out of buildings avoiding a tail. If someone wanted to follow me by cab, let him.

I was at the office in less than fifteen minutes. Black stains ran down the outside of the normally stark white building, giving it a cage-like appearance. Ken met me at the door and practically pulled Rose and me into his office. A slight smoke smell lingered, but the walls were clean and nothing in the office appeared to have been affected by the fire.

"How's your apartment, Ken?" I said.

"Not cleared for occupancy yet," he said, "but that's not important. Things are heating up," he said. "Did you see the news at noon?"

"No, what's going on?"

"The president announced that the government dairy farms were an astounding success. He claimed the well-run farms could produce a pure product for much less money than independently run farms. The secretary of agriculture showed charts glowing with low-cost production figures for feed, equipment, and supplies. He even insinuated the more government farms there were, the lower the cost of milk. He also set the stage for government-run truck farms next."

"This morning, I made a chart of the people we know are involved and assumed who else might be," I said. "I used political donation records as well as news releases showing legislators, businesspeople, and lobbyists together. I have the feeling they are so secure they aren't careful when they meet."

"The vice president called me this morning when he heard about the fire," Ken said. "He wants to meet with us tonight. I called Jay last night. He'll be flying in for the meeting. Now let's take a look at your list."

Ken hadn't considered a few people I thought were suspicious. "I knew your fresh eyes would be a plus," he said. "I never would have considered Jennifer Loose to be mixed up in this. What makes you consider her?"

"Let's see," I said, going back to my notes. "She's a representative from Iowa, right?"

"Yes, and I always thought she was pretty straight. I've never come across her name involved in anything questionable."

"In January, her husband and children were on a ski vacation in Vail. Their pictures were all over the papers, causing me to wonder where Representative Loose was spending her time, especially since Congress was on break. Seemed like she should be with them. I pulled all the names of people you said were definitely involved and plugged Jennifer's name in with each of them. A picture of her and Richard Crose having dinner together showed up in a little local newspaper in Chicopee, Georgia. Although it didn't look like anything was out of the ordinary, could have been a business dinner, I checked hotels in the area and found they had registered, separately, of course, at a small bed and breakfast in Chicopee. Coincidentally, he's an agricultural equipment lobbyist."

"They could have been there on legitimate business. Did you determine if there was an event or legislation pending explaining why they were there? Maybe one of the services picked up the picture and ran it elsewhere."

"Checked. Couldn't find a thing on either. It could be just a tryst, but who knows what's up in Chicopee?"

"The companies Crose represents are big players," Ken said. "If Jennifer's involved with him personally, you can bet she's involved politically. I want you to go to Chicopee and poke around. See what you can find out. There has to be something to take an operator like Crose to that location. I'll stake a lot that it's not just personal. He doesn't really care who finds out his personal business. He's as sleazy as they come and doesn't care who knows it. His wife divorced him last year, so he has no reason to hide anything."

"Maybe Jennifer does, though," I said.

"I really hope you find she's not involved. She's been one of the people in this town who has been able to maintain her family and stay true to her constituents." Ken turned back to Rose. "Make a reservation to Chicopee for Valerie, tomorrow, as early as possible, and try to get her back the same night." Then, turning back to me, he asked, "Will that be enough time?"

"Should be," I said, "at least to find out if there's anything significant going on and if it was a personal or business issue with Loose."

It seemed that Ken cringed a little. "You okay?" I asked him.

"Yes, fine."

But he didn't appear fine. I looked over at Rose and she looked away quickly. What was going on here? Ken was defensive about Jennifer Loose. Was it that he was disappointed to think she was involved? He seemed to have a high opinion of her. Or was it more? I'd ask Rose when I had a chance to speak to her alone. Of course, she was protective of Ken and hadn't known me for long. Maybe I shouldn't put her on the spot. Better let this one go, at least for now. I didn't doubt I'd eventually find out what was going on.

"I know you'd probably like to spend some time with Jay while he's in town, but we need this information," Ken said.

"No problem, business first," I said, and meant it.

"Jay's arriving at Reagan International at five, and we'll go to our meeting from there. Are you ready to go, or do you need to stop at your apartment first?"

"I'm all set," I said. After only a couple days, I was comfortable meeting with high-ranking officials without worrying about my attire. "Where are we meeting the VP?"

"We'd better leave for the airport," Ken said. He waved his finger in front of his mouth as if to shush me.

I got the hint. He must be afraid the place was bugged, so why didn't he tell me this before? I didn't say anything else until we were on our way to the airport.

"Why did you let me go on like that if you thought the place might be bugged?" I asked Ken.

"You misunderstood my caution. I didn't want Rose to know where the meeting was," he said. "Ned Campbell, my tech guy, checked for bugs after the fire. One can't be too careful."

"Why didn't you want Rose to know the location of the meeting?" I said. "She's your trusted right hand."

"Oh, I know, but I try to keep her from knowing everything. If she knew all, she might have to tell, or more likely be convinced to tell. She's so loyal she could be hurt holding out. As this heats up, the less she knows, the better."

"I see, but I think you're too late. Rose has a real handle on this." I thought Ken was being a little melodramatic. He couldn't think someone would use torture, or was it far from the realm of possibilities?

I hadn't thought about my mixed feelings about seeing Jay tonight; hadn't had time. I knew he'd stay at Nan's and we'd most likely be together, but we hadn't had much contact since the trip across the country. Maybe we were both just busy, but maybe not. Could be there wasn't as much feeling there as I'd thought. I'd be gone tomorrow morning for the trip to Chicopee and didn't know how long Jay was staying in DC. I hadn't asked Ken, because it seemed to me Jay should have let me know he was coming, especially if he had strong feelings for me. I didn't know if I felt as strongly as I had on our trip. Out of sight, out of mind, I guessed. It was possible he felt the same.

My mind was brought back to the present when Ken pulled up behind the line of cars parked at the US Airways terminal. "Would you mind checking out the baggage area? It's inside the center door over there? I don't see Jay outside, and I hate to start circling if he's almost ready."

"Of course," I said, jumping out the passenger door. I felt way too excited, my heart pounding. I had to stop myself from an all-out run to the door. I guess my feelings were still a little more fervent than I'd thought a few minutes ago.

I saw Jay as soon as I walked in the door. He was standing near the baggage conveyor belt and looking the other way. He walked closer to the belt and picked up a black duffle. From the size of the bag, he wasn't staying long. What surprised me more was the fact I couldn't stop my heart from racing, and I mean like the home stretch of the Kentucky Derby: all out.

When he turned and saw me standing there like an idiot, not able to move, he practically ran, dropped his bag, and grabbed me off the floor, gathering me into his arms and kissing me, taking away any bit of breath I had left. So much for my thoughts of not having feelings for him. He set me down, looked at me with eyes I could easily read, and hugged me close to him.

"I can't wait until after the meeting tonight," he said.

I smiled. "Guess we'll have to." We left the airport hand in hand and got into the car with Ken. I sat in the back, knowing Jay and Ken would want to talk before the meeting.

They filled each other in with information they'd gained since their last conversation, and I listened. I knew most of it. When it came to Jennifer Loose and Richard Crose, Ken asked me to give Jay the details.

"So, where's tonight's meeting and who will be there?" Jay asked.

"The VP, of course, and anyone else he invited. Since he called it, I didn't ask," Ken said.

"Where?" Jay said.

"It's actually at the VP's house. Can you believe that?" Ken said. "He thinks that meeting right under everyone's eyes is the best way to remain secretive. Who would invite people who were conspiring to an open setting where all could see?"

"He's probably right," Jay said, laughing.

We drove to 34th Street and Massachusetts Avenue to the Queen Anne style, three-story white house on the grounds of the United States Naval Observatory. It was usually referred to as the Admiral's House, previously being the house of the chief of the Naval Observatory. In broad daylight, Ken drove up to the gate of the home of the vice president and lowered the window.

"Mr. Bentz, the vice president is expecting you," said a Secret Service agent. "I'll need to see your identification, Mr. Benson and Ms. Jacobs. You may park in the drive. Your car will be valeted and you'll be shown to the library."

"Thank you, Hansen. It's good to see you again."

"And you," she replied.

The vice president was in the library. He stood and asked us to be seated when we entered. The same people who'd attended the first meeting at the B & B, Beverly Leach and John Banyon, as well as Representative Engle, were there. Jay and Representative Engle were the only new attendees. I wasn't sure why, but I'd thought there'd be more people. After being served coffee, tea, and cakes, the server left and the vice president began.

"Since the announcement by the president about the success of the government-run dairy farms today, the conspiracy by government officials and others to take over the food supply in the United States is moving ahead with incredible speed," Daly said.

The "C" word had been used by the vice president, I thought. Others had been rather careful not to use that word prior to this.

"It's time to bring this to the American people. They need to know the facts," he continued.

"How do you propose we do that, Mr. Vice President?" Ken asked. "Through the paper? We've been as strong in our language as we can without positive proof and without giving specific names. Valerie's been digging and may have found at least one other person in the legislature I was surprised may be involved. We might know for sure by tomorrow."

"I was approached by the secretary of the interior last night," Daly said. "She's been suspicious of where some of her budget had gone. She was told twelve billion earmarked for discretionary funds for her department was needed to keep the country safe from terrorism. The president met with her in person. I'm not sure if he's involved in this deception, if he's too busy or preoccupied to see what's going on, or if others are able to play him, but if I had to guess, I'd say it's the latter."

"Would it be possible for Valerie to meet with the secretary?" Ken asked.

"Of course," the vice president said. "I'll set it up for tomorrow. There's no time to waste."

"Valerie's traveling to Georgia tomorrow. She'll be back in town tomorrow night. Will that work?"

"I'll set it up," he replied. "Can you meet her at her home?"

"Of course," I said.

"Make sure you're not followed," the vice president said. "On second thought, can you go right to your apartment and meet with her there? It will be easier for her to get there unnoticed. When the president approached her, she didn't question his decision to take the funds, so there would be no reason for anyone watching her."

"I'll be careful," I answered.

"Jay, what can you add?" Ken said.

"My people have been investigating what businesses are providing the government farms with equipment and supplies. We've narrowed it down to about half a dozen companies and four dairy supply businesses. Three feed groups also hold exclusive contracts.

"Do you have the names of the specific companies?" I said.

"Using the brand names Valerie saw at the farms and some well-placed questions by our people to companies' sales contacts, we narrowed it down to Candor, Lavelle, Serpentine, Janiper, Caldwell, and James. The dairy supply companies were Chase, Vanguard, Labelle, and Tuxedo. We can't say definitely that any one of them is involved in an illegal arrangement at this point. Some might be diversions."

"What about the names of the feed groups?" I said.

"The feed groups were cooperatives," Jay said. "We're working on obtaining the members' names. We need to get the actual approved budget expenditures in order to determine who's getting paid and the exact amounts. If someone with access to those figures can get them to us, my people can determine if the costs are legitimate."

"Do you have the names of the cooperatives?" I asked.

"Not with me, but I'll get them to you," Jay said.

"I'll speak to Dan Hansen on the Budget Oversight Committee," Engle said. "I know he'll get me what you need."

"I think we'd better meet again in a couple days, but let's make it a neutral location. Jay, can you stick around for a few days? I have some other questions for you, and I'd like you involved in what will take place over the next week or so," Daly said.

"Of course, Mr. Vice President," Jay said.

"Then let's adjourn for tonight. Oh, and Ken, can you write up something a little provocative for tomorrow's paper? I want these worms to start squirming. And you seem to be able to find us great places to meet. Will you take care of that, too? Just call with the details and speak directly to Carrie in my office."

"Sure," said Ken.

Ken dropped Jay and me at Nan's apartment. She wasn't home from work. There was a note on the table not to wait on dinner for her. She didn't expect to be home before midnight. As soon as Jay read the note, he encircled me with his arms and pulled me to him.

"I've hardly been able to talk to you for fear I'd be on the next plane. I couldn't stand being away from you," he moaned, pulling me closer. The next two hours were a wonderful blur.

"I'm starving," Jay said finally.

"It's almost eleven. I have to be up by six."

"Come on. We have to eat. We'll go down to the corner restaurant. We can even call ahead and order."

"Okay," I said. "Order me a burger. I'm going to jump in the shower."

"Get right on it," he said.

Our dinner was ready when we arrived at Tables, only a block from the apartment. When we left the restaurant less than half an hour later, a man with a baseball cap pulled down over his face ran toward us. Jay pushed me ahead of him and told me to run. I didn't budge. He turned toward the runner. As the man reached him, Jay shoved his knee up into the man's stomach. He doubled over. Jay pulled him up, pushed him against the building, and said, "May I help you?" All those years of throwing hay bales and working on the farm had made Jay exceptionally strong. His Special Ops training probably didn't hurt, either.

I couldn't believe it. Was Jay totally paranoid? Why did he think the jogger was a threat to us?

"Why did you do that? I was just running," the man said, stopping between words to gasp for breath.

"I don't think so," Jay said. "You can tell me, or we can go to the police station."

I knew that was a bluff. Jay had no intention of wasting time. If the guy was a paid gun as Jay suspected, he wouldn't want to go to the police.

"Okay, okay," he said. "I was just hired to follow you and let this guy know where you were."

"And who is this guy?"

"I don't know. He told me to call him with this prepaid cell every three hours around the clock and let him know where you were."

"You're going to check in now and tell him we had dinner and just went into the apartment. Do you understand?"

"Yes." He followed Jay's directions.

"Now," Jay said. "You'll give me the prepaid phone and disappear. I will never see you again. If I see you, you'll be in jail. Do you understand?"

He practically threw the phone at Jay and ran away. Jay did have a commanding presence, and I suspected the stalker was still running. We wouldn't see him again.

"Amateur," Jay said. "I'd have thought they were more connected, able to hire some experienced people."

We returned to the apartment. Nan was there, and I left Jay with her to catch up. I excused myself and turned in, knowing I'd have to be up by 6 a.m. to catch my flight.

CHAPTER 16

n the morning, Jay insisted on accompanying me to the airport via cab. The flight to Atlanta was fairly quick, about an hour and a half. I rented a car and drove the forty miles northeast to Chicopee, a fairly small town situated south of the Chattahoochee River and the Appalachians. In small towns, the local diner was a great place to get an overview of the area, and it was still breakfast time. Perfect. The gossip would be flowing from the locals who frequented the place. If there were any people as open as farmers, it was small-town folk. They told all. The Main Street Diner was about three-quarters full when I arrived.

I took a stool at the counter and ordered a coffee, eggs, bacon, and toast from a friendly blond who was happy to help me. "New in town?" she asked.

"Yes, I'm a writer, just visiting. Seems like a quiet little town."

"Neat," she said. "But I don't know if it will be quiet around here for long."

"Oh?"

"Yeah, there've been people all over the place lately, running in and out of town."

"What's going on?"

"Well—" she began.

"How about getting to work, Tilly?" a voice came from the kitchen.

"Sorry," she yelled back. "Be right there."

She turned and collected an order from the open window to the kitchen and delivered it to a booth. By then, there were others coming in, and she took their orders as well. Soon she was back to me with my coffee.

"So, what's going on?" I asked lightly.

"Oh, I'm not exactly sure, but I'm told some of the locals are going to make a bundle of money, shracking or something like that."

"Hydrofracking?" I asked.

"Yeah, that's it, fracking. Some people are really upset, afraid the farmland will disappear, but others are happy about getting a lot of money from the gas companies, I guess. Got to go; I'll get in trouble. Good luck finding a quiet place."

I listened to other conversations but didn't hear much of interest. As I finished my breakfast and was ready to find a real estate company in town, another great place to find out what was happening, an older gentleman sat next to me. He was grumbling under his breath.

"Worked all my life, and now the government's going to take my land," he said.

I ordered another cup of coffee. "Problems?" I asked him.

"More than a problem," he said. "Not from here, I take it?"

"No, just visiting. I'm actually a journalist with a Washington paper. Anything you'd like to tell me about the area?"

"Not sure it would do any good."

"I'm willing to listen."

"The whole area's about to change, and not for the better. The gas companies are coming in and buying up or leasing all the land, going to drill for gas. When I told them no, the law came in and took my land by eminent domain. I never thought it could happen here, in this country. My family has used the land for five generations, always grown fruit. Now the government has decided it needs gas more than food. Somebody is making a lot of money from all this. You can bet on that." His voice had risen as he talked.

"What makes you say that?"

"There've been senators and congressmen all over the place. Some of them bought up the land then sold it to the oil and gas companies. They've been gobbling up the land for the past three years. Didn't just happen yesterday."

"Got any specific congressmen or senators?" I tried to be nonchalant.

He lowered his head, turned it to me, eyes squinting. "Who are you?" he said.

"Can you keep a secret?" I asked with a smile. I'd found someone who could help me. I didn't want to blow it.

"Let's take a booth," he said, moving to an isolated area of the diner.

After we sat down, I shook his hand and said, "I'm Valerie Jacobs, reporter from DC, *Washington In Depth*, looking into the rapid decrease of family and privately owned farms."

"Harold Lemming," he said, returning my shake. "What brought you *here*?"

"One of the people we suspect is behind the takeover of land came here in the spring with a legislator we didn't suspect. I came to see why they were here." I try to be honest with people. I've found they're more likely to be forthcoming.

"If you're talking about that Loose woman, no pun intended, and that arrogant pinhead Crose, I'm guessing they were here to meet with gas company executives who were here the same week. They own some of the land that borders the acreage the gas companies already own."

"How do you know that?" I asked, a little incredulous that this man knew exactly what was going on.

"Why shouldn't I know?" he said. "It's public record who owns what land, and although it's under a different name than theirs, it was pretty clear who owned it. They're the ones who dealt with the real estate agent."

"I see." I tried not to act as excited as I was at finding this honest man who had the connection I needed.

"Why don't you come to the real estate office with me when I finish my breakfast? She can fill you in. What paper did you say you worked for?"

"*Washington In Depth*," I said.

"Ah, Ken Bentz," he said.

"You know the paper?"

"Not until about two years ago, when I started checking into all this. If he hired you, you must know what you're doing."

Hope so, I thought. I paid the bill and we walked across the street to Family Real Estate.

The real estate agent was what many would call stunning, with long auburn hair and penetrating blue eyes, a figure that killed, and the height and carriage to give her credibility. I was sure she could make a sale by simply introducing herself to prospective clients, especially men.

"Miss Valerie Jacobs, my daughter-in-law, Margaret Lemming."

My jaw dropped as I looked at Harold, who was smiling that he'd surprised me. "So happy to meet you, Mrs. Lemming."

"Call me Margaret."

"Valerie is a journalist with *Washington In Depth*." Mr. Lemming smiled and raised his eyebrows, looking over his glasses at his daughter-in-law. She returned his smile and grabbed a folder from the top drawer of her desk.

"Mind if I have a look at your credentials?" she said to me.

I showed Margaret my ID and soon found that the woman was much more than good looks. She knew the business and she knew what was going on in the area.

"I'm not telling you anything you couldn't find in the public records if you knew exactly where to look. This is a list of the owners of record of the land that's been sold in this country over the past three years. You'll note the majority is owned by LLCs, S corps, and C corps. This will give you a list of all the officers of the corporations." Margaret handed me a stack of blue sheets. "I've gone one step further, listing next to each corporation officer their relative who is a state or nationally elected official, those who are supposed to be working for the American people. They're actually working to enhance their own wealth."

Looking at the list, I recognized almost all of the confirmed conspirators plus others. Ken wouldn't be happy to see Jennifer Loose's name. "I appreciate you trusting me with this information. It must have taken you months to obtain these facts. Have you shared it with anyone else?" I said, more than a little surprised she'd entrusted it to me.

"Dad wouldn't have brought you to me if he didn't want me to share this information. My husband, his son, has worked the family fruit orchards all his life, as his ancestors did. If there's any way we can turn around what's happening, I'm willing to try it. We planned to bring our family up on the farm, not on gas fields.

"I'm trusting you because we've tried everything we could think of within the law to no avail. I don't know you personally, but my father-in-law has flawless judgment when it comes to character, and the fact that you work with Ken Bentz cinches it. You might be our last chance. I'd appreciate you not using my name, however. Might not help my business, you know, and I wouldn't be able to keep on top of what's going on if I weren't in this business."

"I always protect my sources," I assured her. "We're going to do what we can to bring what's happening to the public. The facts you've given me will help. I have to get back to Atlanta for a 5 p.m. flight. Is there any way you'd have time to drive me out to your farm and around the area so I can see firsthand what I'm writing about?"

She turned to her father-in-law. "Will you come, too, Dad? I may not be able to answer all Miss Jacobs's questions."

"Of course," Harold said.

Margaret drove to open country, fields of blackberries, blueberries, peanuts, peaches, tomatoes, and corn. Lush crops and beautiful country. Rolling hills replaced totally flat land as we pushed farther north.

"What will happen to the land if they allow fracking?" I asked.

"They'll tear it all up," Harold said. "Make a mess of it. Probably ruin our water supply. Then there'll be no going back. No water, no crops, no people."

"Dad might be exaggerating a little, but we don't really know what will happen. There've been problems, especially in Pennsylvania, where fracking has been ongoing. The chemicals they used contaminated the water supply. The officials of the company never accepted responsibility for the sicknesses people developed."

"What's the name of the company applying for permits to frack here?"

"Champion Gas Company," she replied. "But it's probably a subsidiary of a larger company. It's sometimes hard to determine the parent company."

I took notes so I could follow up.

"I want you to see one more thing if you have time," Margaret said.

I checked my phone. "How long will it take us to get back to town?"

"This is on our way. We'll head south now. We'll be back in town by three."

"I should be able to make it to the airport for my flight."

We drove a little farther, and Margaret pulled onto a dirt road not visible from the main highway. The lane was rutted, dry—I could taste the dust. The vehicle straddled the ruts and thumped along. I thought about the night Jay took me to the computer barn, as I now called it. About a half mile down the road, a gate blocked our way. Margaret stopped, jumped out of the car, and opened the gate. She closed it after driving through.

When she returned to the car, I said, "I take it we're not supposed to be here."

"I didn't see any no trespassing signs, did you?" she replied. "No one will be here yet."

I let well enough alone as we continued. About two miles in, the trees lining the road ended, and there was a clearing as far as I could see. Large trucks lined one side of the area. On the other, trucks, side by side, lined the edge of a large pad of cement. In the middle was a row of large green metal box-like structures about ten feet tall with pipes leading from the boxes into the ground. The opposite end of the pad was lined with flatbeds holding white plastic barrels.

"What is this? What's in the barrels, water?" I asked.

"This is fracking equipment complete with barrels of chemicals," Margaret said. "Champion is all set up and ready to go."

"I thought fracking hadn't been approved in Georgia yet."

"That doesn't stop them," Harold said. "Where do you think the big mucky-mucks have been going? Champion wants to show them what's going to happen when the drilling is approved.

"What're the chemicals for? I thought it was hydrofracking."

"Water is only one ingredient," Margaret said. "Try to get a list of the exact chemicals and answers are hazy. Some use benzene, a carcinogen, or diesel fuel. But there are hundreds of others. How would you like that going into your water supply? They also push fine white sand into the mix. It takes about three million tons of sand to drill one well. That necessitates about fifty semi-loads. Can you imagine the wear and tear on our little rural roads with that kind of truck traffic? Evidently that's not one of the problems anticipated with fracking. And that's not counting the tractor trailers required to bring in the chemicals needed."

"Are people afraid of the effect on the water supply?" I asked.

"Have you had a chance to do any research on fracking?" Margaret said.

"Not a lot. I did look into the Pennsylvania problems. Seems they had some difficulties with leaks, runoff into streams and rivers, necessitating cleanup."

"That was one of the worst results," Harold said. "People are making a lot of money. They don't care about the consequences on the land and future generations, as long as it's not where they live."

"We'd better get going. A shift will come on in about an hour," Margaret said.

"What are they doing if they don't have permission to frack yet?" I asked.

"They're fracking," Harold said dryly.

"Do we have time for me to take some pictures?" I asked.

Margaret picked up an envelope from the seat and handed it to me. It contained pictures of the fracking area, not quiet but in operation.

"You're kidding. They're already fracking?" I said, flipping through the photos.

"This is where they bring the government officials and investors to show them how safe fracking is and how little the process affects the environment." Margaret laughed. "The pictures are dated, and nothing was altered. A professional photographer took the photos. She gave them to me to pass on to our local paper's editor, but he wouldn't publish them. The photographer has a studio in town, and she'd be fine with you using the prints. If you decide to publish them, I'd like you to give her credit. Her credentials and phone number are on the envelope. I know you'll need to talk to her before using them. She asked me to hold on to them in the hope I might find someone to get the word out."

"I appreciate this, Margaret, but I don't understand Champion leaving this place unguarded. It's incredible."

"Not only a feeling of superiority, but overconfidence as well," Harold said. "These people think no one knows they're here. Can you imagine? They not only think small-town, rural Americans are ignorant, but blind and deaf, too, unable to see and hear the semis traveling out to the middle of nowhere."

"Unbelievable," was all I could say.

CHAPTER 17

There'd been no time to see Sandra Pearson, the photographer, before I returned to DC, but there'd be time to contact her by phone the next day. Jay was waiting for me at the airport in a rental.

"The vice president changed your meeting with the secretary of the interior tonight. We'll be meeting elsewhere." He drove us to the next, what I considered clandestine, meeting.

"Don't we have to pick up Ken?" I asked.

"No, he'll meet us there. He wanted us to arrive separately tonight, hopefully staving off attempts to follow any one of us."

"I have a lot to tell you about what's going on in Georgia—and, I imagine, in other areas of the United States. What do you know about fracking?" I asked.

"Done some research. The real expert at home is Keith Jackson. Each of the people working on research for me at the barn chooses a different topic, either by interest or background knowledge. Keith would be the one to ask any questions about fracking. I take it that Chicopee's a fracking site."

Jay drove out of the city and took route 66 toward Annandale. Exiting shortly after, he pulled onto a long two-lane country road. We traveled about three miles without seeing any buildings. At the end of the road was an eight-foot-high wrought-iron gate with barbed-wire fencing stretching on both sides. There were rolled raw barbs along the top, much like at a prison. Wooden guard stations stood at both sides of the gate.

When we neared, two uniformed Marine guards advanced, carrying what I recognized as close-quarters battle receivers. I'd done a piece on the armed services about a year before. My research led to weapons commonly used by the military. The Marine Corps Forces, Special Operation Command, had recently adopted this weapon.

One guard signaled Jay to move forward. He had come to a complete stop when he saw the Marines.

Jay pulled the car forward, and lowered the driver's side window.

"Name and business, sir."

"We are here for a meeting, Master Sergeant."

"Are you a Marine, sir?"

"Two thousand six through two thousand ten," Jay said. "Lieutenant Jay Benson.

"Welcome. May I see proof of identity for both of you and your invitation?"

What invitation? I thought, but Jay slipped a paper from his pocket and handed it to the Master Sergeant, who stood at attention and saluted Jay.

He then turned to me. "Hello, Miss Jacobs. Good to have you on board."

"Thank you," I replied.

The Master Sergeant turned to Jay and told him to follow the road straight to the house.

"Were you in Special Forces?" I asked Jay.

"Yes," he answered. I knew by the shortness of his reply that this wasn't the right time to question further.

We followed the road another half mile. A mansion came into view. No way could it be called a house. The road became a circular drive. A mammoth double door stood at the center of the mansion, with four marines flanking it. When we approached, they all stepped forward, their guns over their shoulders. Jay stopped the car. The marines marched forward, two to each front car door. They opened them and asked us to get out.

"Lieutenant Benson and Miss Jacob?" one of the marines asked.

"Yes," Jay said.

The marine saluted.

"Your car will be taken care of. Step inside the door and you'll be escorted to your meeting. Please do not attempt to wander anywhere other than where you're led."

"Of course," Jay said.

The entry hall was mostly white, shiny marble with a large and winding black staircase in the center, providing a stark contrast. Artwork, including museum-quality paintings and statues, lined the perimeter of the ballroom-sized room. I pictured men and women of high economic or political stature, dressed in their finest, holding champagne glasses with upraised pinkies, visiting and schmoozing, waitresses and waiters taking used glasses and replacing them with fresh champagne. I bet this place had seen many of those parties, maybe even as far back as the '20s, when prohibition hindered the upper-crust politicians from visiting the speakeasies for fear of being caught in a sting and losing the support of their teetotaler voters.

My mind stopped wandering when the vice president appeared from a door to our left. "Come join us. I'm glad you were able to return from Georgia in time to meet with us, Ms. Jacobs. Hi, Jay, good to see you." He acted like an old friend of Jay's.

"Hello, sir," Jay said, extending his hand to shake the vice president's.

"Please, call me Val, Mr. Vice President. It's good to see you again." I reached to shake his hand.

"Then you must call me Dan," he replied.

"That would be difficult for me, and I think disrespectful," I said.

"Then you may call me Dan when I'm no longer vice president, which may be sooner than the next election if things keep moving in an accelerated direction."

"That's a deal," I said. "But let's hope it doesn't come to that."

Dan led us into a library, larger than the whole of our local one in Madden. Books lined the room, floor to ceiling, three stories high. Rolling ladders facilitated reaching the books at the first two levels, and the third level was on another floor with a staircase for access. The bookcases were dark cherry wood. Cherry tables and leather-cushioned chairs provided seating in the center of the room. Small, individual lights were placed down the centers of the tables—for research, I imagined.

The vice president led us through the library and into an adjacent room, a luxurious living room with leather-upholstered couches and chairs, cherry coffee tables, and other smaller tables scattered throughout the room. All the people in the room were those who'd been at the other meetings. There was one man I didn't know, but I assumed he'd be introduced eventually.

"Our hostess for the evening will be here shortly," said Daly. "We'll wait until then to begin."

"Do you know who the mysterious hostess is?" I whispered to Jay.

"Haven't a clue."

"Good to see you got back in time," Ken interrupted.

"I wouldn't have made it back," I said, "if I hadn't been given pictures taken by a local photographer. If I'd had to stay to take photos myself, I would've missed the flight."

"I'm glad you made it. There'll be some pretty big news tonight. I'll want you to fill everyone in on what you found on your trip," Ken said.

"What happened with my planned meeting with the secretary of the interior?"

"She was involved in a car accident and is in the hospital. She might not make it."

A door opened. A woman walked in and shook hands with the vice president. He turned and said, "This is Penelope Strauss, owner of this magnificent property."

Strauss was about five and a half feet tall with an average build, probably in her mid-forties. She wasn't a beauty, but far from ugly. Wearing jeans, a T-shirt, and work boots, she looked like she stepped off a tractor. There was even a little hay sticking out of her short, dark, curly hair. A touch of gray framed her temples.

"Sorry for the appearance," she addressed all of us. "Have to make hay while the sun shines, you know. Have you started?"

"We waited for you," Dan said. "Would you like to start?"

"Heavens no. I asked Carly to bring us some lemonade and sandwiches. Let's eat, then we can begin. I don't believe I've seen you before," she said, turning to me.

"Hi, I'm Valerie Jacobs. I'm working with Ken. And this is Jay Benson."

"Ah, yes. I've heard about you and Jay. Glad to have you with us."

I felt a little qualm at that. I'd heard that from almost everyone. Glad you are with us or joined us or on board, or whatever. I was an investigative reporter, and while, because of my background, I couldn't help root for farmers, I knew I had no special powers to help them. What if I failed to obtain the information needed to stop the takeover of the farmland? I'd never been comfortable with people depending on me. It was clear government people and some big businesses were taking over the land, but I needed to connect the evidence to convince the American people. And was it too late to stop it? What would Nate and Jess do?

A teenage girl entered the room carrying a tray of sandwiches, and behind her followed a woman, probably in her sixties, with a tray of glasses and pitchers of tea, lemonade, and water.

"This is my mother, Candace Rappaport, and my daughter, Carly," Penelope said to Jay and me. Evidently, everyone else knew the family. I'd thought Carly must be a maid. I didn't expect the family of someone owning a place like this to serve guests.

Penelope must have seen the surprise on my face. I never was any good at hiding my feelings, which wasn't always a plus for a reporter. "My dad didn't believe in having someone else do what we could do ourselves. He believed it would be a slight to our guests not to serve them. I agree. That doesn't mean we don't have people to help us. We need it with this large of a place, and if we have a big affair, we have helpers serve our guests."

The sandwiches and glasses were placed on the table, and we all helped ourselves. "If anyone would like anything stronger, it's in the next room. Help yourselves," Candace said.

When everyone had their plates, we sat at the table and got started. "Ken, why don't you lead us tonight. I'd like to hear about the Georgia deal first," Dan said, looking in my direction.

I had just bitten into a sandwich, so I had to raise my finger to the vice president of the United States, signaling him to wait. I didn't really do that, did I? Oh my God, I did. I chewed as fast as I could while getting my notes out of my bag on the floor.

I gave them the full report. Thankfully, I'd written it up on the plane ride back to DC. Then I passed the pictures around for them to see.

"I knew they'd do something like this," said the deputy secretary of agriculture. "Champion applied for permits to start hydrofracking near Chicopee, Georgia, in April. They were told to wait to do anything until they received a firm permit. I received word from my contact in Chicopee that the company had purchased the land, not leased it as they'd indicated. They leased the land within five miles around the drilling site, too. Because the prices to farmers for their products in that area were so depressed, the growers jumped at the chance for money to keep them afloat. Champion has a great line about how safe the drilling is and makes anyone who disputes their claims look like fools, jealous because they aren't able to lease their land to the company. Some who have gone against them have also had other problems. I wouldn't be surprised if they were generated by the company."

"So, what can be done? They didn't wait for permits to drill, as was the deal. We have proof," Jay said, pointing to the pictures.

"Can you prove these photos are genuine?" Dan asked.

"I'll speak to the photographer tomorrow to ascertain exactly how they were taken, but while I was there, I saw exactly what's shown in the photos. The drills were not running at that time, but as you can see, the photos show them running and new loads of chemicals and sand being brought in."

"I know a photo expert in town who can ensure they have not been tampered with," Ken said. "I've used him before."

"Good," Dan said. "Valarie, when you speak to the photographer, ask if she's willing to come to DC to testify to the authenticity of the photos and to what she saw, if people are charged in the future."

"Yes, Mr. Vice President," I said. I made a note.

The vice president asked Ken to speak next. "By now, everyone has probably heard about the fire at the paper. What wasn't provided to the news was that all my files about the takeover were stolen."

There were multiple gasps.

"I thought they were burned," Jay said.

"No, there was not much destroyed. The fire department put it out before it entered my office. I believe the fire was set to cover up the theft. The arsonist didn't count on the fire being smothered so quickly."

"That means whoever hired the arsonist knows what we know," Leach said.

"Not exactly," Ken said. "The files in my office were inaccurate. I have everything on my laptop, and I never leave it anywhere. I suspected there might be an attempt to find out what I knew and exactly who was involved in the investigation, so I planted information we learned months ago. No one is mentioned by name. When they looked at the files, I imagine the culprits had a good laugh about how little we knew. They should relax a little, maybe make some mistakes, or come out in the open more. I didn't plan on them starting a fire, though, and I can tell you it pissed me off."

"Those of you who don't know our situation are probably wondering why we live in a fortress," Penelope Strauss said, looking at Jay and me. "I'll start at the beginning and make it as short as possible.

"My husband Hans and I used to live in southeastern Pennsylvania on a family farm that had been in his family since the 1700s. Some of our neighbors decided to lease their land to a fracking company. We didn't blame them, mind you. They needed the money. We all had dairy farms, and the price we received for our milk had dropped. Because most of them had mortgages, they would have gone out of business without the added income. To make a long story a little shorter, our water was contaminated, so we could no longer water the cows. Had to sell the herd. The land could no longer be farmed. Luckily, we had no mortgage, so we walked away."

The Deputy Secretary of Agriculture was next. "I'm afraid, as the vice president indicated, the process of eating up the farmland is escalating. In the last month, 200,000,000 acres of farmland have been taken by eminent domain by federal, state, county, and local governments. Five hundred thousand family farms have been sold—not to other farmers, but to government officials, either privately or through their government positions. Five hundred thousand acres of farmland have been sold to private industry, and ninety percent of that land has been purchased by foreign government entities. A hundred thousand acres of land have been leased, mostly 30- to 99-year leases, to domestic entities and foreign countries. If this trend continues, we'll lose control of the majority of our land by year's end."

"Do you have a breakdown of foreign countries involved? Although all the figures are astounding, that concerns me the most," Dan said.

"Yes, I have it broken down," Leach said. She passed a packet of papers to each of us. "You'll see the greatest purchases and leases have been executed by Canada, the Netherlands, Germany, the United Kingdom, and Portugal, with Saudi Arabia, Qatar, and China increasing their purchases recently. I've also included a graph showing the farmland taken out of farming or out of the hands of individual United States citizens in the past twenty years."

There was complete silence, except for the sound of turning pages. No one said a word until Penelope Strauss said, "Want that 'something stronger' now?"

Everyone agreed to a drink while we let the new statistics settle.

The vice president took the lead. "It's time to go public with everything we have. When we do, there's no telling what'll happen. I'm going to hire a private security company to protect each of you.

"I want the junior senator from Michigan, Senator Bennett Slalom, to explain how he was approached by someone he thought was a lobbyist."

"Be happy to," Senator Slalom said. "I was approached by Sasha Lowenstein, who said she was a lobbyist for a national agricultural organization recently incorporated, the Call for National Farms Association, or CNFA. According to her, the purpose of the organization was to educate the nation about the lower cost of food produced by government farms and how the concept of national farms would make their lives better. She stated further that this would ensure the American people owned their food sources, since the government belonged to the people.

"I'd already attended a few meetings explaining the government's national agricultural production, so I knew the propaganda style being used. What was new was this: Lowenstein offered me what she called a 'special ownership' in this organization. Because I was a senator, I could have a *special* share in the government profits. After all, it was only right, because I was working hard for the people of the country, I should be given special consideration."

Slalom continued, "When I asked what was expected of me for this special consideration, her answer was, 'Oh, Senator, nothing at all. Your votes for the approval of certain legislation necessary to help the American people are all that's needed. Nothing more than you're already doing.' As soon as she left, I wrote her exact words so I could relay it to this group. I couldn't imagine the cost of food in the future if bribery was being used on multiple government senators and representatives.

"I asked what would happen if I didn't vote on a piece of legislation the way the CNFA thought I should. She countered she had no doubt I'd vote in favor of what would help the American people become prosperous.

"When I asked what specific legislation she was talking about, Lowenstein told me there would be a bill brought to the floor in the Senate called the Trevor-Gains Agricultural Project. She strongly encouraged my support.

"I've been trying to get a copy of the bill without success. It's being kept under wraps. It's obvious it has enough votes to pass through the House, because Lowenstein had no doubt it would reach the Senate shortly. Votes anticipated from the Senate chamber must be close if they're resorting to asking junior senators for support. We're pretty much ignored unless we're needed. What I must know from you," Slalom said, motioning his hand toward us, "is how I should handle this. There's no way I'm selling my votes, but I think we have a possibility of outing them to the general public if we play this right. I'm willing to do whatever's necessary—wear a wire, or whatever—to stop these people from taking our freedom away. I came to Washington to serve all the people, not a select few."

"As we all have," the vice president said.

"Won't they be ready for something as simple as a wire?" Jay said.

"I think they're so overconfident at this point, I doubt it," Ken said. "Can we count on one of our friends in the FBI or CIA coming up with a plan to help us with the appropriate equipment?"

"I'm not sure," the VP said. "But I do know a couple retired people who've kept up on the latest technology and will help when I explain the situation. I'll contact them, and we'll meet again tomorrow night. Remember, though, we can't do anything illegal. Our whole deal is to keep our rights and not take anyone else's rights away, even the people we think are trying to take our freedoms. Can we meet at your apartment, Valerie?"

"Um, I guess so. Are you sure? The woman who rents the apartment has a pretty nosy doorman. Nothing much gets by him."

The vice president laughed. "David can go a little overboard," he said.

"You know him?"

"He's one of us," Jay said blandly, not looking at me.

I didn't reply, just looked at Jay with a question unsaid. I wondered who else he knew was 'one of us.'

By the time we left the home of Penelope Strauss, my mind was whirling. "Don't you think you could've told me David was part of this group?" I asked Jay.

"I could have, but it wasn't necessary. Everything in its time."

I turned to Jay, my face turning red. "This attitude will stop right now. I will not be kept out of any part of this operation if I'm expected to work on it."

"There's the old Val I know," Jay laughed.

"Stop laughing," I said. "I'm serious here. If you want me doing this, I won't be kept in the dark. Do you understand?"

"Got it," he said.

When we pulled into the gate to the apartment, David stopped us. "You have a visitor," he said, looking at Val.

"Who?" I asked, concerned.

"Annie Jacobs, your niece," David said.

"What's Annie doing here?" I said aloud.

"She didn't say, Ms. Jacobs."

"Let's go find out. Maybe she wanted an advance look at her potential DC home," Jay said.

When we walked into the apartment, I knew something was horribly wrong. Annie sat at the dining room table, head in her hands.

"What's happened, Annie? Is it Mom?"

"It's not Mom, Val. It's Dad."

"Nate? An accident? How bad is he hurt? Why're you here?" I sounded more like Annie than myself. I was confused. What could be wrong?

Jay moved closer to Annie. "What's going on?" he said, his hands on her shoulders.

"Mom and I didn't want to tell you on the phone," she said, looking at the floor.

"You're scaring me, Annie. Tell me. Is Nate hurt?"

Annie took a deep breath and blurted, "Dad committed suicide last night. He's gone."

I stood, not moving. This couldn't happen. Nate was strong. He was depressed and he was drinking too much, but suicide? Never. "Stop, Annie, that couldn't happen."

Jay caught me as I crumbled. No tears. I had to find out what had happened, but I felt like I'd been kicked in the gut. My legs went numb. I bent forward and held my stomach with my arms. I heard a bloodcurdling scream, then realized it was coming from me. He couldn't be dead. He was my big brother. He'd done everything for me—he was more of a father to me than our dad had been. Nate had brought me up, made sure I had everything I needed and wanted. "Why?" I asked Annie. Jay led me to the couch, then walked back to the table where Annie was sobbing.

What had I been thinking to react this way? Poor Annie. Nate was her father. Was. Was. Of course, Annie was devastated. Jay was leading her to the couch beside me. We hugged, and I thought she was going to break my neck. We clung to each other, but I still had no tears. Just disbelief. Jay sat on the other side of me, his hand on my back. He hadn't said a word, but his face paled. Annie stopped crying. She'd probably been crying for hours. Her face was blotchy, her eyes swollen. Did Jess let her come here alone?

"Where's Jess?" I said.

"She's home. Marion's staying with her until I get back in the morning. Mom insisted either she or I had to tell you and Jay. Since she had to take care of Grandma, she said I should come."

"She must be devastated," Jay said.

I'd almost forgotten he was there. Turning to him, I let go of Annie and hugged him. "What's happened?" I said. "How could this be true? I feel like I'm in a nightmare. It can't be real."

Questions and answers back and forth and crying, mostly from Annie, took us until after midnight. Nan had returned home sometime before eleven and joined in the shock.

Addressing Annie, Jay said, "What flight are you on in the morning?"

When she told him, he called the airline and booked us on the same flight.

"I'll call Ken," I said.

Ken was compassionate and told me to keep him informed when I'd be back in town. He would let the others know I wouldn't be available for the foreseeable future.

"Val, may I speak to Jay?"

I put Jay on the phone. Annie and I trudged into the bedroom to get her settled so she could get some rest and fill me in on the details.

CHAPTER 18

I stayed with Annie until she fell asleep. I still hadn't cried much. Three in the morning, and I hadn't been asleep yet. I went into the kitchen for some milk and found Jay sitting at the table, head down. I hadn't taken time to think how this would affect him. In spite of their differing opinions about involving me in the farming affair, he and Nate were close friends. "I'm sorry," I said.

"What for?"

"For thinking about only myself. I know you must feel horrible."

"You have nothing to be sorry for. I hope you can forgive me."

"What for?"

"For getting you and your brother involved in this."

"You don't think he committed suicide either, do you?"

"Of course not. Even at his lowest point, he wouldn't have done this to Jess, Annie, or you."

"Then what do you think happened? Me taking this job got him killed, didn't it?" I couldn't live with the thought I might have been at fault for Nate's death.

Jay stood and walked around the table, embracing me. No real tears yet. "Val, no matter what happened to Nate, he loved you, and nothing you've done caused his death. There are some bad people out there, and no matter what we do, we can't control their actions. We can't always protect the people we love."

I knew Jay must have been thinking about his younger brother, who'd died in a car accident when he was sixteen, driving too fast on a curve right after he got his license. He flew over a bank and down into a deep ravine. It took a crane to pull the car up, and by the time they'd medivacked him to Albany Medical Center, an hour away, he was dead. Jay knew what it was like to lose a sibling, and realized there was nothing he could do to change the situation or make it easier for me.

But there was something I could do. I could find out exactly who killed Nate. I could grieve later. I'd hunt the people down who killed my brother, and I'd make sure they got what they deserved.

"It's okay to cry," Jay said. "I'm here for you and your family. Let it go, Val."

"Don't have time to cry," I said, pulling away from Jay. Grabbing my laptop from the table, I brought up Safari, needing to see what was being said about Nate's death. I started with Madden's local paper, then moved on to papers and TV stations in the area to see if they'd picked up the story. I felt something and looked up.

Jay was staring at me. "What's wrong? I need to know what's being said about Nate's death. When I get home, I want to be ready to hit the ground running. I'm going to find out what happened."

"Val, the way you're acting is not how you respond to your brother's death. You need to take time to feel."

"I'll feel when I want to feel," I snapped. "Right now, there's no time to waste." Returning to the screen, I didn't notice when Jay left the room, and to tell the truth, I didn't care. Blood was blood, and I would find out what happened to my brother. If I was to blame for his death, I had to know.

CHAPTER 19

My gut wrenched. When she wasn't crying, Annie's face contorted in her attempt to hold back tears. If it hadn't been for Jay, I wouldn't have been involved, and Nate wouldn't be dead. We hardly spoke on the ride to the airport, the flight, or the car ride home from Albany.

Jess was walking from the barn to the house when we pulled into the driveway about 10 a.m. We had made record time. I looked for Nate. What was I thinking?

Jess obviously hadn't had any sleep—eyes dark underneath, slouched shoulders, mouth visibly downward at the corners. Annie jumped out of the back seat and ran to her. They hugged and cried. When they finished, I hugged Jess but couldn't find any words to say that would comfort her.

"Tell me what happened," I said, more like a journalist than the sister of my deceased brother.

Jess stepped away a little and asked, "Are you alright, Val?"

"Of course *I'm* alright. Nothing happened to *me*. I'm still alive. The one who Nate and you always took care of, brought up, protected, and gave everything to, is fine. I'm alive. I'm fine."

Jess looked at Jay and then at Annie.

"So what's wrong?" I addressed Jay and Annie. "I'm fine." I went into the house ahead of them and ran upstairs to my room, past Mom, whom I couldn't face. It was my fault. It *was* my fault. I'd insisted on getting involved in spite of what Nate wanted. Why hadn't I listened? My brother would still have been alive.

I went into my room and cried until I couldn't cry anymore. Exhausted, I fell asleep.

A knock on the door woke me. "Val, it's Jess. May I come in?"

I was still groggy, then remembered what had happened and wished I didn't. "Of course."

She sat on the bed next to me. "You can cry, you know, Val."

"I did cry. Now I'm done. I want to find out who did this to Nate. Don't you want to know what happened? I mean, I know it's my fault when it comes down to it. If I hadn't been involved in this ag thing, he would be alive. He didn't want me to do it, but as always, I didn't listen. I've been poking around, and they think by killing Nate they can stop me."

"Val, what are you talking about? You know Nate committed suicide, don't you?"

"I'm sorry, Jess. I don't think he did. I think he was killed."

Jess's hands began to shake. "I never would have thought that of him, but the police said . . . if you're right, if someone killed Nate, is Annie in danger? Oh my God." Her whole body shook.

"It's okay, Jess." I held her. "I'm not going to let anything happen to Annie. Don't worry."

"What is this all about? Who's involved? Who killed Nate?" Jess said.

"I'm not sure, but I'm going to find out. Annie will not be in danger. I'll make sure of that." I wasn't sure how I'd make sure, but I would. It was the least I could do for Nate, who had always done everything for me.

"I want to talk to the police," I said. "His friends are not going to believe he committed suicide. He wouldn't give up. I'm going to make some calls, make sure all of us are protected. The only thing you should be thinking about is Nate's memorial."

"We aren't having a memorial yet," Jess said. "I need to talk to Annie and you together, fill you in on some things Nate told me. Then we'll all help find out who killed him."

"No, Jess. You can't involve Annie, and *you* can't do anything. I'll take care of it, Jay and I, and all of the others already working to determine what's going on in this country. We'll get to the bottom of it."

"If you think you can keep us out, you're wrong," Jess said. "Nate was my first love, my only one. He was not only my husband. Nate was my best friend. If you think I'm not willing to risk my life to avenge his, you're crazy. Let's get Annie up here. I want to talk to both of you."

I'd never seen Jess so strong. She always seemed to take a back seat to Nate. Whatever he said, she pretty much went along. I'd always thought it was because he was the dominant partner. Maybe they'd discussed things and she agreed with him. Perhaps she was stronger than I'd thought.

"Don't move. I'll get Annie," she said.

I didn't budge.

After Annie settled on the bed, Jess began to pace back and forth. We waited.

"Nate had a drinking problem, so it's a natural conclusion that he committed suicide, the end of many alcoholics. Everyone around here knew he was an alcoholic, so anyone interviewing his friends would not be surprised at suicide. Nate didn't talk to me like he used to, so I thought maybe I'd just lost total touch. But now, Val says your father may have been murdered." She looked at Annie.

Annie sat still and listened, not letting us know what she was thinking.

"Annie, what I need to know from you is—has there been anyone around here asking questions?" Jess said.

"What do you mean? No more than the usual neighbors." Annie hesitated and squinted. "There was a guy who stopped by the other day when you left for work early, said he needed to talk to Dad and you about a life insurance policy Dad had purchased last week. Said he needed your signature, Mom."

"Your dad didn't buy a life insurance policy. Didn't believe in it," Jess said.

"Did he give you the company's name?" I said.

"I wrote it down. It's on the desk in the kitchen, pink post-it. I'll get it." She ran out of the room, probably glad to have something to do.

"Maybe he did purchase a policy, to help you and Annie. Maybe he thought something would happen to him, or . . ."

"Don't even think it. I agree with you. He didn't commit suicide. We're going forward on that premise until someone proves otherwise," Jess said.

Annie was back with the note: "Carrier's Life Insurance Company," she read.

"Never heard of it," Jess said.

"That's an Albany number," I said. "Let's call."

Jess picked up the phone and called. "Hello, my husband passed away and I was told a salesperson from your company was asking for my husband and me two days ago. I'd like to speak to that person. My husband's name is—was Nathan Jacobs."

"On hold," Jess looked up, cradling the phone with her shoulder.

We waited in silence.

"This is Jessica Jacobs. That is correct. My husband passed away two days ago. I want to know who took out a life insurance policy on him."

She listened, then spoke again.

"That's not true. I never spoke to you before, and I certainly did not take out an insurance policy on him. My husband didn't believe in insurance. I want your name and your supervisor's name. I'll be giving them to the police, and they'll get to the bottom of this."

Jess wrote on the post-it that Annie had given her, ended the call, then threw the phone on the bed.

"What the hell's going on?" she said. "The man on the phone is coming out here now to show us the paperwork. This is crazy."

"Anyone home?" Jay's mom yelled from the bottom of the stairs. Around here, good friends didn't knock, or if they did and didn't get an answer and knew you were home, they came in to check.

"Be right down," Jess said.

Marion had brought her famous meatloaf, baked potatoes, carrots, and a chocolate pie, Jess's favorite.

"You shouldn't have, Marion. I don't think I can eat," Jess said.

"Well, you're at least going to taste." Marion hugged Jess. "I'm staying right here until you three have had some lunch." She set the table and made sure we all took a small plate of food.

After lunch, she washed the dishes by hand while Jess called the sheriff's office to determine when she could expect more information. She knew there would be an autopsy, even though suicide was suspected. It was procedure; the sheriff had explained that to Jess. The girl at the desk told her that Undersheriff Carson would be out to the farm that night. It was expected the ME would have completed at least a preliminary autopsy by five o'clock.

"We may know by tonight," Jess said, ending her call. "The sheriff will come out himself. I'm thinking the insurance representative should be here within an hour."

"What's happening?" Marion said. "I didn't mean to eavesdrop, but Nate didn't kill himself, did he?" Without us answering, she continued, "I knew it! He never would have done that to his family. Sorry. You don't have to say a thing. I'll get out of your hair." She turned, hugged Jess, and left before any of us could respond.

"I'm going to take a shower," I said. "You okay, Jess? Annie?" I wanted to give them some time alone. I went into the living room, hugged Mom, and told her I was sorry. She gave no response, but tears slid onto her cheek. After wiping them away, I flew upstairs, jumped in the shower, and cried while I stood under the steaming water.

CHAPTER 20

I walked out to Jay's house after my shower. It was only half a mile, and I wanted to spend some time with his family. Annie and Jess needed to spend time together, and I didn't want to be there when the sheriff or the insurance agent came. I just wasn't ready to face strangers about Nate's death.

Jay brought me back to the house about eight. The sheriff's car and a late-model Lincoln were parked in the driveway.

"Would you mind coming in with me?" I asked Jay. "I could really use your support."

"Are you sure Jess and Annie will want me there? After all, Nate's death may have something to do with the ag business he was adamant I not involve you in. Jess probably doesn't want to see me."

"I'm sure they won't mind. Neither Annie nor Jess blamed us. As a matter of fact, Jess indicated a desire to find out what happened to Nate, to make sure the killer receives justice."

When we walked in, a man in a black suit looked at me and said, "Is this a joke?"

"What?" the sheriff asked.

"That's the woman who took out the insurance policy on Mr. Jacobs's life."

My mouth dropped open. "I've never seen you before. Who are you, anyway?" I said.

"You know very well who I am, young lady. I'm George Vanderpelt of Carrier's Life Insurance Company."

Who addresses someone in her twenties as "young lady"? Who even used that expression anymore?

"This is Nate's sister," Jess said. "She did *not* take out the insurance policy. She hasn't even been in the state. She's been in DC. You're mistaken."

"Please, sit down, Mr. Vanderpelt and Ms. Jacobs." The sheriff looked at Jay with a question.

"This is Jay Benson, our next-door neighbor," I said.

"Yes, I know Mr. Benson," the sheriff said.

"Sheriff, there's something wrong. As Jess said, I've been out of town and I would have no reason to take out a life insurance policy on my brother."

"I am *not* mistaken," the insurance man said. "You are the one who came to my office and asked about the life insurance policy, but you said you were Mrs. Jacobs, Nathaniel's wife. I told you I'd have to have your signature and that of your husband before the policy could be finalized. I came here, but your daughter said you were at school."

"Are you telling me I look old enough to be her mother?" I said. Annie smiled slightly. Under different circumstances, she'd be howling. "I'm telling you, I wasn't even in the state."

"She's right," Annie said. "You asked me about my mother." She pointed at Jess. "She teaches at the local school."

"Well, I'm telling you that *she* is the one who came to my office in Albany." He pointed at me with a jerk of his arm.

"Sheriff, I will be glad to give you names of people in Washington, DC, who knew my whereabouts on the day in question. What day was it, Mr. Vanderhuff?"

"George Vanderpelt," he said. "The day was last Tuesday, July 25, as you very well know."

"Let me get my notebook," I said. I dove into my bag, anxious to prove where I'd been. When I flipped through to July 25, I back-stepped a bit. "That's the day I flew to Chicopee, Georgia. I spent most of the day with two people, and my airline tickets and car rental receipts should supply you with ample proof of my location."

"I don't know how you did it," Mr. Vanderpelt said, "but unless you have a twin, it was you."

"Do you have your airline stubs with you?" the sheriff asked. "And Mr. Vanderpelt, this may be a moot point if, as you say, the life insurance paper did not have the necessary signatures to make it effective."

"That's why I came. Nathaniel Jacobs did sign the papers."

"May I see the signature?" Jess asked.

Vanderpelt looked at the sheriff with his eyebrows raised.

"Why not?" the sheriff said. "I don't see any harm in that. Are you saying that the policy is effective because Mr. Jacobs signed it?

"It looks like Nate's signature," Jess said, "but I don't think he'd have signed it in a million years. I told you, he was against insurance."

"This is quite a mystery, then," the sheriff said. "When did Mr. Jacobs sign the policy?"

"The day I came to the farm. Last Friday, when Ms. Annie Jacobs told me her mother was at school. She directed me to the barn to get Nathaniel's signature."

"Annie, was there anyone besides your father at the barn, or did you see him sign the policy?" I asked.

"There was a salesman or someone at the barn. I didn't recognize the truck."

"Did you actually see Nate in the barn," I said.

"No, but I thought he was there. His pickup was parked near the barn."

"He could have been anywhere with another vehicle," I said. "He has four-wheelers and tractors. I bet the other person whose vehicle you saw at the barn signed it. Did you see him at all, Annie?"

"No, just the truck."

"What can you remember about the other vehicle, Ms. Jacobs?" the sheriff asked.

"It was a black Dodge, one-ton dually," Annie said.

"Did it have New York plates?" Sheriff Carson continued.

"Yes, the newer ones, orange with blue lettering."

"I'll check into it. Now, Mr. Vanpelt?"

"Vanderpelt," he corrected the sheriff.

"Is this life insurance policy a valid one or not?" Carson said.

"It is."

"Who is the beneficiary and how much will she or he receive?"

"The beneficiary is Ms. Valerie Jacobs, and the amount she'll receive is one million dollars."

Jay had been silent until now. "That's ludicrous," he said. "I know Nate didn't take out a policy and name Valerie the beneficiary, but I think I do know what's going on. Let me call Ken, Sheriff, but I need to speak with you alone first."

The sheriff and Jay stepped outside, and within a few minutes, Carson came back in the house. "Mr. Vanderpelt, I'd like you to come to the station in a little while to give us more details. Is that possible?"

"Of course," he said. He looked at me and smiled, and the sheriff asked him to wait while he talked to me.

"Ms. Jacobs, I'd like to speak with you alone."

I led him into the living room where he was able to ask me questions openly. "Jay has filled me in with what's going on in the capital. I'm giving you a pass for the time being. I'm going with the idea that someone is trying to frame you to stop your investigation."

I couldn't help but think he knew about this whole thing before, in part because he referred to Jay by his first name. Ordinarily, a police officer would refer to him as Mr. Benson.

"I appreciate that," I said.

"Jay vouched for you, so I can give you a little time, but if it turns out you did take out the policy, nothing will stop me from coming after you. Do you understand?" His voice had changed and was totally firm.

"Of course. I would expect nothing less," I said.

CHAPTER 21

The next morning, I flew back to DC alone. I hadn't told Jay I was going because I knew he'd insist on coming with me. Like I needed help protecting myself. Annie drove me to the airport. I didn't reserve my seat until I arrived in Albany. I timed it so I'd be there just in time for the 9:20 Southwest flight to Baltimore, no time for anyone to track me. They might be watching Reagan International, but wouldn't expect me to fly into Baltimore. Annie wanted to come with me, but I convinced her Jess needed her more right now. I promised to get her to DC as soon as possible, well before she was scheduled to start at Georgetown.

"You know I'm following you in a few days, don't you?"

"I wouldn't be surprised, but make sure you're careful. Don't tell anyone but your mother you're coming. Keep yourself safe. Can you ask Jess's brother to come to the farm for a visit so she won't be alone?"

"Actually, Uncle Jack just retired, so I'm sure he'd come. I think Aunt Jill is still working, so he'd probably welcome something to do, and she'd be thankful to have him out of the house for a while. I guess he's going crazy, doesn't know what to do with himself."

"Great. With Jack there, I won't have to worry about Jess. Can you fill him in on what's happening, or shall I call him?"

"I'll fill him in, but I'm sure he'll want to talk to you, too. This will be right up his alley. He'll be thrilled to help."

"You take care." I hugged Annie goodbye and went upstairs to security. I only had fifteen minutes to get through, but there weren't many travelers. When I moved to the TSA agent at the podium, she looked at my ID and boarding pass. She hesitated and asked me to step to the side.

"Is there a problem?" I asked. "I was just given the boarding pass downstairs."

"Just step over here, Ma'am," she said.

If I didn't get through security within the next three minutes, I was going to miss my flight, to say nothing of the fact she'd called me "ma'am." Did she think I was fifty? She must have had my name on a list or something.

"My flight is boarding now," I said. "If you can tell me the issue, I'm sure it can be cleared up quickly." I spoke a little louder than I'd meant to, but it turned out to be a good thing. The agent pulled an iPhone out of her back pocket and pushed a number, but shoved the phone back in her pocket when another TSA agent approached. From his stripe, I could tell he was a lieutenant, probably the one in charge.

"What seems to be the problem?" he addressed the agent.

"I wasn't sure the ID was legitimate," she lied.

"Let me see it," he said to me. He ran an instrument over my ID and directed me to the line with the least people waiting. "Looks fine," he said, giving the agent a look. "Stop in my office before you leave today," he said to her, "and remember, you're not allowed to make personal calls during your shift."

"Yes sir," she replied, and continued checking IDs. He stood next to her during the time it took me to get through the line, her brow sweating and her face pinking.

I had to run for the gate, but made it at the final boarding call. I was sure the agent was being paid to alert someone I was returning to Washington, but if I was lucky, I'd be in Washington before she was able to use her phone to call. Or, maybe I was just imagining things. I tended to get paranoid when so much was happening.

When I arrived in DC, I didn't see anything or anyone unusual at the airport. I'd called Ken when I got on the plane, and he'd arranged for Ethan Scott to meet me at the curb.

"I'm sorry for your loss," Ethan said as soon as I met him outside the baggage area.

"Thank you," I said. "I'm going to find out who did this."

"I thought . . ." he trailed off.

"My brother did *not* commit suicide," I said.

He didn't say anything, just looked at me questioningly. Probably thought I was in denial. "Ken asked me to give you this envelope," he said. "I believe it's the latest information. There's also an article Ken is running in today's paper. It will blow everything wide open. Ken wants your take on it. He respects your opinion and journalistic skills, and so do I," he said.

I opened the envelope and started reading. "Wow," I said. "Does he have proof that will hold up?"

"You know he wouldn't run it if he didn't," Scott said. "Representative Engle said this is critical. The American people have to know what's going on so they can make up their own minds."

"So, what's going to happen when the paper comes out?"

"The vice president and Ken are going to speak to WAFR at *Washington In Depth*'s office to coincide with the release of the paper today. He's bringing in people who've been directly affected by the takeover. Each of them will confirm the validity of that portion of the article referring to his situation."

"Wow, and the politicians and businesspeople behind the takeover are going to let this happen? Do they know?"

Scott smiled. "Of course not, and I don't think they'll find out. The only ones who know about it are the vice president, Ken, and the owner of WAFR. She's not even telling the camerapeople where they're going. Nadia Pearson, the owner of WAFR, will conduct the interviews live. Once they get started, pardon my expression, the shit will hit the fan big time."

"No pardon needed. I grew up on a farm. That was one of the milder phrases. What time did you say it was starting?"

"Twelve thirty. Everyone's already here. Flew in yesterday and the day before, staggered them, even though we don't think the conglomerate knows anything about their identity, too arrogant to think we know much. We aren't so overconfident that we think we *do* know everything, but today should bring out the big guns. The conspirators will either go underground farther or make some big mistakes trying for damage control.

"I'm guessing all the news agencies will be over them like glue. Hopefully some will fear getting caught and offer to talk, whistleblower status. If we can get to the right person, it will be all over."

"You're not really thinking this'll be it, are you?" I didn't think Ethan was naïve enough to think people used to power would crumble so easily.

"Of course not, but Ken's hoping there'll be one or two on the lower rung of the conspiracy who will be scared enough to talk, be willing to turn in their associates."

"Want to go to your apartment or directly to the paper?"

"The paper," I replied. "By the way, why didn't Ken call me about this? I hope he knew I'd come."

"Ken has respect for you. He'd never have asked you to come back when you had a death in the family."

"Of course, I should have known."

By the time we made it through traffic and to the office, it was nearly twelve. Scott dropped me at the paper and drove on down Cambridge to find a parking place. When I walked in, I saw Kate and David Fisher and Carrie and Steve Dawson. "It's so good to see you," I said, shaking hands all around. Ethan was filling me in."

"What's going on?" David asked. "Ken called yesterday afternoon and told us to be on the 8 p.m. flight to Washington."

"You can tell Ken's not a farmer," Kate said. "He doesn't know how hard it is to get someone to cover the work at home. We were lucky David's brother was visiting. He was nice enough to tell us to go ahead and he'd handle the farm. What's this all about?"

Ken appeared from his office. "I'm expecting Mitchel and Amy from Nebraska any minute. Then I'll explain everything. In the meantime, anyone need lunch?"

"I'm starving," I said, so fast that everyone turned toward me. "Sorry, but I don't think I've eaten much in the last few days."

"I can understand," Ken said. "Rosemary, would you order us an assortment of sandwiches and salads from Jonathan's?"

"Of course," she replied. "Any restrictions or preferences?" she addressed everyone.

After we all replied with headshakes or "no," she disappeared into Ken's office. Shortly after, Mitchell and Amy arrived by cab. After the usual greetings and introductions, Ken began.

"We're going live on WAFR at 12:30 to address the American people and tell them what we know—only the facts as we know them. Let them draw their own conclusions. The vice president will address the American people immediately prior to our broadcast. After giving them the overall picture of the conspiracy, he will warn of future announcements about the plan to take over the farmland in the United States. That's when we'll report."

"You're doing the talking, right?" Amy looked at Ken.

"After the vice president, I'll start," Ken said, "but I want each of you to speak when it's time."

"I don't know that I can do that," Amy said, her voice shaking.

"I have nothing prepared," Carrie said.

"That's the whole idea," Ken said. "Unlike how the conspirators think, the American public can see through deceit. If you had rehearsed lines, they'd think it was just like a reality show, practiced to make them believe what you were saying. I'll ask you to give detail from your own experience. There's not one of you who can't answer my questions. You're living this. Just imagine you're sitting in your kitchen, talking to friends."

There was silence.

Ken continued. "No makeup, no rehearsal, if you stammer, it's alright. Just talk from your hearts. As I said, you've been living this. There's nothing you don't know about your situation."

"You won't be asking us anything not directly related to our situation in Utah?" David said.

"No, and if I ask you anything you're unsure of, ask me to clarify or say you don't understand or don't know. Be one hundred percent honest. Our goal is to educate the American people by giving them the facts, not try to influence them in any way. Because, after all, it's their decision. If people don't care where their food comes from, who takes advantage of them, or how much they pay for it, we don't have a problem. But, if the majority thinks they deserve honesty from the elected officials and in those they do business with, they will care."

"Where do we do this? It doesn't seem there's enough room here to fit cameras, camerapeople, and all of us," Amy said, still sounding worried.

"We'll do fine," Ken said. "Let's get organized." Ken asked the men to help him, and they moved most of the furniture to the side. We sat in chairs around the old printing machine.

We'd no sooner gotten settled in our places according to how Ken was going to ask us questions, when the cameramen showed up, two of them with huge cameras. Walking in behind them was the owner of the station—a former investigative reporter, Nadia Pearson, highly respected by other journalists and the public.

Behind her, the vice president and two Secret Service agents entered. Ken introduced Dan Daly to Nadia, then each of us. Mouths dropped open at the sight of the VP. There was a visible uptick in tension from the visitors, sitting up straighter, hands shaking or clasped tightly, shifting in their seats. The agents stood next to the vice president until he asked them to step back out of the camera's view. "No point in putting you at risk," he said.

"We'll stay with you, Mr. Vice President," the taller agent said, leaving no room for discussion.

Nadia directed the vice president to the empty chair near the center of the group. The agents stood behind him. A number of wires were plugged into the walls, and the TV crew brought in lights on tall stands. Nadia passed us the mic so we could try it out. "Don't worry," she said. "Just talk normally and not too close to the mic. You'll come through fine. No need to raise voices. The lights will be bright, but try not to squint. You have about five minutes."

"Wish I'd dressed better," Amy said. She wore gray dress slacks with a white shirt that fit her slim figure perfectly. Of course she looked wonderful compared to me, still in my cargo pants and wrinkled, sleeveless shirt from the plane ride. The men were dressed in jeans, T-shirts, and caps—the farmer uniform.

"We wanted everyone in what they usually wear," Ken said. "No pretense here. Just be yourselves."

"All right, everyone," Nadia said. "Make sure you're in your place. Ted, turn on the lights." The cameraman complied, and everyone froze as the room brightened, causing us all to squint. Then all the lights went out.

"Everyone stay where you are," Ken said. "It's just overload. I'll check the circuit box." He moved to the back of the room and into his office, where the board was located.

"Not the circuit breaker," Ken said, returning to the group.

"Three minutes to air, Ken. Shall we go to plan B?" Nadia said.

"Better," Ken said. "While your guys take care of that, I need to check outside. Mitch, Dave, Steve, come with me."

"What's plan B?" I asked Nadia.

"The camera boys have gone out to hook up the generator in the truck. Ken anticipated trouble. We're always ready with backup power, especially when we film in these older buildings. The wiring isn't updated. Ken also wanted to be prepared in case there was a leak and the conspirators tried to stop the broadcast."

"One minute," Nadia said. The camerapeople were back in the building and hooking the generator into the equipment. Ken and the others hadn't returned.

"Don't worry," Nadia said. "Ken will be back in time."

How could she be so calm? Must be part of the job. It was one thing writing stories for a paper or online, and another entirely appearing live spontaneously. I couldn't do it.

She'd barely finished the sentence when Ken and the others walked in the side door and took their seats.

"Twenty seconds. Everyone in your places?" Nadia said. "Don't hit the lights until exactly 12:30," she addressed her cameramen.

Lights on. "Good afternoon, all," Nadia said. "Today we have a special broadcast for all Americans. Grab your phone and call anyone you know who might be interested in learning what some of your congressmen, senators, executive office members, and businesspeople are doing with your money and what they plan to do to you. After our initial address, the people who will be speaking today are ordinary citizens like you. The only difference is that they were affected sooner. They've been researching and learning about what their government officials have done.

"I'd like to present the vice president of the United States, Mr. Dan Daly."

"Good afternoon, fellow Americans. I felt compelled to advise you some of your elected officials, business enterprises, and foreign entities have been perpetrating a hoax on you, the American electorate. You voted for your executive and legislative representatives, trusting that they would follow your wishes and do what was in the best interest of the country. In my opinion and in the opinion of others, you are being duped. There is a conspiracy afoot to take over the country's land, food supplies, energy resources, and water supplies, to place them in the hands of a few who will make a profit while you lose those resources. You will be hearing more specific details in the coming days so you can make up your minds if you are as concerned as we are about the actions being taken. Nadia," Daly said, handing the mic back to Ms. Pearson.

"Thank you, Vice President Daly," Nadia said. The vice president and the Secret Service agents exited the building.

"I'd like to introduce you to Ken Bentz, the editor of *Washington In Depth*, a Washington, DC, newspaper. He began the investigation into agriculture three years ago. Ken, please start by telling us why you started your investigation in the first place."

Nadia handed a mic to Ken. "I'll be as direct as I know how to be with you, the American people. I suggest you take notes or DVR this presentation so you can refer to it later, as you check the facts we give you. I was at a political dinner three years ago, on July 4. I'd been asked to attend by a United States senator friend. He wanted me to circulate and listen. He wouldn't give me any hint as to what I was listening for, just that he was concerned about what he thought might be taking place. No other clues. I did as he asked, because he was as far away from an alarmist as one could be—a laid-back guy, you might say.

"What I heard sounded like a movie. As I circulated, high-ranking administrative personnel, senators, and representatives talked to businessmen and women. What they said led me to believe they thought it would be a good idea to take over agriculture in this country. The reason for this was not clear that night, but having researched and investigated and confabbed with people around our country over the past three years, I've found that reason. The conspirators planned first to take over the food supply in the United

States, then charge exorbitant prices to the public, thus making themselves rich and powerful. What could be more formidable than to control the food supply?

"The conspiracy has not yet touched most of you. I'd like you to hear directly from people who have already been affected by the takeover. I'd like to introduce Carrie and Steve Dawson. Steve, will you begin by telling the public why you lost your farm?"

"It started when the county government took over the water flowing through our land," Steve began. "We were no longer able to use the water without paying the government officials. Now, we want to pay our way, so we were, at first, willing to do what was asked. Then we found out the reason for the diversion of the water—so the county governments could sell the water to other states. Politicians sold us out for money. They sold out their own local communities for money. As if that wasn't bad enough, when farms started going out of business due to water shortages, guess who bought the farms? I'll tell you who bought them." Steve's voice rose, and he sounded angry.

"Let's let Carrie continue, shall we?" Ken said, patting Steve on the shoulder, trying to soothe him.

"The same politicians who charged for the water and their friends in business bought the farms, at the same time telling the farmers they were doing them a favor. We have names, if you'd like them now," Carrie addressed Ken.

"I don't think we'll have time for that tonight," Ken said. "We can publish those in the paper. But let's hear from Mitch from Nebraska. He has a different story, but with similar results. Then we'll listen to the Fishers from Utah."

Mitch told the abbreviated stories about the milk-processing plants going out of business, the rising transportation costs, and the foreign investors buying United States land. The Fishers added to the Dawson story. Then Ken took the mic back. "I have just one more thing to add. Others who have been researching and investigating this conspiracy have been followed, and their families have been put in harm's way. Today, in an attempt to stop this presentation to the American people, the power was cut to this building."

We all turned toward Ken, shocked, although I'm not sure why. I, of all people, having been run off the road while traveling with Jay, shouldn't have been surprised.

"Luckily," he continued, "Nadia and her crew from WAFR were prepared with generators. Otherwise, the bad guys would have won this one. We want you to know, no matter what happens, we will not stop our search to bring you the truth unless you tell us to drop it. Now, I'd like to finish by asking my colleague, without whom much of this information would have been available, to speak to you. Val?"

Many thoughts went through my head in the seconds before I answered Ken, one of which was, "How could he do this to me?" Then I knew I was all in. I had to do this, especially after the text I'd received from Annie just before the show.

I took the mic and faced the camera, all fear leaving me. "Five days ago, my brother, a man who brought me up and had never done a wrong thing to anyone, was murdered. It was made to look like a suicide, but I received word from my niece just before this presentation aired that the sheriff has found irrefutable evidence that it was homicide, made to look like suicide. There have been no arrests yet, but I want the person who did this to know there is no way you are scaring me off. There is no doubt you have taken away the person who was closest to me. It will not be for nothing. I will not stop until you are all exposed for what you are. That's all." I handed the mic to Nadia, who spoke next.

"You have heard what these people had to say," Nadia said. "You may let them know what you think by emailing, texting, or writing the studio to my attention. Thank you."

She looked over at us. "And, we're off air."

CHAPTER 22

"Knowing that you'd want to get home as soon as possible, I've taken the liberty of reserving flights for you for this afternoon," Ken said, addressing the Dawsons, the Fishers, and Mitch and Amy. "And I'd like you out of here before our adversaries have a chance to find you. Call me if you have any adverse effects as a result of the broadcast. The public will need to know if there are any repercussions against you.

"I didn't ask Nadia to tell the public to contact her station with their opinions, but I was glad she did," Ken continued. "The response will let us know if the people are behind our continued investigation. I'm guessing we should have a reaction by tomorrow morning. I'll let all of you know as soon as I hear from Nadia. We've rented a van and driver to take you to the airport. Again, I appreciate all of you giving up your lives for the day to address this issue."

"After all you've done, it's the least we could do—although, I thought I'd soil myself when I had to talk," Amy said.

That was enough to break us into laughter, releasing tension, a suitable closing for the day. Ken and I said goodbye to everyone, and I asked him if I could talk to him briefly.

"Why didn't you ask Jay to come?" I said.

"Why didn't you tell Jay you were coming back to DC?" he said.

"I'm not sure—just wanted to be alone, I guess. I've had a bit of a struggle dealing with my brother's death. My reactions weren't exactly normal."

"We never know how we'll react until it happens to us, and who's to say what's normal?" he said. "I didn't tell Jay because I didn't want any leaks."

"He wouldn't tell anyone," I said. Ken didn't trust Jay? How could that be? "I don't understand."

"There've been leaks, and I don't know where they're coming from. Someone from the conspirators' side obviously knew what we were up to. The electrical wires were cut only to this building. We've had other incidents at the paper. Either someone's listening to everything we're doing or having us followed, or someone I've put trust in is trading information to our enemies. I have to find the source."

"Well, I can tell you that I've known Jay all my life. Farming is everything to him, and he's a person you can trust. He does what he says, and he would never betray this cause."

"I want to believe you."

"Did you distrust me, too? Is that the real reason you didn't call me?"

"I wouldn't lie to you, Valerie. I've trusted you since I first met you. I don't think you could lie without it showing. I didn't call you because I thought you had more serious matters to deal with. I called the others personally and asked them not to tell anyone where they were going. Nadia didn't tell any of her people their destination, and even drove the van herself so she wouldn't be giving any of her people directions verbally, thus allowing someone to listen."

"I still would put my life in Jay's hands. You can trust him, Ken. I promise you."

"I consider that a glowing recommendation, and I'll seriously weigh any reservations I have before making a judgment. But I'd like you to contemplate the possibility that there's someone among us we can't trust. Be watchful. Now, Ethan is waiting inside to drive you home, and I won't take no for an answer. I'd like to tell you to sleep in tomorrow morning, but I'll need you here early. I'll contact Nadia first thing to determine the response from the general public."

CHAPTER 23

It couldn't be my alarm. It had to be the middle of the night. I reached for my cell on the bedside table—4:30. Who the hell? Jess's cell. "What's wrong?"

"Val, turn on your TV," Annie said.

"You called to watch TV?"

"Just turn it on," Annie said.

"Okay, okay, just a minute. What channel?"

"Any channel." Was she going crazy?

Then I saw what she meant. I left it on one channel for a few minutes, then flipped through the other channels. On every news channel, there were clips of last night's newscast. I finally left it on TNN, the most pro-administration station I could find. If this was at all being believed, this was the place to find out. I watched.

"And the closing was particularly moving, when Valerie Jacobs spoke," Maya Borg, the morning anchor said. My speech played. I hadn't realized my eyes were filled with tears while I was talking. I was so busy being angry I didn't know there was also grief showing.

"Oh my God," I said.

"Haven't heard you use His name lately."

"Very funny."

"Just wanted to be the first to hear your reaction."

"Thanks, Annie. Love you. How are you doing, and how's your mom?"

"Love you too, Valerie. We're doing fine. Should I come down there and help? Mom could come, too."

"No. Don't come yet. I'll call if I need you. Talk to you tonight, or as soon as I have any more information. Love you."

"Aunt Val, be careful. I bet there're a lot of people mad at you, a lot of powerful people. We can't lose you, too."

She never called me Aunt Val. "Don't worry, Annie. I won't take unnecessary chances."

I showered, dressed, and walked into the kitchen with the intent of fixing coffee. Nan was already at the table, and handed me a cup when I walked in. The TV was on. "You're quite a celebrity," she said, an edge to her voice I couldn't quite identify.

"Very funny. Have they said anything about people's reaction to the address?"

"Only that the network's computer system crashed because of all the emails, tweets, and social network posts."

"Are you going to tell me if they believed what we said, or do I have to call the station?"

"You can try if you want, but I doubt you'll be able to get through. The phone lines are jammed, too."

"So?" I said. Nan was playing coy for some reason, making me wait for answers.

"Overwhelmingly calling for an investigation. There are demonstrations planned in New York, Washington, Philadelphia, and every other major city in the United States. There have never been demonstrations planned so quickly and so organized—according to WAFR, that is." Nan sounded skeptical.

"Wow. I've got to call Ken. See what our next step is."

"I'd say you did what you meant to do. Now the public will take over and do what has to be done." Such a flat voice for Nan.

"You don't know how powerful these people are and how much money they have poured into this conspiracy. They're not going to give up. We're going to have to keep investigating."

"If you say so," Nan said.

"Coming home early tonight?"

"I'm hoping so. I've been up since three working on this brief. Planning to be home by five. Want to grab some dinner, or have dinner here? I can pick it up on the way home."

"Sounds good," I said. "I'll try my best. Call you if I can't make it. We haven't had much chance to talk lately, so it would be good to catch up."

"See you tonight," Nan said.

I couldn't wait to get to the office and talk to Ken about our next step. I took a cab and practically ran into the office. When I closed the door behind me, Rosemary sat toward the wall. I thought she was talking on the phone, or listening rather. As I moved closer to her, I realized her head was in her hands and she was crying.

"What's wrong, Rosemary?"

"It's Ken. He was run down by a hit-and-run driver early this morning."

"Oh my God! Is he . . . gone?"

"No. He's hanging on, but not by much. The doctor said it would be touch-and-go for the next twenty-four hours. Ken wouldn't let me stay, wanted me to get back to the office and help you run things."

"Run things? I can't run things. I work for Ken. I don't know how to run a paper. I'm going to the hospital. Where is he?"

"You can't go. He can't have visitors."

"How did you get in to see him?"

Rosemary hesitated. "I was with him. He'd gotten a tip to meet someone at the southwest entrance to Dumbarton Oaks. The caller wouldn't give his name. I thought it sounded dodgy, but Ken wasn't about to pass up the possibility of procuring a whistleblower. I shouldn't have dropped him off. I should have stayed, but he insisted."

"I don't get it. Don't you live on the other side of Georgetown?"

She looked at me. "Oh, I'm so sorry," I said. "Sometimes I'm pretty thick. Are you okay? Were you hit, too?"

"No, I'm fine. I'd gone into Starbucks to grab a coffee. If I hadn't needed my caffeine fix, I might have seen the car coming, or maybe it wouldn't have run him down if I'd been with him—you know, a witness."

"And maybe you'd have been hit, too. Do you think it was intentional?"

"The detective who questioned me said there were no skid marks. The driver tried to hit Ken. It wasn't an accident. I'm sure it was all because of last night's broadcast."

"What time did this happen? It's only nine now. What time were you coming to work?"

"We left my apartment about 5 a.m. He would have left by 3:30, but I told him Starbucks didn't open until five, and there was no way I'd go to work without my blonde roast. If we'd left earlier, I bet they wouldn't have been waiting for him. He'd be all right." She started crying again.

"I'm sorry, Rosemary, but you don't have time to feel guilty, any more than I have time to grieve my brother. Ken is still alive, and there's no way he'll give in. There are more people involved in this than we know, and we have to find out who they are. That's the best thing you can do for Ken right now. So, in the words of my mother, you need to buck up and get to work."

Rosemary looked up at me like I'd slapped her face. "How can you be so cold?"

"I don't know. If that's what you think it is, maybe I'm just an unfeeling person. I'll break down later, when I've nailed the bastard who killed my brother."

"I'm sorry," she said. "You're right. Where shall we begin?"

"Are you sure Ken wanted me to run things? You know more about it than I do."

"He said you should take over until he gets back and that I'm to help you with whatever you want."

"Okay then. I guess I have no choice. Let's start with our list of contacts. Warn everyone that was on the news show last night, especially those who spoke. Include Nadia and her cameramen—they may be at risk as well. A text is probably quickest."

"I did anticipate we'd have to contact everyone," she said, showing me a list.

"Let them know Ken has been attacked and is in the hospital, so they should be watchful. We'll contact them as soon as we know anything about Ken's status."

"Of course. What about Jay?"

"Leave him off the list for now. I'll contact him," I said. Ken had planted a seed of doubt about Jay in my mind. I'd have trusted him with my life before Ken's comment. I'd lived next to Jay all my life. We grew up together. But still.

I picked up my phone and went into Ken's office for some privacy.

"Hi Marion, Jay around?"

"He's in the barn, but he'll probably pick up. He was upset when he found out you'd gone back to Washington without telling him. When he saw the broadcast last night, I thought he was going to explode. He was hurt you hadn't told him about it."

"Actually, I didn't come back for that. I came back to find out who killed Nate. I had no idea there was going to be a broadcast until I got here. I've had a little trouble dealing with Nate's death, and I probably haven't been myself."

I heard a click on the phone. "Hi J—"

"What the hell are you doing, Val? Going back to DC without telling anyone, then doing a broadcast that could get you killed. Have you lost your mind? Don't you *think*?"

"Number one, I don't have to tell you every move I make, and like I told your mother, I didn't know about the broadcast until I got to DC. And why would you say that I could get myself killed?" I was getting more suspicious of Jay by the minute, and how dare he talk to me like that?

"Look, if you can stop yelling at me for a minute, I called you for a reason. Ken is in the hospital, the victim of a hit-and-run. I thought you'd want to know."

I waited for his reaction. He took a deep breath. "Should I come down there? I'm worried about you. I'm sorry."

"I'll call if I need you. I may need some information from you."

"Anything you need. Is the paper shutting down until Ken gets on his feet?"

"I'm running it until he gets back," I replied, and waited, and waited, and waited for his reply.

"Do you think you should do that?"

"You think I can't handle it?" I said.

"That's not what I meant. I was just . . ."

"I have to go, Jay. A lot to do."

"Be careful, Val."

I hung up.

Rosemary and I set up a plan of action. Our first order of business was to have a meeting with the principal players of our investigation. It would include everyone located in DC and the surrounding area. It was set for two days later. It would be the most secretive meeting yet, with everyone involved congregating in one place. The only person missing would be Ken. I decided I did trust Jay, in spite of what Ken had said, and would invite him, but I didn't let him know the scope of the meeting. I felt the all-encompassing meeting was necessary due to what had happened to Ken. We needed to move up our plan before the conspirators had a chance to move on with theirs.

Because I wasn't overly confident my plan could be accomplished, I decided to contact Representative Engle and run it by him. He was a stickler for detail, and I knew he'd see any flaws. He was in session but called me back about five minutes after I'd texted him. The senator said he'd come to the office when he finished at the Senate. He arrived at noon with lunch for the three of us.

"Wow," I said, "didn't know you were bringing lunch."

"No big deal. Hope you still like hotdogs with sauerkraut. I remember you and Beth eating them Saturday nights when you were at the house."

"Love them," I replied. "Rosemary?"

"Not on your life, and I mean that. Your life will be worth nothing putting those so-called meats and chemicals in your body. I'm surprised at you, Val. Besides, I always bring my lunch—all organic and none of that processed food for me."

I wasn't intimidated. "Thanks," I said, and took a bite. "Delicious."

"Glad you like it. Guess you'll have to eat Rosemary's portion."

"Don't mind if I do."

We had everything laid out on Ken's desk. "We need you to take a look and see if our plan is feasible."

"Val, I'm sorry about Nate."

The hotdog lost its taste, and I set it down. I'd actually forgotten about Nate for a couple minutes. How could I? I was enjoying a hotdog while my brother was dead because I had to dig into this deal.

"Sorry," he said. "I shouldn't have said anything."

"It's not you. I'm handling it. Let's look at the plan."

After discussing the feasibility of my choice of meeting places, he convinced me it would be less suspicious to meet at my apartment, or I should say Nan's apartment, under the guise of a charity meeting. "I'll set up a special meeting of a charity I sponsor and invite the others. Let me handle it. Just give me the contact list. No one will think twice about a charity meeting. I'll have my secretary contact everyone."

"Thank you, Mr. Engle. I'll try to talk to Ken before the meeting and have an agenda we can follow with our next moves. I think we need to shore up what's next to ensure everyone's on board. Can I ask you a more personal question?"

"Of course."

"I wouldn't repeat this if Ken were not laid up, but I need your advice."

Representative Engle remained quiet, waiting for me to speak.

"Do you trust Jay? Ken's not sure of him at this point. I was going to tell him about the meeting but not let him know its scope. What do you think?"

He hesitated before answering. "Valerie, I know you've known Jay your whole life, but people do change. Did you have much contact with him after high school?"

"No. I didn't even come home summers once I left for college, and I took a job in the city right after college. So, no." I waited for him to continue.

"You probably should trust your intuition. If you feel confident doing so, invite him. Your thoughts?"

"I guess I feel devious not asking him. He was involved before me."

"If you have doubts, you can say you only asked people in the DC area for this particular meeting."

"I guess I can look at it that way," I said.

CHAPTER 24

The next two days, Rosemary and I worked on an agenda for the planned meeting at the apartment. Ken continued to improve according to our calls to the hospital, but he still wasn't allowed direct calls or visitors. Rosemary crossed in front of Ken's desk and turned on the TV.

"What's going on?"

"You'll see. And you won't believe it."

"As promised," Bill Hutt of WMHY said, "the real story behind Valerie Jacobs, the investigative reporter who claimed her brother was killed by higher-ups in a conspiracy to take over the country's farming industry. It turns out that Ms. Jacobs is actually a suspect in her brother's death. She purchased a million-dollar, double indemnity life insurance policy on her own brother just days before his death. She stands to collect two million dollars—that is, *if* she can prove it wasn't suicide, thus her insistence her brother's death was a homicide. And, of course, *if* she's not convicted of his death. Certainly brings into question any of the rubbish she and her group were spouting last night, doesn't it?"

"It's started sooner than I thought," I said.

"These people will stop at nothing," Rosemary said. "First they kill your brother, then they try to kill Ken. Now they're trying to destroy your credibility."

"No problem," I said. "My name will be cleared soon, and I have to believe the people who know me will not believe that shit. Sorry. I revert to old habits when I'm pissed."

"Rosemary, call all the people involved in exposing the conspiracy and warn them. Don't worry about notifying the politicians and others in and around Washington. They'll know what's going on, but call the people in Utah, Nebraska, and anyone else out of town. Let them know that if they want out, it's okay. We can't protect them from here. Their credibility will be hit next. Use the burners Ken bought."

"Of course. I'll let you know their responses."

I called Jess to let her know what was coming.

"Already heard," Jess said. "TNN picked it up. All the neighbors are calling and stopping by to tell us they're behind us, all of us, including you. They didn't know whether to believe your report last night until TNN reported you were a suspect in Nate's death. They knew then you were right. My uncle is already here, too, and he wants to talk to you." She put Jeb on the phone.

"Val, I'm coming down there, taking the ten o'clock flight tomorrow morning. I'm booked at the Hyatt near the capital."

"You can't. You have to stay on the farm and protect Jess and Annie. I couldn't live with myself if anything happened to them. I can handle things here."

"You remember Curt and Gail Congdon? They were on the force with me."

"I do," I said.

"They're on their way here right now. Will be at the farm in about twenty minutes. They'll stay here as long as necessary."

"I appreciate you coming. Thanks, Uncle Jeb. I'll meet you at the airport."

"I look forward to seeing you and learning more. I'll make sure you're safe, in the background, of course."

Nothing further of any consequence was reported in the news the rest of the day. Rosemary said all the farmers involved were still in one hundred percent. The feedback they got from neighbors was horror that the perpetrators would try to destroy my credibility. They didn't believe it for a minute. Said they'd be ready for whatever hit them next.

I was sure our adversaries were planning their strategy but hadn't expected the forthcoming reaction. There'd been a tremendous backlash against TNN, with 90 percent of the Twitter feedback negative, especially after our local sheriff was interviewed and said I was out of the state on the day I was supposed to have signed the life insurance papers and when Nate was killed. He further commented that his investigator was close to discovering the identity of the man and woman who'd impersonated Nate and me, initiating the purchase of the insurance policy. An arrest was imminent, he noted.

I hadn't asked Nan if she was good with having the meeting at the apartment tonight, and was unable to reach her. I was told she would be in court until after six. That would be too late. She'd told me when I moved in that I should treat the apartment as if it were my own, so I hoped she wouldn't mind.

As soon as Rosemary and I put the paper to bed, truly a joint effort, she checked with the hospital about Ken's condition and picked up his laptop that he'd fortunately given to Rosemary before the hit-and-run. We headed to Jonathan's in Rosemary's Prius, where we picked up the food Rosemary had ordered earlier and continued to the apartment. At the security gate, I let David Nare know about the night's meeting.

"See your tail?" he asked. Rosemary started to turn around, but I put my hand on her arm to caution her.

"Yup," I said.

"Usually, after you're in, they take off—probably figure you're in for the night."

"Good," I said. "But I supposed they'll tail the others here tonight."

"Everyone's covered for tonight. There'll be no tails to this location."

"How can you be sure?"

"Believe me, no one will be followed tonight. The ones who usually do the tailing are going to be busy answering calls to other locations. By the time they realize what's going on, it'll be too late, and everyone will be safely back in their own homes."

"Will you be coming in for the meeting?"

"No. I have a lot to do here. I'm part of the decoy operation. You just get everything settled so we can return to our normal lives."

"We'll try. Oh, by the way—Nan doesn't know about the meeting, so you might want to inform her so she's not shocked when she walks into her apartment and sees the representatives, the vice president, and others," I said.

Rosemary drove into the garage. I grabbed a luggage cart from the stairwell, loaded the food onto it, and we went up the elevator to Nan's apartment. We'd just finished setting the food out on the kitchen counters when the first visitor arrived. "Only 6:30," I said.

"Hi, Penelope. I'm afraid we're not very fancy, but please help yourself to some food."

"Good food is good food," she said. "Looks like Jonathan's. That's as close to homemade as you can get without standing in a kitchen all day. It looks great, and I'm famished. Please join me, Val. I want to talk to you before everyone else rolls in. You too, Rosemary."

I hadn't planned on eating before or at the meeting, too nervous to be hosting, but I fixed a plate with some veggies and dip and some spinach salad. Then I joined Penelope and Rosemary in the dining area.

"I visited Ken today," Penelope said.

"I thought he couldn't have visitors," I said.

"That's what we wanted everyone to think," she said. "But he insisted I tell you and Rosemary. We're trying to determine who the leak is, and Ken can do more if everyone thinks he's out of commission for now. I put on a show when I left the hospital, crying. Anyone who knows me is going to think that's definitely out of character. I knew I was being followed, got the license plate, and sent it to a friend of mine in the police department. Dave and his people are taking care of it."

"Who do you think the leak is?" I asked, not certain I wanted to hear the answer.

"Not sure," she said, "but we know it's not someone in DC. It's got to be someone in the Northeast."

"You mean in upstate New York," I said.

"Sorry, Val. Can't be sure of who, but it looks that way."

"I'm not questioning your conclusions, but how do you know?" Rosemary asked.

"Pings," Penelope answered. "We're monitoring the major conspirators, and every time they're contacted we can tell the source of the calls, texts, and emails. In the last two days, there've been numerous calls from burner phones to various players, coming from the general area of your farm." She looked at me. "We can pinpoint within about ten miles with our equipment."

"I told Ken I didn't believe Jay would do this. I still feel that way," I said. "But I should tell you he's coming into DC tonight. I didn't tell him the agenda of the meeting, but I think he'll be here. I don't know when his flight's due. But really, what would Jay get out of joining that group? He's always believed in a free market and people being able to farm the way they wanted, whether it be a small family farm or a larger, individually owned facility."

"Val, I like Jay. I hope Ken's wrong, and he's opening his mind to try to come up with others who could be doing this. He brought Jay into the fold, so to speak. He wants to be wrong about him being a traitor, and he respects your opinion and knows you believe in him."

"I should tell you my sister-in-law's uncle Jeb is flying into DC to keep me safe. He's a retired New York City police detective, and after he saw the newscast, he insisted. I couldn't talk him out of it. He'll be staying at the Hyatt near the Capitol."

CHAPTER 25

The vice president was the next to arrive. Everyone else followed within twenty minutes. Daly called David at the security office. "All's good. I thought this might work."

"No one followed us. We have one more on his way up. You'll be glad to see him."

Was it Jay? I thought. The doorbell rang. Rosemary was closest to the door and answered it. I could see her mouth drop open as Ken walked in.

The phone rang, and I looked at the vice president as if I needed his permission to answer. He nodded.

It was David. "Nan and Jay are here. I need to speak to the vice president."

I handed the phone to Daly. He listened, eyes squinting. Looking concerned, he said, "No, don't try to stop them. Thanks for letting me know."

"What's wrong?" I said to the vice president.

"Could you and Ken step into another room for a moment?"

"Of course," I replied, feeling my eyebrows knit toward my nose.

When Ken closed the door, he said, "Nan and Jay are on their way up."

"I thought he might come in tonight," I said.

"They were looking very close," he said, slowly looking at me.

"There're lifetime friends," I said.

"Closer than friends," the vice president said slowly.

I didn't answer, but looked at him, then Ken. "I think David has misinterpreted a friendly gesture," I said.

"Maybe so, but you need to be wary. I'm not asking you to make any decisions. I still want to give Jay the benefit of the doubt. I just want you to be prepared for anything, both to do with the crisis and personally," Ken said.

"So how do we handle this tonight? Do we talk freely in front of them?" I asked, not believing my coldness. I put on my reporter voice and my unbiased, unfeeling attitude, no emotions. This was business. I'd deal with my personal feelings later. After all, I wasn't a child.

"We don't have a choice," the VP said.

Ken gave a slight knowing smile. He knew the drill, knew I could handle this.

We returned to the group. No one asked any questions. They wouldn't think of questioning the vice president.

I turned to the door when I heard the click of the latch. I could do this, although I reminded myself that Nan, my best friend, could always read me. I'd be the best actress tonight. I started to the door, and when it opened, I hugged Jay and welcomed him, smiling broadly at Nan at the same time. "I'm so glad you made it," I said to Jay. "Nan, I hope you don't mind. We're having a meeting here tonight. Can you join us?"

Nan looked stunned for a moment, probably by the number of people in her apartment. She'd always recovered quickly, though. "Love to," she said, exploring the room. She obviously was not surprised by most, but when her gaze met Engle, her eyes widened. She must be tangled in this, I thought. She wasn't surprised by anyone except him. Right then, I knew Nan was part of the conspiracy, but I'd be damned if she'd know I had any idea. I couldn't help but wonder if Jay and Nan were actually close, but there was no way I would react. It was possible Nan was the leak, and yet I never left any of my material where she could access it. How would she know what was going on if she wasn't involved with Jay?

"Come in, guys—we're just about ready to start." I turned to the others and said, "You all know Jay, and this is Nan, my best friend." I put my arm around her back and gave a little hug, smiling. "She only knows what was broadcast on TV. Anyone want to fill her in?"

Jay looked at me as if I'd committed a crime. "Maybe she won't want to know," he said.

"We can trust Nan completely," I said, looking stunned at Jay. "You know that."

He stared at me. Was I not covering my feelings well enough? Or was Jay genuinely surprised and not comfortable including Nan?

"Your endorsement is good enough for me," Ken said. I knew we were about to hear anything but the truth. I didn't know if Ken had suspected Nan before, but I couldn't help feeling he must have trusted me explicitly to have confidence I wouldn't discuss anything with Nan.

Jay was completely quiet, head down part of the time, while Ken filled everyone in. Ken recited, word for word, the misleading information stolen from his office. Jay was obviously aware of the deceit, but said nothing. The others, except Nan, of course, were aware something was up, but didn't question Ken about the misinformation.

When Ken finished, the VP said, "Well, I think we can cut things short tonight. It sounds like we're doing fine. I don't foresee any urgency in our actions. There's no sign the plan has been amped up. Why don't we meet again in a month? Ken, will you take charge of setting that up?"

"Sure, Dan."

There were confused faces, but no one said a thing. They had complete faith in Ken and the VP. I don't think Nan saw any confusion. She was trying not to smile, probably feeling we knew nothing of the accelerated plan to take over the farms in our country.

"I'm sorry—I have to leave, too," Nan said. "I have a dinner meeting tonight." Nan grabbed her coat and was out the door, probably going to report what she'd found to whomever she reported to.

I turned to say something to the VP and Ken, but they both held up their hands. Ken opened the apartment door, went to the next apartment, and came back with four men carrying wands and bags of equipment. They scanned the apartment for bugs as Ken and the VP engaged the rest of us in nonsense conversation. When they completed the sweep, Ken said, "It's safe to talk."

Jay asked to speak. "I'm pretty sure Nan is involved in the conspiracy, and I don't mean on our side. I met her in the garage, and she asked questions and even tried to seduce me, telling me she was sorry to be the one to let me know Val was seeing someone else, said she was home late every night when I was back in New York. She shocked the hell out of me."

"She was right about me being late every night. It's been a busy time."

"I knew she was lying, Val."

"I hope so, but this isn't about us," I said, my face reddening because we were talking in front of everyone, including the vice president, about our personal life.

"Right," Ken agreed. "Let us tell you all exactly what's really going on. Then we'll deal with Nan's involvement and get you a different apartment, Val. You can't stay here now, but we don't want Nan to know you are on to her. Dan figured the leak was coming from Nan or her family back in New York. Didn't you say her parents lost a lot of money and wouldn't be able to hold on to their farm?"

"Yes, Nan told us they were having problems, but I can't believe they'd be involved . . . oh my God. She couldn't have been involved in Nate's death, could she? She's known him since she was a child. And trying to frame me for his death? We've been almost like sisters forever."

"We don't know yet," Ken said. "I have an acquaintance at her firm. I'll give her a call right now. Although the firm represents many of the businesses involved in the takeover, my friend is not in favor of all the food in the country being controlled by a few people. She's one of the first people who came to me with her suspicion something wasn't right. I knew you were living with Nan and she was working there, but I never connected that a first-year would be given any major information."

Ken stepped out of the room and made his call. He was only gone a few minutes.

"Nan, it seems, was given her job with her law firm, Baker, Conway, and Schmidt, because she was willing to get involved in the land takeover. It was felt by the higher-ups they could use her because no one would suspect a fresh young lawyer of being jaded enough to conspire."

"So she's probably gone back to her firm to give them the good news that we have nothing?" I said.

"Imagine so," Ken smiled. "By the way, you did a good job of covering what you knew. Must have been difficult."

"You don't know," I said.

"I have more information," Dan said. "My group and I have narrowed down the businesses involved, and with the information Val gathered in Georgia, we know more of the politicians implicated. I think we're ready to go public with names on tomorrow night's broadcast. We're going primetime. The only decision to make, and I want it to be a group decision, is do we go with the politicians tomorrow night, and follow up with the businesses involved, or vice versa?"

I think the politicians will be more effective," Jay said. "After all, more people know the politicians as opposed to the individual companies. I'm guessing some of the companies may even be from abroad?" Jay questioned, looking at the VP.

"True," he replied. "More than you might think, which makes this all the more frightening for our country."

"We have to keep working," Ken said. "We have to keep this in the news every night to keep the American people interested. We're talking big resources to slam and slander every one of us. Is everyone ready for it?"

Nods all around. The VP said, "Tomorrow night's broadcast will be from the observatory. Nadia is all set up for it."

"I don't know," Ken said. "I'm not sure you should come out again. I'm afraid the president will make you step down. That won't be good for your political future, and you won't have access to as much information. I'm surprised nothing was done after yesterday's address. Were you called in?"

"Not a word from the White House. I've pretty much been kept out of any important meetings for the past few months anyway. The president doesn't have a clue, but I'm sure some are suspicious. I don't know how much he's actually involved or if he's oblivious.

"I'd love to see his face when I name the politicians involved. Then, if he makes me step down tomorrow night, I'm free to go on air anytime I want and tell what I know. How will it look if he tries to get rid of me? It'll give more credence to what I've said. There are worse things than being a whistleblower for the American people. If it ruins my political career, so be it. What am I worth to the country if I'm not honest?"

CHAPTER 26

Jay and I awoke at about 6 a.m. after turning in early the night before. I didn't want to face Nan, not knowing if I could pull off acting like her best friend. I thought about the possibility that she could have had something to do with Nate's death. It seemed impossible, but then again, all of this did.

Jay seemed to read my mind. "Let's shower and go for breakfast. We won't have to see Nan. I heard her come in about one this morning. I'm sure she won't be up early."

We walked to the diner around the corner from the apartment and within forty-five minutes consumed a huge farmer's breakfast, fried eggs, corned beef hash, toast, and lots of coffee. "How can you stay so thin and eat so much?" Jay said.

"Must be all the activity, although lately it's been more mental than physical. Uncle Jeb is arriving at Reagan International at eleven. Any way you can pick him up? Dave offered me his car. I'm sure he won't mind if you take it instead. I have to get to the paper and help Rosemary."

"Sure. Where's your uncle going to stay?"

"He has a room at the Hyatt for now, but he'll move in with me. Ken's finding me a two-bedroom. Guess he knows someone. Seems to have unlimited connections. I don't want to talk to Nan until Dan announces the facts to the world tonight. I should tell you, too, I had some doubts about your involvement with Nan, but I stuck up for you in front of everyone else. I received a text from Ken this morning. There were still pings coming from near our farm, calls to the people involved in the takeover. Do you know if Nan's family is involved or have any idea who the traitor could be at home?"

"I don't. I completely trust everyone who works at the barn, and I can't believe Nan's brother or parents are involved. I'll check into it, though. Financial difficulties can cause some to do the unthinkable. I wasn't totally surprised by Nan. I know you've been friends forever, but she's out for herself and always has been. You may have been a little blind to her ambitions. She wants it all and obviously doesn't care who she hurts getting it."

"Maybe you're right. I know she's ambitious and has taken a few questionable shortcuts to get where she is, but I wouldn't have contemplated her going this far." It was surprising how much confidence I had in Jay's loyalty when in his presence.

"I'm going to contact the people who work at the barn today and ask if they've encountered anything or anyone suspicious, even the slightest hint," Jay said. "Val," he added, reaching across the table and taking my hand, "I want you to be careful today. You're the main target after the broadcast the other night. Until last night, they thought Ken was down for the count. If they can put you out of commission, they might think it stops."

"I'll be careful. Why don't we get the car from Dave, and you can drop me at the paper before you go to the airport."

"Sounds good," Jay said, putting thirty dollars on the table.

We left the diner, hand in hand. Across the street, a man leaned against the building, engrossed in his cell phone. As we walked by, he slid his phone in a pocket and followed us. Jay tightened his grip on my hand and pointed to a coffee shop. We entered through the front door. Jay left me waiting in the long line, then pointed to the men's room, but walked past it out the back exit. I remained in line, ordered two coffees, and sat at the counter facing the window at the front of the store. When Jay drove up in Dave's car,

I exited the front door, jumped in the passenger seat, and we were off, the tail left standing on the sidewalk, already on his cell as Jay steered around the corner.

"He'll probably get our plate number," I said.

"I don't think so. Just happens something's hanging out of the trunk."

After circling the block, Jay dropped me in front of the paper. That was odd. The door was locked. Rosemary was always the first one at work. I searched my bag for the key. Maybe she went upstairs to Ken's apartment, or maybe she'd spent the night with him.

After turning on the overhead lights in the outer office, I walked into Ken's workplace. Shock couldn't begin to explain what I felt. Rosemary lay sprawled over the desk, torn papers grasped in her hands, eyes wide open, not moving. "No," I screamed. "Don't be dead. Rosemary!"

I touched her neck, but couldn't feel a pulse. I grabbed my phone and called 911, then pulled her onto the floor and started CPR. Nothing. I'm not sure how long I tried before a man appeared in the office. He said he was an EMT who'd heard the 911 call on his scanner. He felt for a pulse. "She's gone," he said.

He bent down next to me. "It's too late. Are you alright, Ms. Jacobs?"

I must have passed out, because when I awoke, the EMT had disappeared—to the hospital with Rosemary, I thought, trying to concentrate. How did he know my name? I partially regained focus. A woman holding a stethoscope on my chest knelt beside me. I tried to stand.

"Lie still," she said.

"Rosemary," I choked, sitting up. "I couldn't save her. Everyone around me is dying."

She stared at me. "Ms. Jacobs, I don't understand. We'll transport you to the hospital." Two attendants navigated a stretcher into the office.

"Not hurt," I said, sounding groggy. "Where's Rosemary? Where did he take her? Please tell me she's not dead."

"You were the only one here when we arrived."

A bulky man pushed into the office past the ambulance attendants. "Detective Spencer," he said. "What's happened here? We received a call about a suspicious death. I don't see a body. It wasn't removed, was it? There's a procedure to be followed," he continued, looking at the woman who was helping me.

"I'm Carla Houston, EMT. I know procedure, Detective Spencer, is it? I heard the call and arrived about five minutes ago. Ms. Jacobs is under the impression a woman she calls Rosemary is dead. However, when I arrived, I found only Ms. Jacobs lying on the floor. She's in shock."

"She's also covered in a substance resembling blood. She needs to come to the station. Her clothes are evidence, and she'll have to be questioned. The Crime Scene Unit is on its way to cover the office and surrounding area. Don't touch anything."

"I know procedure, Detective. I'm not sure she's medically able to go with you. She should be examined at a hospital. Do you know who she is?" Houston said, looking at me.

"Should I?" the detective said.

"She's Valerie Jacobs, a reporter involved in the biggest story in the news today. She's with a group that's exposing a conspiracy to take over the nation's farming and food industry, among other things if I understand it correctly. There could be more to this."

Spencer turned his attention to me. "Are you the one who called in a suspicious death?" When I didn't look up and answer immediately, Spencer spoke louder, "Ms. Jacobs, where's the body?"

"*She* was on the desk," I whispered.

"There's no body here," Spencer said.

"She was lying on the desk. I did CPR until an EMT arrived."

"I'm telling you, there's no body here. You are obviously covered in blood, so I have no doubt something happened here. Perhaps your accomplice moved the body. You need to come with me."

"I have to make a call, let my boss know about Rosemary."

"You can call when we get to the station."

"But you don't understand."

"Not really," Spencer said. The detective pulled me up, handcuffed my hands behind my back, and signaled for another detective.

"Take her downtown," Spencer said. The officer led me toward the door.

Houston turned to me. "There was no one here when I arrived, Ms. Jacobs. Do you know the name of the other EMT?

"No, he didn't give his name, said he was an EMT and Rosemary was dead."

"Who can I call for you?"

"Call Representative Engle's office and tell him what's happened. Use my name and his assistant will put you through."

Spencer cut in. "You will not interfere with this investigation, and you will not call anyone, Ms. Houston, or you will be arrested along with Ms. Jacobs."

"I'm being arrested? For what?" I said.

"I'm transporting you to the station until I determine what happened here. If you come willingly, we may be able to clear this up and let you go home. You are covered in blood, so until the crime scene unit has completed the investigation, I can detain you."

I looked past the detective, imploring Houston to make the call.

"Don't worry, Detective, I don't need any trouble with the police," Houston said. "I'm not about to make any calls, but I will issue a complaint with the police department about you not allowing needed medical care for this patient." Spencer turned without responding to Houston. When the detective led me out the door, Houston made eye contact with me. I was sure she'd make the call.

When Jay and Uncle Jeb returned from the airport, they'd look for me and wouldn't stop until they found me. They'd get to the bottom of what happened to Rosemary. Even if Houston was too afraid to make the call to the Senator, they'd find me.

The detective didn't say a word as he led me to the unmarked car in front of the paper.

"Which precinct do you work out of?" I asked.

He didn't answer, just led me to car, shoved me in the backseat, and walked to the driver's side.

"Where's your partner?" I asked. Something wasn't right.

No answer. I panicked. I raised my shackled feet and banged the meshed, metal partition between the back and front seats. I growled, "Let me out of here." No answer. I was being kidnapped. This wasn't a policeman, at least not an honest one.

"You're making the biggest mistake of your life. People will look for me, powerful people, and they won't stop until they find me."

Laughter sounded from the front seat. "You think you're working with powerful people? You have no idea what power means."

I was quiet, hoping Houston made the call to the senator. He would contact the vice president, who'd put everything in motion sooner than tonight. What would happen if she hadn't made the call? Maybe she was in on the conspiracy. Possibly the 911 call never went through to the proper authorities. I'd have to escape on my own, not depend on anyone else to rescue me. The plan to foil the conspiracy was more important than any individual. If I failed to survive this, Jay, Ken, and others would carry on the fight. But I had to persist, had to be the one to discover the identity of my brother's killer. I needed to live.

I lay on my back, bent my knees as close to my chest as possible, and with as much power as I could muster, kicked the side window with both feet.

More laughter sounded from the front seat. "You have no chance of breaking that window."

"You have no idea how strong a farm girl can be." All those hot summer afternoons of unloading hay and early mornings at the gym were about to pay off. I repeatedly let my boots strike the window with all my might. Finally, the window shattered.

The laughing from the front subsided. The officer, or whoever he was, stepped on the gas, but only momentarily. Traffic suddenly braked ahead, and the car came to a complete halt, surrounded by traffic. I had already pushed the top of my body out the window and was screaming so loudly the man in the passenger seat of the car to the left jumped from his vehicle and rushed to me. My driver moved to the passenger seat, exited, and ran down the street.

"I was kidnapped!" I yelled.

The man pulled me out of the car. Not realizing the source of the blood on my shirt, he said, "I'm so sorry. I should have been more careful."

"It's not mine," I said. "So grateful for your help. He kidnapped me, not a real policeman. Please, your phone?"

"Of course," he said, "but are you sure you're okay?"

I gave him Jay's number and he called, holding the phone for me. "I'm okay, but they've killed Rosemary and someone tried to kidnap me. Did you pick up Uncle Jeb?"

"Yes. Are you sure you're alright, Val?"

"I'm fine. This man helped me. You have to call the vice president, but if you can't get him, call Representative Engle. If there's any way to move up the national announcement scheduled for tonight, do it. Things are coming apart. The conspirators have stepped up their game. Where shall I meet you?" I asked Jay, not wanting to say where we'd meet with the stranger listening.

"Let me talk to the man who helped you," Jay said.

I handed over the phone.

"I'm Lieutenant Bradley Lefkowitz, US Marines, and my driver, Sergeant Greg Perry, is with me. What can we do to help?"

I could still hear Jay's voice on the other end.

"Lieutenant, you've just met Valerie Jacobs. She's working with a group to stop the takeover of private land in the United States."

"I recognized her from TV. I'll help however I can."

"Yes, sir," Bradley said, and clicked off. He checked the police car and found keys for the shackles and handcuffs.

Throwing the keys to Sergeant Perry, who released me, he said, "Traffic is letting up. We'll take you where you need to go."

What choice did I have? Covered in blood, I couldn't very well take a cab.

When I asked the men to take me to the vice president's residence, both turned to the back seat as if to say, are you serious?

"That's right," I said. "It looks like we've been busted. The perpetrators of the conspiracy know we're further ahead in our investigation than they thought. Hopefully, we can reach the public with the rest of the evidence before they kill us."

"No one will hurt you," the lieutenant said. "We'll stay with you and protect you. No problem. You don't realize how many people are behind you, especially in the services. Many of us knew something was going on with the food supply, but no one could put his finger on it. Do you want to call your friend again? We're about fifteen minutes from the vice president's."

"Thanks," I said. "My uncle just came into DC. This wasn't quite the welcome I'd planned for him." I called and told Jay where we were.

"Don't go there," Jay said. "We're on our way to the place farthest from town where the group met. Everyone will meet us there. I can't tell you more on the open line. Do you remember how to get there?"

"Yes. I think it'll probably take us at least an hour from here.

"Let me talk to the Lieutenant, Val."

I handed the phone to Lefkowitz.

"Yes, I know the area. Yes, sir, I can do that."

Lefkowitz clicked off, turned to Perry and said, "We have to stop at the next gas station."

The driver pulled into a Hess station. Val could see through the full glass windows as Lefkowitz talked to the clerk. The worker pulled out a cell phone and handed it to the marine. The lieutenant stepped nearer the windows so the clerk couldn't hear.

"We're going to try a roundabout route just in case," Lefkowitz said when he returned to the car.

Perry checked the rearview mirror constantly. There were no problems, and we pulled into Priscilla's about an hour after I'd talked to Jay. The marines guarding the entrance opened the gate and signaled us in, not even stopping the car to check IDs.

We were rushed into the house—no checking ID's there either. The car was taken by one of the marine guards from Priscilla Strauss's and parked who knows where. Lefkowitz and Perry looked at each other in confusion.

"Don't worry," I said. "You'll know everything I know in a few minutes. You may be surprised how high up this goes, but you'll understand the urgency if you don't already."

Jay met me inside the library. He took one look and said, "You're hurt. You didn't tell me you were injured."

"I'm fine—not my blood."

"Lieutenant, Sergeant," Jay said, offering his hand.

"Lieutenant Bradley Lefkowitz."

"Sergeant Greg Perry. Glad to meet you, Jay. And good to be able to help such a worthy cause. We're anxious to learn more."

"Glad to have you on board," Jay said. "Let's go to the conference room. Everyone else is here already." He looked at Val.

"Does Ken know about Rosemary?" I said.

"He does, and he's so angry I'm not sure we can contain him for the next hour."

"How are we going to air from here within an hour? We'll have to get to a studio, and I can't go in like this," I said, lowering my head and raising my arms.

Priscilla came around the corner and signaled me to go with her. She led me to a bedroom. "These should fit," she said, handing me a shirt and slacks. "Put your clothes in this paper bag. The police will need them."

"Don't worry. We can broadcast from the house. Nadia has her crew here, and the vice president is putting the finishing touches on his speech. We're going live at four before we're *all* busted."

"I'm surprised the military hasn't been called out by the president and that we're still alive," I said.

"If they could find us, we probably would be in jail at the least, or maybe at Guantanamo as enemies of the state," Jay said. "Our only hope is to come out totally to the public with the names of everyone we know is involved. If we've missed anyone, we could still be in trouble."

The five walked into the conference room, joining the others who filled the chairs around the large conference table. More chairs were brought in. "Over here, Val," the vice president said. "I want you sitting next to me. These crooks have to know that you're alive, well, and still after them."

"Where's Ken?" I asked.

"He stepped out for a bit," Priscilla said. "We were filling everyone in on what's happened over the last twenty-four hours, and it was too much for him to take in front of everyone. You know how private he is. He doesn't like to show his emotions."

"Val, I'm so sorry you found Rosemary like that. It must have been horrible," the vice president said.

"It doesn't seem real," I said. "Or maybe it wasn't. Has her body been found?"

"Not that I know of," Priscilla said.

The vice president started speaking. "We'll be going on air in fifteen minutes. It's time to give the American people names and more facts. I'll announce what politicians are involved and give more details to the public. If we're still on the air after that, Ken will be on my left and explain how he was mowed down by a hit-and-run driver and left for dead. Val will sit on my right and tell how she found Rosemary, how Rosemary's body disappeared, and how she'd been kidnapped. Val, I know you've had a hell of a day, but I want you to write this up into an article that will be printed for distribution in the morning in case we're pulled off the air before we can get all the facts out."

"Pardon me, Mr. Vice President, but how could we be taken off the air?" I said.

"The government has the ultimate power. The president could declare martial law and take over the airwaves with one phone call. Let's hope those involved in the conspiracy aren't watching. Four is an odd time, but that's why it was picked. Enough people will see it that the word will spread, and we might get enough information out before we're cut off.

"Val, you'll have to print the paper from here."

"How will I do that?" Val said.

"You can type it on the computer and we'll put it online in the morning. I doubt the president will kill the internet to the American people. There'd certainly be a revolt if that happened. We live in a society where people must get their news.

"We also have people standing by ready to distribute written copies of the story to all the major newspapers across the country. We aren't taking a chance the president and his associates are smart enough to keep the country online."

The whole story would explode in about five minutes. We could all be thrown in jail and never heard from again, but we would have done our best to save our country. That was the important thing, not a few individuals.

Priscilla could read Val's face. "Don't worry, honey, we're safe here. No one will be able to penetrate this compound. It's like we're invisible while we're in this house. They won't be able to figure out where the broadcast is coming from. They'll see the end result on televisions and radios across the country, but they won't know the source. We'll be bouncing all over the world."

"But the vice president said we might get shut down."

"The only thing they can do is declare martial law and take over the stations. How do you think the people of the United States would like that?"

"They'd better not try it," I said. "We'd have all kinds of cred."

The vice president began, "Fellow Americans, I am Dan Daly, Vice President of these United States, and I'm coming to you with another message you need to hear. I'm not speaking to you as the vice president, but as a fellow citizen who does not believe in what's happening in this country. As many of you have heard, there is a movement to take over the farms, farmland, and food-growing industry, as well as the water and energy sources we all need in order to live. The people trying to do this include government officials, business leaders, bankers, stock market leaders, foreign entities, and even some farmers, as hard as that is to believe.

"Ken Bentz, editor of *Washington In Depth*, and I spoke with you a short time ago and gave you a heads up. We have the names of specific politicians, businesspeople, and companies involved in this conspiracy. We will list those names in just a minute. If, for any reason, the government cuts this programming off, you can find those names at the *Washington In Depth* website.

"If the internet is cut off, you will be able to receive a written form that will be distributed through a network spanning our country—that's *our* country, *yours* and *mine*. It does *not* belong to government officials who believe themselves to be above the law or to businesspeople whose money they feel entitles them to break the law. Remember, if people more powerful than I see fit to cut off communication to the American people, you can be one hundred percent sure this conspiracy has credence. If you can't find the names of those involved on *washingtonindepth.com*, there will be hard copies released in the morning.

"You will be able to view the list of people for whom we have concrete proof of involvement to take over the nation's food, energy sources, and water supplies. It will show on a running roll on the right side of your screen beginning . . . now. I'm turning this over to Ken Bentz. Ken."

"Thank you Mr. Vice President. I want the people of this country to know what can happen when a journalist exposes the wrongdoings of people who think they are above the law. When I left my apartment building on Monday, the morning after the last broadcast, I was run down and left for dead by a hit-and-run driver. Police investigated and suggested I might pretend I was worse off than I was. They were unable to ensure my protection. Therefore, I've been living off grid for the last few days while Val Jacobs took over the work. She will tell you what happened to her today. Val."

"Hello," I said. "Today I found one of the loveliest people I've ever met lying across her desk, dead. She was Ken's assistant, so she has been working hard with the rest of us, only longer than any of us here, except Ken, of course. Her body disappeared and I was kidnapped. I was rescued with the help of two marines who showed they loved their country as much as the rest of us.

"Please let your politicians know you will not stand for a few taking over this country. The price of food and energy, as well as everything else depending on those industries, will be too much for the average person, even people with above-average incomes. The few people who own everything will not care if you don't have enough food or don't have jobs as long as they have their money. Greed is rampant. The time has come. You need to stand up now and not allow these people whose names are running on this program to succeed. Otherwise, it will be too late.

"Ken, the vice president, and the rest of this group will continue working to expose wrongdoing. We will welcome those whose names are running here to change what they've been doing and join us right now. We'll run the names from the list of those willing to give up the takeover, if we hear from them tonight. Some may have been tricked or blackmailed into the conspiracy and will welcome a way out. To those who decide to continue trying to get rich on the backs of the American people, know that we are not giving up. Thank you for your time, and let's hope we will all survive. Mr. Vice President, do you have anything else to add?"

The cameras moved toward the vice president. "I don't know what will happen after this broadcast. I suspect I may not be vice president in a few hours, so I will tell you it has been a pleasure serving the people of the United States. I will continue serving in any way you deem appropriate. The best to you, and the best to our country."

CHAPTER 27

The entire address was broadcast without interruption. The president summoned the vice president and Ken to the White House immediately following the broadcast. It took two hours for them to deliver the facts to the president. He expressed what appeared to be genuine shock and vowed to do whatever was necessary to reverse the situation. He was on the air at nine the next morning stating as much to the American people. Whether that was possible remained to be seen, but with the president apparently behind us now, there was a better chance.

The president claimed to be oblivious to the conspiracy. With so many politicians and, as it turned out, cabinet members, involved, they were able to keep the president busy on other matters so he wouldn't suspect what was actually happening. I wasn't confident he had no involvement.

Over the next week, five cabinet members were dismissed and three arrested by the Justice Department using the information Ken and the vice president provided. Politicians were on TV twenty-four seven, trying to cover their asses and get as far as they could from those we listed on air and in the paper. To listen to them, you'd think they didn't serve (a term that could only be used loosely) in the same chambers with their fellow senators and congressmen.

Businesses and banks from coast to coast expressed their horror that any business would be involved in such an endeavor to hoodwink the American people. They actually used the word hoodwink, like it was a little joke instead of the conspiracy it was. And those whose involvement was proven in black and white by Ken and our group articulated their profound apologies and fired some low-level staffers, blaming them as the responsible parties.

Although the story was out and no one could deny the facts, the American people did not seem outraged. Many believed it didn't affect them. It affected only the farmers, and some felt if small farms couldn't make money, they *should* go out of business. What did it have to do with the rest of the population? Times changed, and people had to change with those times. After all, the politicians said food would be cheaper and that would make everyone's lives better.

"Can people really believe these editorials?" I said.

"They can if it makes their lives make more sense," Ken said. "Did you really think the first wave of our exposure would do the trick?"

"I did," I admitted. "Naive of me?"

"Most definitely, but you don't have the experience or years I have. It's easier for people to believe that those guilty of trying to defraud the American people have apologized for their indiscretions and are willing to change direction. We are a forgiving society. After all, who hasn't committed an indiscretion?"

"How are you really doing, Ken?" I said.

Knowing I was referring to Rosemary, he said, "She knew the risks, but if she's really dead and we ever find who killed her, you may have to lock me away, or I'll be in jail the rest of my life."

"You're not convinced she's gone?" I said.

"Not until we find her. I'm holding out hope someone wants to use her to blackmail me into not pushing this investigation further. Time will tell."

"How's Jay doing?" Ken said. "More to the point, how are you doing? Were people back home upset with you and Jay when they found out you'd turned your friend Nan in?"

"Jay's as upset as I am that the American people aren't rallying and demonstrating to stop the government farms and takeovers. After their initial response, they seemed to give up. He feels the lives lost are not even being considered. Misuse of government funds and overreaching of the laws don't seem to be a concern of most people. I suppose you'd say Jay's young, too, and was overly optimistic the people would jump on board."

"I'm not saying you're wrong. It's just I've been around almost twice as long as you and I'm probably jaded."

"My Uncle Jeb wants to stay in town and help any way he can. He doesn't want me staying alone. Do you have any problem with him?"

"He's right. The conspirators are going to come full force at you, me, and anyone else involved. They will continue to discredit us. They will gain momentum and get a second wind. Is there anything in your past, short-lived as it is, they can turn around and make you sound shady or just immoral?"

I didn't answer right away.

"That hesitation makes me a little uneasy."

"Well, nothing big, but I wasn't exactly a teenager that my mother was proud of."

"What are we talking? Drugs, drinking, sex?"

"I'm not really comfortable talking about this with you."

"Are you going to be comfortable with it being splashed in the headlines?"

"You're kidding, right? They aren't going to look that far back, to a few little high school indiscretions?"

"Oh, they will, believe me. And they'll exaggerate. Spill. I'm sorry you're not comfortable with it, but you need to tell me everything that anyone else knows so we can get ahead of it."

"I guess my mother was right—everything you do comes back to bite you."

"Probably. Let's get this over with."

"I was never arrested, so there are no legal issues. I did party quite a lot, drinking in high school and some drugs in college, no hard stuff."

"Is there anyone who would like to see you fail? Someone you were unkind to through your younger years?"

"No, I was pretty much friends with everyone. Didn't want to miss any parties."

"All right, then there's nothing we have to get ahead of. Let's discuss our next research area. I'm happy your uncle will be staying with you. He seems to have made quite a reputation with the New York City Police. A little questionable on his methods, though."

"He's retired now, so he said he'd be happy to help with anything we need. He's a pretty good strategist and worked undercover for some time, a job he loved. He's a bit of a frustrated actor, so he loved doing undercover. He doesn't have much fear, which I suppose could work either way."

"I have an assignment for him, but I'd like to talk to him first," Ken said. "No offense, but I want to make sure he'll do things on the up-and-up."

"No problem. I've always thought of him as an ethical man. When do you want to see him?"

"How is this afternoon?"

"I'll call him as soon as we're done here."

"Call him now. Then we'll talk."

Val called Uncle Jeb and set up an appointment with Ken at four that afternoon.

"Now, let's get to work," Ken said. "I'm sending Jay back home. He needs to look at all his people and make sure they're not part of the leak. Nan was definitely in bed with the conspirators, but we think there may be more in your area of the country. They're probably not the only ones, either. I need you to talk to Pete Engle to find if he has any more information on politicians he suspects. We have maybe one more day before they get their act together and come after us."

"What do you mean?"

"I have a friend at the *Times*. He called me today to let me know the Justice Department will be issuing warrants for Jay, Senator Engle, the vice president, you, and me."

"What for?" I asked.

"We are being accused of treason—punishable by death, of course."

"Are you kidding me?" I said, not able to hide the horror I felt.

"The warrant says we have released confidential government information without permission, that we have obtained this information from leaks in the government, and therefore we are no different than Snowden—who, by the way, the jury is still out on."

"How do we fight this?" Val asked. "I don't particularly want to go to jail."

"We get out ahead of it. Tonight, WAFR is doing a documentary on our findings to date. They have also been given the information about the tentative arrests. They will point out the Justice Department has no legal rights in this case, because we obtained the information from individuals who are not government employees. Those people have agreed to come forward and are being interviewed live on the air tonight."

"Aren't they worried about being falsely charged, too?"

"Nadia has guaranteed us access to her station's attorneys if we are actually charged."

"I hope you're right, Ken."

"Let's worry about getting all our ducks in a row, not things that haven't happened yet."

"We're bringing in the people from the Midwest for the broadcast. Will you take a van and meet them at the airport at 4 p.m.? They should all be there by then. Get them settled at the Hyatt. I've made reservations. I'll meet with your uncle and let him know what I want him to do," Ken said.

CHAPTER 28

In DC, the week passed relatively quietly. No warrants were issued for the investigators, Ken, me, or anyone else. On Saturday, Ken, Senator Engle, Beverly Leach, and I were able to fly to New York and attend a party at Jay's farm, hoping to find the source of the leaks. We split up and circulated, trying to unobtrusively listen to as many conversations as possible. Jay and I happened to meet near the keg about an hour into the party. "Anything?" I said.

"Nothing that sounds suspicious, but many expressions of support," Jay said. "Look who's here." He nodded his head toward the driveway.

"Katy Johnson? What about her?"

"Look who she's talking to. They look pretty intense," Jay said.

"Bart Kelly? So what?

"Bart's one I thought might be involved with the conspirators, or at the very least, be receiving money for information. He's in financial trouble. With all the farms going out, his farm supply store is struggling. Rumor has it he's been flush lately and is planning to relocate to the Caribbean. He's purchased a house on the beach on Grand Cayman. I can't imagine him having the money for such an investment. Let's make a move to get closer, get a better listen."

"Not necessary," I said. "Look who's right behind them, listening to every word."

"Ahh! Dad's on the job." Jay laughed. "Dad never did like Bart. Says he was an arrogant pimple."

"Can't say your father ever minced words," I said.

"Let's get back to circulating. Anything else you learned this week that should make us suspect anyone else?" I said.

"We need to look closely at Nan's family."

"You mean they're showing up?"

"Evidently, Nan hasn't shared with her parents that she's been accused of conspiracy against the American people."

"Has she actually been charged with anything?"

"I'm guessing she won't be. The fact the law firm hired her because she was naive and knew about farming should be punishment enough for her. She has a pretty high opinion of her abilities, and to be hired for ulterior motives should about do her in. The law firm fired her immediately when they were accused of being in on the conspiracy, and blamed it all on her. She won't be hired as a lawyer anytime soon, at least not at any reputable firm. She's also lost her apartment, because the firm was paying for it."

"So her family was not in on the conspiracy?"

"I doubt it. I've been asking around as much as I can without raising suspicion that I'm investigating them specifically. They're in the same financial straits as every other farmer."

"Well, let's get to it," I said, giving Jay an intimate touch on his shoulder.

No other leads surfaced at the party. An investigation of Katy Johnson turned up nothing of any significance—probably a personal confrontation. She was the one that followed the money. If she thought Bart could give her more than she had in her current situation, she'd sniff it out.

Ken, Representative Engle, Bev, Jay, his family, and I met back at Jess's house after the last guest left. I felt nauseous as I thought I should have been saying Nate's house, but I'd never be able to say that again. He was gone, and I was sick that I'd been responsible.

"Sorry," Jay said. "I was sure there'd be chatter we could use."

Ken's phone rang, and he excused himself from the kitchen table. He wandered into my mother's room, unintentionally scaring her. She screamed.

I ran in. "It's okay, Ma. This is my boss. We're working on a story for his paper in Washington." Fear showed in my mother's face, but she stopped yelling. She looked at me. "Carrie?" she said.

"No Ma, it's me, Valerie, your daughter."

A few tears slid from her eyes. "Where's Carrie? Mother will be mad at her if she doesn't get home before midnight."

"Mom, Carrie's been gone for a long time now." Carrie was my mother's sister. Relatives said I inherited her fair skin, dark curly hair, love of excitement, and disposition. I never knew if the disposition comment was meant as a compliment, but suspected it was not.

"I know. She's going to get in trouble. Do you have a car? We'll catch up to her. Get the Buick out."

"Mom, Aunt Carrie died twenty years ago."

"No! No. Stop saying that," she said. "Carrie died? What happened? Take . . . take me . . . to the funeral home," she said between sobs.

"No, Mom, it was a long time ago. The funeral was held twenty years ago."

"Stop saying that," she sobbed. "Why won't you take me to the funeral home?" She was trying to push herself up on her elbows, grabbing the rail of the bed, her eyes wide with fear.

Ken came closer. "Hold a minute, please," he said into the phone. Turning to Mom, he said, "We'll take you in a few minutes."

"What are you talking about?" I asked.

Mom lowered herself back onto the bed and seemed to settle. Ken took my arm and guided me to the next living room. "It's alright, Val. My mother had Alzheimer's. I've learned from experience you might as well agree with what she's thinking. It's not going to do any good to argue. And it will only frustrate you and her."

"I wasn't arguing. I was just telling her the truth. I should lie to her?"

"It's not lying, Val. It's calming her down. She's living in the past. There's no reason to upset her further. People with Alzheimer's relive their past. My mother experienced her mother's death many times. It was horrendous to see her suffer, until I learned how to make her sessions a little less painful. Distract her. I found she forgot quicker and wasn't in pain for long."

"I haven't spent enough time with her. It's all been on Nate, Jess, and Annie. When this is over, I think I should come home for a while. Give Jess a break, if that's alright with you."

"Of course. I have to finish this call. Where can I talk?"

"In the next room to your left."

"I'll be out shortly," Ken said.

I looked at my mother, who'd gone to sleep, and realized I had a lot to learn about Alzheimer's. It was time I started. "As soon as this is over, I'll be back to stay for a long time," I said to Mom.

Jay came into the kitchen, and Ken joined us.

"That call was regarding our plan to follow the money. The financial people have found some accounts in the Caymans that look suspicious. I want you and Jay to leave in the morning for Grand Cayman. I'll have all information ready for you. There's a flight out of Albany to Miami at 10 a.m., and then on to Grand Cayman. I'm sorry I can't give you more time at home, but you need to talk to people in person, and I can't go right now. I'm still trying to find out what happened to Rosemary, and a couple taking a vacation won't be questioned. You do have passports, right?"

"I do," I said, my eyebrows raised toward Jay.

"Yes, I have one," Jay said.

"I'm not very good in the finance area," I said. "Not sure I'd recognize discrepancies, even if we can get into the accounts."

"I can handle that part," Jay said. "Studied some finance at one point."

"Of course you did," I said, and laughed. "Jay studied everything."

CHAPTER 29

Jay and I had just boarded the plane from Miami to Grand Cayman when he turned to me and said, "Have you been to the island before?"

"No, I've never been to any of the islands. Been too busy to go on vacations for the past few years. You?"

"Yes, my latest visit was last winter for a week."

"Mmmm," I said, "with someone?"

"Yes," he said, and smiled like he was going back to that week.

I had to admit I was feeling what some might consider jealousy. I'd never been jealous before, but if I had, I thought it might have felt like this. I didn't say a word, just looked at him. It was none of my business what he did last year before we had anything. And what did we have, after all? Nothing we'd even talked about, no commitment, although I did feel what I thought might be close to love for him. Maybe he didn't feel the same.

"Aren't you going to ask me who I went with?" he said.

"No, it's none of my business, really."

"I was hoping you'd be a little jealous."

"Why? We've always been friends, but to be honest, I'm not quite sure what we are now? Are you?"

Jay bent over in his seat, laughing.

"What's so funny? Was what I said humorous? I didn't mean it that way." I was angry with myself for sounding a little annoyed.

Jay turned to me and took my hand. "Val, I love you. I don't think I could love anyone any more than I love you. You're the most honest person I know and, I think, a person not sure of her feelings. Am I right?"

"I've never been in love before," I said honestly.

"Not even puppy love in high school? I thought you said you had a couple of relationships when you were in California."

"I was fond of both of them, but I wasn't in love. I liked them, respected them as people, but not in love. I think what we have is love, but since I've never experienced it before, I'm not positive. I miss you when you're not around. When you kiss me or touch me, my stomach feels like it's in my throat. I ache for you. But the last thing I want to do is tie you down."

"Some people like that," he said with a snicker.

"I don't think I would, at least not literally," I replied.

"I thought we might scout out a place to come on a real vacation," Jay said. "And I'd like to talk to you about where we're headed as soon as this whole mess is over."

"I think we're all going to need an extended vacation."

"We'll get in early evening, so the first thing we need to do, orders from Ken, is get a good night's sleep," Jay said. "In the morning, we start at the Grand Bank of the Caymans. Ken has given us a letter of introduction, and I have $100,000 in cash in my carry-on. He thought that would be enough to get us in. It's not much by Cayman standards, of course, but we are a young couple who has supposedly started a business for which we'll need a bank for deposits on a monthly basis."

"What kind of business?"

"Import/export, of course. That could be anything, but we're starting with antiques. Of course, we can hint that some of our top customers are specifically looking for antiquities, those that would not normally be sold. We are to learn the process for depositing money. Then, we're to make contacts with other bank customers who might be interested in purchasing antiquities.

A few hundred dollars placed in the right hands is supposed to open some doors. We just have to find out whose hands to place the money in."

"This actually sounds like fun," I said.

"Don't enjoy it too much. We're a little on the edge here. We don't actually want to do anything illegal. Don't want to wind up in a Grand Cayman jail. I'm not sure how much power the people we're working with can wield."

"I wrote an article on banking abroad with the goal of hiding money some time ago. Maybe what I learned could help us." I pulled my MacBook out of my carry-on and brought up the article for Jay to read. He hardly glanced at it.

Before I knew it, the plane was descending and I was looking at one of the most beautiful places I'd ever seen. The whitest sand, the greenest water, and I could see to the bottom of the ocean. I'd only ever been to the ocean on the northeastern and western coasts of the United States. There was no comparison. How could it be so clean? And what beautiful houses, or should I say mansions, most with pools.

I felt Jay looking at me. "Fantastic, isn't it?" he said, smiling.

What a perfect setting. Too bad this was work, but not until morning. We had several hours before we had to turn in, and Jay said we'd make every minute count.

Going through customs was quick, with airport staff extremely helpful. This island knew how to welcome people. Cabs lined the road outside the airport, but Jay grabbed the bags and walked across the road to the land transport area. He stopped at a van marked Ritz Carlton.

"You're kidding," I said.

"Ken said we should stay at the Ritz, make a big impression, look the part."

"The Ritz must be the most expensive hotel on the island," I said.

"We have the rest of the afternoon and the evening before we have to think about what we've come for. I think we should enjoy it. As you saw on the way in, this is a beautiful place. I plan to show you a good time, and before you say we shouldn't, remember, since we've expressed our feelings for each other, found something we've never had, we haven't had time to have a relaxing dinner, a stroll on a beach, or just talk about us. Tonight's the night."

I didn't argue. I took his hand and boarded the van.

It was only a short drive. "It's right on the beach!" I said.

"As I remember, you love the beach, right?"

"No place more peaceful. Let's change and go for a walk," I said, peering at the calm ocean.

The beach went on forever. Neither Jay nor I talked much, just walked hand in hand on the silvery sand. "Want to head back for dinner?" Jay asked.

"I have worked up an appetite," I said.

I showered the sand away and dressed in a flowered sundress and heeled sandals. While I was dressing, Jay called the concierge and made reservations at a bistro, The Surge, about a block from the hotel.

"What a quaint little place," I said when we got there.

"Yes, it's survived the building all around it. The food is delicious and the owners are as friendly and down to earth as the people at home."

"You've been here before?" I asked.

"Yes, many times. Once a year since graduating high school, other than when I was in the service, I've come here. I save all year long to spend one week in luxury and peace."

"Wow, you surprise me. I never thought of you as someone who would enjoy this type of vacation," I said.

"I hope you're ready for more surprises," he said.

A woman, probably in her fifties, approached us. "Welcome back, Mr. Jay. You've come early this year, and this time with a beautiful young lady."

"I'd like you to meet Valerie Jacobs," he said.

"Good to meet you," I said.

"This is my friend, Antoinette LaFrance," Jay said, as Antoinette and I shook hands.

"And I see the way you look at her. She is very special, no? Welcome to The Surge," she said.

"It's wonderful to be here," I said. "I'm just learning about Jay's fascination with the island."

"My husband and I enjoy getting to know everyone who comes in, but Jay is special to us." She opened the door next to her and shouted, "Pierre, come see who's here!"

"You know I cannot come out of the kitchen now. Send them in!"

When he saw Jay, Pierre said, "Ahhh, Jay my boy. How are you? Why are you here so early? You always come in the middle of your winter, and you've brought someone with you this time." Pierre took my hand, drew it to his lips, and kissed my wrist, bowing his head but making eye contact.

"This is Valerie, a very special friend," Jay said.

"It's nice to meet you, Pierre," I said.

"And you," Pierre replied. "Now, go sit. I will cook, and we will drink and talk later, no?"

"Of course, Pierre," Jay said.

Antoinette took our order. I noticed that ours was the only order she'd taken. "You seem to be very close friends," I said to Jay.

"Antoinette and Pierre are about as good as they come. They treat everyone who comes in the door the same, the wealthiest visitors or the poorest inhabitants on the island. They close the restaurant on Mondays and work at a soup kitchen."

"I can't believe there's a need for a soup kitchen on this island. When we were flying in, all I saw were what would pass for estate houses at home, and pools with most of them."

"Who do you think waits on all the rich people? When recession hits the United States, Europe, and Asia, it affects everywhere in the world. People lose their jobs here, too. Some of them lose their homes. Even wealthier people need help sometimes."

"There's a lot I don't know about you, isn't there?" I said.

Jay smiled. Antoinette served our food. I thought she might join us, but she said, "Enjoy," and returned to the kitchen.

"She'll let us eat, then she and Pierre will join us for after-dinner drinks," Jay said.

"Are you reading my mind now?" I said.

"Yes," he smiled.

When Antoinette and Pierre joined us, they brought Grand Marnier. After drinking a few, Jay and I strolled back to the hotel, helping each other. I was feeling so relaxed I had to lean into his side.

"Let's take a walk on the beach," Jay said.

"Is it safe? It's pretty late."

"You're with me. I wouldn't let anything happen to you. I want to show you something. The lights from the houses on the beach will guide the way."

We walked past the hotel pools and onto the sandy beach, the water glittering in the moonlight. Looking in both directions, I saw that the beach was dimly lit, first by the faint Ritz standing lights, then farther down by lights from other hotels and houses along the beach.

We had walked maybe half a mile north when Jay said, "Val, let's sit here for a while." He led me to a gazebo in front of a huge palatial house facing the ocean.

"I'm not sure we should. We'll be trespassing."

"No, I'm sure it's fine."

"Is everyone that friendly here?"

"Sit down, Val. I want to ask you something."

I stopped breathing, and it must have been evident to Jay that I was apprehensive. I actually gasped a little.

"Have a seat," he said, smiling and speaking more gently than I ever remembered. He pointed to the molded white marble bench.

He took my hand and looked straight into my eyes. "Val . . ."

Maybe I had the wrong idea. I was very relaxed from the wine and Grand Marnier. I didn't see a ring anywhere. Maybe I wasn't thinking clearly. I hoped I wasn't.

"Val, are you listening?"

"Yes, I'm sorry. I think I had too much to drink."

"Val," Jay began again, "I want you to look out at the ocean."

I complied and again took in a deep breath. It was beautiful, truly breathtaking. The moon shone on water that was so calm, it looked like a shimmering washboard, and at the horizon, a play of various pinks still showed from the day. I couldn't speak.

"Val, this can all be yours."

"What?" I said, truly confused.

"Turn and look at the house. Walk with me." Jay took my hand and walked me to the huge wooden door.

"Jay, no one is home. Do you know who lives here?"

"I do. It's fine." Jay took a key from his pocket, opened the door, and led me through. He disarmed the alarm and turned on the lights.

It reminded me of Priscilla's house, the spacious entry with a huge circular staircase leading to the second floor. Jay reset the alarm and led me upstairs.

I followed him blindly, not knowing what was going on. It must belong to a friend, I thought. Jay was trying to give me a taste of the good life, trying to impress me. I followed him, relaxing a little, probably due to the alcohol I'd consumed.

When we reached a bedroom at the front of the house, he opened the drapes that faced the ocean and unlocked the doors to the balcony off the bedroom. "Come look," he said, and led me to the balcony. The same view, only more resplendent from this height.

Jay led me back to the bed and took me in his arms. I willingly followed. Between the view and the drinks, and my love for Jay, I followed him. Our lovemaking was probably the best ever, both of us giving all we had.

I awoke first in the morning, rose from the bed, and wrapped myself in a blanket. With the effects of the alcohol gone, my doubts returned. It was cool, and the doors to the balcony were still open. I crossed the bedroom and looked out over the ocean from the balcony. Amazingly, there were no hotels or other houses visible from my vantage point. The balcony protruded in front of the other structures on the beach. Mind-boggling, I thought, and then wondered again who owned the place.

Distracted, I didn't hear Jay as he came up behind me, encircling me with his arms. I felt so safe. Then I remembered why we'd come to the Caymans. "Don't we have to hurry to the bank?"

"No, the banks don't open until ten. It's only six. Let's shower and dress. Then I'll give you the tour."

"Our clothes are at the hotel."

"No, I had them transferred here. They're in the closet, over there." He pointed to the far point in the large space that was the bedroom. "The bathroom is to the right of the closet. There're towels and robes."

I stepped into a bathroom that was bigger than my bedroom at home—and I had one of the largest in the old farmhouse. A shower the size of five was in one corner, with more showerheads than I'd ever seen in one space. A large, white marble sunken tub filled the area under bay windows overlooking the ocean. Marble everywhere—the walls, countertops, and floors, all pristine white. Two plush white robes hung on the back of the door with white terrycloth slippers on the floor behind it. Stacks of towels sat on a green glass table adjacent to the shower. Whoever owned this place had more money than I could ever imagine.

After our shower, Jay showed me around the mansion. It was not fully furnished, but what was there was simplistically elegant.

"Now, are you going to tell me who owns this place?" I said. I'd shown more patience than I was usually able to muster. I'd reached my limit.

"Val, I want you to know that I love you. I've always loved you. I want to spend the rest of my life with you. Here."

I almost missed the last word, but I did hear it. "We could never afford to live here. I think I'd be happy spending the rest of my life with you, too, but it doesn't matter where. I know you love the farm, and we could work out something so we could live near it. I'd have to travel a lot, but with the internet and other communication devices these days, we could work it out."

"Val, I don't love the farm. I don't want to work for the rest of my life like my mother and father did. I'm not going to end up with arthritis, bad knees, and a bad back so I can't enjoy life. I want to live here. And we can afford it. This house is mine. I knew the only way I'd get away from the farm was to make enough money to take care of my parents and myself for the rest of our lives. Otherwise, I'd never be able to leave without feeling the guilt."

He looked around. "The enjoyment here is endless. We can travel all over the world. You don't have to work. I don't have to work."

"But where did you get . . . oh my God, you're one of them. You're working against the farmers and the American people. Just so you can enjoy *yourself?*" I had difficulty breathing, and my body didn't feel like it was part of me. I bent forward, hands on my knees, trying to catch my breath, afraid I'd pass out. It was like I was outside of myself, looking at a scene in a movie. I should have paid more attention to my doubts. I should have listened to Ken. He was right to suspect Jay. I was too close to the story, the biggest mistake a reporter can make.

"So *we* can have a life. Do you know how many people just do what they want? I don't really care about anyone else but us. That's the American way. The American people don't even care about what's going on. Have there been demonstrations? Not many after the initial burst. Has anyone petitioned the government to stop what it's doing? No. People are only upset for a moment, then they forget. No one really cares."

I stared at Jay, feeling like I was having a dream, a nightmare. That had to be it. I shook my head but didn't wake up. All the doubts I'd had about him being involved in the conspiracy came back. My mind was on fast forward. Nate's arguments with Jay about me getting involved, the trip on the way back from California, being run off the road, Jay acting secretive then trying to explain it away later, Ken's doubts. I had put all those incidents aside in my mind, instead choosing to believe in someone I'd known all my life and whom I cared about.

"Just how involved are you in the takeover of America's land for your own greed?" I said, feeling the veins in my head and neck throbbing, my face becoming hotter. I felt like I might explode.

"It was my idea. I just had to contact the right people to make it happen. I've been working on it since high school," Jay said, smiling and proud. "I studied how to make this happen." He spread his arms out as if he were encompassing the house, or maybe the world.

"Our classmates as well as the community looked down on farmers. They thought we weren't smart, made fun of our clothing and our parents. Thought we weren't intelligent. In actuality, farmers are some of the smartest people, able to run businesses when the laws and payments they receive for their products were jokes. How many people can run a business that receives less than it costs to make their products? I made up my mind that I would show them all, show them how I could outsmart the politicians, the businesses, everyone. People need food to live. Farmers should be at the top of the pyramid, not the bottom."

Couldn't he see my reaction? He must have mistaken my incredulity for excitement. Didn't he hear what I was saying?

"How many of *your* people at home are involved in this? Was Nate involved?"

"He suspected me, tried to talk to me—and swore if I got you involved, he'd stop me."

"So you had him killed, or maybe did it yourself?" I was trying to speak, but I wasn't sure which of my words could be understood.

"Of course not," he said, stepping away from me, seemingly horrified. "I would never have hurt Nate. I loved him. We've been like brothers. It was hard to hide what I was doing from Nate. He was too smart. I'd never have harmed him, but I don't think he committed suicide either. His death had nothing to do with me."

"Or anyone you are involved with?"

"Possibly, but certainly nothing I sanctioned."

"Well then, it's alright, isn't it?" I screamed. "I need to be alone. I'm going out. Don't follow me."

"You're coming back?" Jay said.

"What for? We're obviously not going to the bank. That was all a ruse to get me here, right? Is Ken involved with this?"

"Are you kidding? Mr. Do What's Right? Or Mr. Oblivious? He has no idea I'm involved. We never have to go back, Val, never. We can travel the world."

"What about your family, my family?" I think I was crying. I had to get myself under control. I couldn't take this personally. Treat it like a story, I told myself. Pretend you're undercover. I was undercover, but not with Jay. I had to contact Ken.

"Life is about us, now. I made this happen for *us*."

"I have to think, take a run on the beach." With my back to Jay, I pulled my passport and phone out of my bag and tucked them in the waistband of my shorts while sliding on my sneakers. I openly slipped my wallet into my zippered shorts pocket, forced myself to breathe evenly. "I'll bring coffee. Do you want anything else?" I knew my voice had taken on a flat tone. I couldn't help it. I hoped Jay didn't notice. He seemed so self-involved he probably didn't.

"I'll order a variety of breakfast food from a diner nearby. They'll deliver. How long do you think you'll be gone?"

"Give me an hour," I said, and walked out the door. If I was lucky, that would be enough time to get myself to a safe place and call Ken.

I ran as fast as I could, south, in the direction of the airport. I could have been in better shape. Sticking to the beach for the first quarter hour, I ran through an access path to the main road behind the oceanfront homes. I thought better of that and turned to run perpendicular to the beach. If Jay started looking for me, he'd try the main road first.

I'd just turned left onto a road parallel to the beach again. I stopped, caught my breath, and stepped into a small park surrounded by trees. No one was around. Too early. I found a bench behind some bushes and reached for my phone with the intention of calling Ken.

A policeman appeared, causing me to jump. "I'm sorry miss, this is a private park," he said. "It belongs to the residents of this area. You don't look like anyone I know. Are you visiting someone here or just running out of your area?"

"I'm so sorry. I didn't realize this was private. I'm registered at the Ritz. I was just taking a morning run and stopped to call my friend, see if he wanted me to bring breakfast."

"I see," he said. "Your name, please."

No point in lying any further, but I was afraid to tell him the truth. I no longer knew whom I could trust.

"My name is Valerie Jacobs. I'm a reporter for *Washington In Depth*." I handed him my wallet with my ID and press pass.

"Sorry, Ms. Jacobs, but the residents of this island value their privacy."

"Oh, I'm here on vacation, not working." I smiled at him. "I definitely don't have time for running while I'm working."

"Okay, then, but I'll have to ask you to move on."

"Of course," I said. "Is there a coffee shop nearby?"

"Around the corner," he said.

"Thanks, have a great day. Who could help it in this place?" I said, and smiled at the policeman. He didn't respond.

I hurried to find the coffee shop. It was larger than it looked from the outside. It wasn't hard for me to find a corner in the back. I called Ken.

"Ken, I don't have long. Jay's admitted he's involved, that he actually started the takeover. He wants me to stay in the Caymans with him and live a life of luxury. Can you believe it?"

"Where are you right now? Is Jay with you?"

"No, I said I was going for a run. I'm in a coffee shop. I'm going to try to get away, but I could use some help. Do you know where I can get help? Should I go directly to the airport?"

There was silence. "Ken, are you there? Please don't desert me. What do I do?"

"Do you want to stay with him?"

"Are you crazy?" Val had to stop herself from screeching. "I don't even know who he is. I need to come home."

"Valerie, I know this will be difficult, but if you think you can pull it off, I need you to go back to Jay. Is he at the Ritz?

"No, he has his own mansion on the beach. Can you believe it?"

"That's even better. Go to the house. He probably has information there. We need to follow the money. Can you do that? Can you convince him you're with him one hundred percent, that you'll stand by him, give up everything?"

"I'm so disappointed and angry right now, mostly with myself, I can probably do anything. I want to bring him back to the United States to face his neighbors and so-called friends that he sold down the river. I can't tell you how much I hate him right now. He says he had nothing to do with Nate's death, but he's a liar. I don't believe him. I have no doubt that he'd kill me if he suspects I'm working against him. He's been planning this since he was in high school.

"Val, you need to stop reacting with your emotions. If we want to stop the conspiracy, you have to think smart. Number one, take the battery out of your phone as soon as we finish talking. Smash it and get rid of it. Tell Jay you lost it on your run."

"That will leave me dark. I'll have no contact with anyone. I don't know anyone on the island." I was panicking.

"I will have someone contact you. She'll be close, and ready to help you when you need it. Her name is Shinara Bennett. I sent her to the Caymans when you said you were going. I didn't trust Jay, and when he told me he wanted to take you to the Ritz, I had her book a room there. She'll find you. Don't try to contact me directly again. That'll be too dangerous. Do you know the address of Jay's house?"

"No, but it's only two houses north of the Ritz's property, on the beach—I think I said that."

"Don't worry, Val. Go to the bank with Jay and keep an eye out for anything that might give you additional names or evidence. Make him believe you're with him. Be in investigative reporter mode, and believe what you're telling him. Can you do that? We need to see the money track. You're the only one who can do that now."

"I'm not a bad actress. I'll do it, and I'll nail him for Nate's death. I can do this. He has betrayed everything he was brought up to value. When will I talk to you again?"

"I'll see you when Shinara brings you back to Washington with all the information. Don't worry about bringing Jay back. I'll take care of that."

CHAPTER 30

"I was beginning to think you weren't coming back. I tried calling but didn't get an answer," Jay said when I ran up the sand to greet him.

"I lost my phone. It must have fallen out of my pocket. I retraced my steps, but someone must have already picked it up. Know where I can get another one?" I reached up behind his neck, pulling him down to me, kissing him tenderly. "I love you, and if you want to stay here and travel the world, I can't think of anything I'd rather do." I wondered if he'd believed I'd turn my back on my family or forget that he had, either directly or indirectly, something to do with Nate's death.

"I was afraid you wouldn't come back, that you'd gone home."

"I don't ever want to be away from you again. Do we still have to go to the bank? I shouldn't have been gone so long. I'll shower and change. Didn't get the coffee, either." I kissed him again.

"I'll get coffee and breakfast and bring it to you," he said.

I let the water run over me and gradually turned it as cold as I could tolerate. I hoped I could do this. I had to do all I could not to cry. I'll do it for you, Nate, I thought.

Returning to the bedroom, I saw the steaming coffee on the table. No sign of Jay. I tiptoed to the bedroom door and listened. I heard nothing. Leaning out the door to the balcony, I heard his voice. I walked onto the balcony and saw him talking to a woman, no one I'd seen before. Was she someone who was in on the plan? I was being neurotic. She probably happened to be walking by the house and he was being his usual friendly self. Ha! I'd take this opportunity to look around the bedroom.

Pulling drawers out and taking care not to move papers around too much, I looked through all the dresser and bedside table drawers. Nothing of any consequence. No names or numbers, at any rate.

I sat on the balcony with my coffee and watched as Jay finished his conversation with the woman. It didn't appear to be anything other than chitchat. When he turned toward the house, he looked up, saw me, and smiled that broad, infectious grin. Today, it appeared to be the grin of the Cheshire cat, not the smile I'd always been quick to return. I managed a little wave and an equally deceiving smile back. There, dammit, I can pretend too.

"Take your time," he said. "We don't have to hurry. I'm going to make a few phone calls."

Because I didn't think I'd be able to sneak downstairs and listen to his calls without being detected, I dressed, poured another cup of coffee from the carafe Jay had left, and returned to the balcony to drink it and think. How would I manage this without any help? If I'd been in LA, at home, or even in Washington, at least I'd know my way around. Here, I was blind.

Jay interrupted my thoughts when he put his hands on my shoulders. I jumped and spilled coffee over the table. "My God, you scared me," I said.

"You were a million miles away. What were you thinking?"

"I was trying to think how to tell Ken I'm not returning to the US," I lied. Wow, I did that easily.

"You don't have to worry about that yet. We can stretch this out a few days, then we'll think of something. Ready to go to the bank? I have something to show you."

"Sure."

"I'm going to show you how many people are with us, so you understand and know you made the right decision."

"I know I've made the right decision to be with you," I said. He didn't need much convincing, I thought. His ego and arrogance were immense. He didn't even conceive I wouldn't do exactly as he suggested. What I did was smile up into his eyes and make him believe he was the only man I'd ever be with. It almost made me laugh to think I could act so well.

"The driver should be here in about five minutes. Let's go down to the garage and wait for him." The garage was on the south side of the house. "Which car do you want to take?" he said, pushing a button that opened all four bays. There were a Mercedes, two BMWs, and a Jaguar.

The first thing that popped into my mind was Jay had taken advantage of his friends, farmers in America, as well as every other American who would be affected by what he'd done. My jaw tightened.

"What's wrong?" he said, sounding alarmed.

"I twisted my ankle when I ran this morning, a sudden pain. It's gone now. Wow, these cars are beautiful."

"I want you to know you've made the right decision."

He must have thought I was terribly shallow to care only about things. He didn't know me at all.

A stout man with longish, graying hair rounded the corner, and I recognized him as Keith Jackson, the farmer from home. I'd seen him in Jay's computer barn, too. He was the fracking expert Jay recommended I consult when I visited Chicopee.

"You remember Keith?" Jay said.

"Of course. How are you, Keith?"

"Thanks to Jay, I'm better than ever."

"Keith takes care of this place while I'm in the States, and he likes to work on the cars. They're his babies, so he drives me around when I'm here. Which one shall we take today, Val?"

"Mmmm." I pretended I wasn't disgusted by Jay's display of opulence. "I've always wanted to ride in a Mercedes." I smiled, while cringing inside.

On the way to the bank, when Jay put his arm around me and pulled me to him, I tried not to tense. I wanted to hit him, but instead, I told myself I had to make him believe I cared or I wouldn't be able to prove he was involved in Nate's death. And that was the most important thing I had to do.

"Oh, I almost forgot to tell you," Jay said. "A new arrival to the island is having a get-together tonight. Lives a little north of the house. She wants to meet some people, and invited us. I hope you don't mind. I said yes. She seemed so nice, and I think you'll get on with her. She owns a newspaper in the UK—Shinara Bennett."

I tried not to react. "If this is going to be our home base, I'll need to get to know people. I'd love to go. But, I don't have appropriate clothes for such an event."

"We'll stop and get you something after we go to the bank."

"Keith, we'll start at the Grand Cayman Bank and go from there," Jay said.

"We're going to more than one bank?" I asked.

"We'll have a few stops, but we don't have to make them all today."

It wasn't far to the Grand Bank. Would Jay show me the list of names of those involved? Would there be any we didn't already know? That would be too easy. Whatever I learned, I'd pass on to Shinara Bennett that night. If I could just keep up the pretense.

I took Jay's hand in mine and smiled at him. Better not lay it on any thicker, I thought. It would make him suspicious.

Keith pulled up to a remarkable marble building. Even the island's banks were outlandish. Jay stepped out of the car and walked around to open my door. He put his arm on my elbow and led me inside. This was definitely different than any bank I'd ever seen. There was a huge lobby, with one desk near the back where a woman sat. When we walked in, she moved around to the front of the desk and walked toward us. "Welcome back, Mr. Benson."

"Hello, Janice. I'd like you to meet a very special person, Ms. Valerie Jacobs."

"Very happy to meet you," she said. Turning to Jay, she asked, "What can we do for you this visit?"

"First, I'd like to see my safe deposit box. We'll need about an hour."

"You will sign off for Ms. Jacobs?"

"I'll add her to my account, with her permission?" He looked at me with a questioning look.

"Of course," I said, trying to look innocent and thinking this was going to be oh so much easier than I'd anticipated. I had to do all I could not to chuckle and wring my hands. How could he trust me unconditionally after what he'd done?

We followed Janice to an elevator. She inserted a key, and Jay put his key in the same lockbox. We stepped onto the elevator, and it lifted us to the fourteenth floor. Janice led us to a small room. Jay and Janice followed the same procedure, but this time, the keys went into a lock on a metal box, number 54367, and Janice pulled the two-foot-square metal box out of the wall. Jay opened the door, and Janice led him and me to another room. The keys were used again, but when they entered this room, there were two comfortable stuffed chairs with a table between them.

"What can I bring you to drink?" she addressed Jay and me.

"I'd like wine from *my* cellar. Val, red or white?"

"Red, please," I said, trying not to gag on the way he emphasized the word.

When Janice left, I said, "I think I could get used to this." Lowering my eyes, I looked at Jay.

"I hope so," he said. "You're going to love it. Who wouldn't?"

Someone who loved her brother and family and country, that's who, I thought. But I smiled at him. "So what did you want to show me?"

After a knock on the door, Jay stood. When he opened it, Janice brought in a tray with a bottle of wine and two glasses. There was also a silver, tiered tray with cheeses, fruit, and crackers.

"If you'd like anything else, please ring," she said.

"Thank you, Janice," I said. "It looks lovely."

Jay looked at me. "Life could not be better than this. I'm so happy you decided to stay with me." He poured the wine and offered me the tray.

"Okay, down to business," he said, after we'd tasted the wine.

Jay opened the box full of papers and folders. He lifted the folders and laid them on the table, handing me a red one. "These are the politicians in the country who are involved with our plan. You'll see we're in good company." He handed me the folder.

I opened it and read, trying to memorize as many names as I could. I couldn't keep my surprise hidden. My mouth dropped open. There were federal politicians as well as state figures, governors, state senators, and legislators, and local politicians organized alphabetically by state.

"I knew you'd be surprised with at least a few," he said with a smile.

I wanted to knock him off his chair, hit him over the head with the wine bottle, or maybe both. But I had to contain myself. "I'm astounded by a few of these names," I said, looking over the list again in an attempt to make sure I remembered them.

"Are you ready for more?" he asked.

"I guess so," I said, smiling at him and looking forward to the day I could see the smirk wiped off his face.

Next was the blue folder. "Business owners involved," he said.

I couldn't say I was very surprised with the businesses involved. They were the ones we'd identified, with a few more I would have expected: big oil, Fortune 500s, chemical and pharmaceutical and insurance companies.

Then came the biggest shock. The yellow folder was labeled "Agricultural Entities."

"These are the files that will make you realize you made the right decision, that you are on the right side, the side of the farmer."

Jay kept pulling files out of the boxes, fifty in all, one for each state.

I pulled the New York State file first and glanced through the sheets in the folder. This couldn't be. Many of our neighbors were listed, even the farmers who'd lost their farms for one reason or another. I set the folder down and asked Jay for the Utah folder.

He handed it to me. They were on the list. Some of the farmers we'd visited were involved, too. I was beginning to understand.

"You started it, then drew your friends in," I said.

"Don't you think it's about time the people who've worked the hardest in this country get what they deserve?"

"Do the politicians and business entities know the farmers started it?"

"Of course not. You know they're the ones who think they know everything. They couldn't possibly believe that the 'dumb farmers' could even think of such a thing. Believe me, when they find out the farmers are the ones who actually own the so-called government farms, water supplies, and leases on gas and oil land, they won't believe it. They think they're invincible, that they've orchestrated the takeover of this country's food supply as well as making money on fracking and the oil industry. They have no clue."

"And what will happen when they find out?"

"They're going to find out very soon."

"The politicians and businesses have the power. What will they do when they find out you've double-crossed them?"

"Nothing they can do. Everything is legal. I don't think you understand what's at stake," Jay said.

"I guess not," I said, now not able to hide my shock and disappointment. "I think I need some air." Jay may have thought what he did was right, but I didn't. Farming was still going to be in the hands of a few who would control the food prices, and while I sympathized with the farmers who'd received low prices for their goods, I didn't think sticking it to everyone else in the country was the way to make their lot better. And Nate hadn't either.

"Of course. Let's go." Jay pushed a button near the door and put the files back in the boxes, and then in the vault. Janice appeared in less than a minute.

"We're finished for today," Jay said, and Janice walked us out of the room, down the elevator, and out of the building.

My head was spinning. This was totally unexpected. I didn't dare ask Jay any questions. I had to get away from him for a while. My brother was dead. Rosemary was most likely dead. They had tried to kill Ken. How many other people had been eliminated?

"I know this is a lot to absorb. You need time to let it all sink in. I know just the place."

I didn't answer, didn't dare. When we got in the car, Jay told Keith to take me to Adriana's Spa on Tricot Lane, then to Andromeda's. "Spend the rest of the afternoon at the spa and shopping at Andromeda's. It will relax you. I'll take a cab back to the house. I have some work to do."

There was no questioning. Just what he said was going to happen, no input from me. I hadn't known him at all. What a control freak.

I couldn't spend the day trying to relax. I needed to run, to think. I asked Keith to take me to a shoe store, where I purchased sneakers, then had him take me to the spa. I told him there was no point in him waiting around. I'd catch a cab to Andromeda's when I was done at the spa and call him when I was finished shopping.

"Jay would prefer I wait for you," he said.

"I'm sure he won't mind. He knows I'm used to taking care of myself. I'm definitely not used to being waited on. Don't get me wrong, it's nice and all, but really, wasting your time seems so . . . wasteful. I'm sure there are things you'd rather be doing. I'll call you when I need you. I turned, not waiting for an answer, and entered the main gym door. I looked out, and Keith was already pulling away from the curb. I waited a minute and walked back out of the gym, sneakers on. I began running. I didn't know where I was going, but I knew I needed to run off some stress so I could continue. I stopped at a Verizon store and purchased a phone to replace the one I'd "lost." I purchased international coverage, then ran on to a park and called Ken. I filled him in on what I'd found out.

"I'm not that surprised. As you know, I'd suspected Jay before, but this definitely puts a new slant on things. Don't take any chances, Val. You shouldn't be calling me. Clear your history as soon as we finish talking. Jay might put on a good show, giving you the idea he trusts you enough to show you his records, but I'm guessing he's not telling you the complete truth. Anyone can put on paper what he wants you to believe. Keep your eyes open, and give any information you find to Shinara. I'll talk with her, and she'll give you further instructions tonight. I have to confirm a few details. In spite of what Jay has told and shown you, you can trust the people that have been meeting with us—except Jay, that is. Remember to clear your history."

"If he finds the call, I'll tell him I called to give notice," I said. "His arrogance will allow him to believe it."

After talking to Ken, I felt better. I hadn't misjudged everyone I'd met. I flagged down a cab, spent about half an hour finding an outfit at Andromeda's, and called Keith on his cell. Jackson answered immediately and said he'd be there in five.

CHAPTER 31

"**W**here have you been?" Jay said, his face red. "Keith said you ditched him."

"What? I didn't ditch him. I felt like running instead of going to the spa, so I said I'd call him from Andromeda's when I was finished. Want to see what I bought, or do you want to be surprised? That's some store. I don't think I've ever been in a store with no price tags. I hope I didn't go overboard. The clerk wouldn't tell me how much anything was."

"You're changing the subject. Where did you go?" Jay said, not changing his irate tone.

"Bought some sneakers, went running, stopped at a phone store to replace my phone," I said, holding up the phone, "then to Andromeda's. What's this all about?"

"I trusted you, let you in on everything. When I assign a driver to you, I expect you to stay with him and go where I've told you to go."

"Are you kidding me? If *letting me in* means I have to give up thinking for myself, then let me out! Don't you know me? I've always thought for myself—not always making the wisest choices, I'll admit, but the consequences were mine, and I had to live with them." My voice grew louder. I knew I was taking a chance going up against someone whom I'd recently learned was an obnoxious controller, but I wouldn't be able to make contact with anyone if he was watching me every second.

His mouth dropped open. I wasn't sure if he was shocked that I'd talked back to him or if he was going to tell me to get out. Either way would be all right with me. I'd find another way to get the information I needed to stop him, but I could hear Ken's plea for me to help. Maybe I'd better try to repair this.

"I guess I forgot myself," he said. "I've been working on this for so long. I know you're with me on this. I trust you." He moved closer to me, took the packages and dress bag, and laid them over a nearby chair. As he hugged me, I felt his body relax in my arms. "I'm sorry. We're so close to the end of this. Guess I'm wound a little tight," he said.

Too bad nothing could come of this. I had always cared for Jay, but when I thought about it, in the past, something always held me back. The side of him he showed on this day told me why. I must have always sensed something wasn't quite right. After all, my brother had tried to warn me. Maybe if I'd listened to him for a change, Nate would still be alive. Had Nate suspected, or even known Jay's end plan?

I pushed away from Jay and said I was going to shower and get ready.

"Want some company?"

"No," I said, and took the packages off the chair and walked away.

"I really am sorry," he said.

I didn't turn around.

CHAPTER 32

Jay left me alone for the next two hours. I was dressed and on the balcony when he knocked on the door. Maybe he was sorry, or maybe just afraid I would walk away and print the truth. Whatever he'd done, possibly he'd cared a little for me. I could definitely use his feelings to get the information I needed.

What had happened to me? I felt nothing, cold. Jay was someone I'd cared for a day ago. Now, if I felt anything, it was close to hate. I'd deal with that when this was over. No time for regrets or self-recriminations now.

I opened the bedroom door.

"You look beautiful," he said. "I'll shower and dress. Can I get you anything first?"

"No, I'm fine, and thank you for the compliment."

I stepped onto the patio and waited for Jay. So many thoughts were going through my mind. How would I manage to get Shinara alone tonight and pass on what I'd learned? How would I keep Jay at bay without appearing suspicious? What did I need to do to bring this information to the American people and not wind up like my brother? At the thought of Nate, I felt rage.

I jumped when Jay touched my shoulders from behind. "Sorry," he said, "I didn't mean to scare you. I'm sorry about before. I do trust you, Val. This has been a long process, getting to this point. I guess I'm a little tired and jumpy myself. Please, forgive me."

"Of course," I said, turning to face him, hugging him as I did. I felt like crying, but knew I had to stay focused.

"Let's go," he said. "We'll relax tonight, forget about everything but having a nice social evening with future friends."

"Sounds good," I said, all the while thinking how difficult that would be for me.

CHAPTER 33

We walked the beach to Shinara's hypothetical home. There must have been fifty steps on the stairway from the beach to the front porch of the house I assumed had been rented by Ken for the purpose of passing on information. The party was in full swing. Approaching, I could hear beach music with a classical twist. Shinara stood out in the crowd in a white, flowing dress that looked more like a gown on her slim body than a beach dress. When she saw Jay and me ascending the stairs, she walked down to greet us. She wore white high stiletto sandals that wrapped around her legs to mid-calf. She was a beautiful woman with long, loose blond curls cascading down her back.

"I'm so glad you came, Jay. And this must be Valerie?" she said, extending her hand. "I'm Shinara Bennett."

"It's a pleasure to meet you, Shinara. You have a breathtaking home."

"Thanks. I've just moved in, so I'm getting used to the size. This is quite a different lifestyle than I'm used to. I'm sure you'll hear it from others at the party, but I won it in a contest in the States—the house and enough money to allow me to live in it the rest of my life. I've decided to keep working, though, so this is the first I've had a chance to spend any amount of time here. I'm on vacation from the small newspaper I own in the UK."

She laughed. "So sorry. I'm going on and on. Please, come have fun. I'd love to talk to you later, Valerie. I hear you're a journalist. I may be interested in starting a paper in the States and would love some advice, if Jay doesn't mind me pulling you away for a few minutes?" she asked, looking at Jay.

"Of course," Jay said. "I see quite a few people I know, so just say the word. Putting his arm around my shoulders, in what I now viewed as his possessive hold, not a caring gesture, he said, "Whenever you get a chance to talk, feel free."

Like it was up to him, I thought. I was starting to dislike everything he said and suspect every action. Too bad I hadn't seen his real character sooner. I again wondered if Nate would still be alive if I'd been wiser. No time to think about that now. Like Scarlet O'Hara, I'd think about it tomorrow. Now I had to play the part.

Jay and I circulated, and he introduced me to bankers, real estate brokers, physicians, surgeons, business owners, CEOs and CFOs. There was one publishing house owner, but obviously no journalists, farmers, or people who actually did the work all of these high and mighty people benefited from. Of course, there wouldn't be any of the regular people here. This was not a real world. I wondered how Ken got all these people together so quickly.

I found myself wondering how Jay already knew so many people on the island. He must have spent quite a lot of time here, not just as an annual tourist. I also found myself wondering if his parents knew what he was doing. If I was honest with myself, I could picture his father being involved, but never Marion. She was too good a person. She would be crushed when she found out. Maybe she already knew. Maybe that was the reason for her severe headaches.

On a positive note, the food was delicious. How was Ken paying for this? I knew some of the people involved in trying to stop the takeover were wealthy, but doubted that many were. Shinara interrupted my thoughts. "Things are slowing down. Would you mind me borrowing Val for a little while, Jay?" She was so upbeat, acting interested in learning about journalism in the States.

"Sure," Jay said. "I see some people I'd like to talk to about a trip I'm planning."

"Let's go to my office. It'll be quiet there," Shinara said.

The office was on the third level of the house. I drew in my breath. The widow's watch room would be the perfect writing space. The south side of the room was all glass, overlooking the green, clear water of the Caribbean. I must have inhaled again.

"Wouldn't it be the perfect writing room?" Shinara said. "This room gave me the idea of how to get you alone. We'd better not waste time. What have you learned?"

I filled Shinara in on all the names I could remember and what I'd learned from Jay.

Shinara reached in the top drawer of a desk and handed me a compact. "It's a camera, for you to take pictures of any records you can obtain so we have the total scope of what's involved. Here's a flash drive." She passed me what looked like a tube of mascara. If you can find his computer, push this button and it pops out. Don't get caught. Ken said you'd figure it out. He has total confidence in you, said he's grown to depend on you over the short time you've been with him."

"Is there anything specific I should search for?"

"He'd like you to photograph the files that you saw at the bank, but only if you think you can get away with it. He also needs the financial records. He thinks Jay's acting as CFO and has ultimate control of all the money. Ken believes Jay to be quite dangerous. He's worried for your safety if Jay finds out what you're doing."

"I'll be careful. When will we meet again?"

"When we want to talk, either of us can use the excuse of a half day at the spa. If we don't need much time, we can always invent a headache, or we could set up a lunch date for the day after tomorrow if you think you can have something by then. Ken wants you out of here as soon as possible."

"That's good with me. Jay put my name on his accounts at the banks. I can tell him I want to study them so I can help."

"Good idea. Won't he want to go with you or be suspicious of your motives?"

"I'll wait until I know he has plans. He knows I like to be busy, and he's so egotistical, I honestly don't think it would cross his mind I'd go against him. He's planning a trip. I'll let you know when I have the details."

"Let's exchange numbers so we can communicate with each other," Shinara said. "Will Jay get suspicious if we meet for lunch?"

"No, I'll tell him you want to take me to your hairstylist. He's always made fun of my non-hairstyle, so knowing I'll be making an improvement, he'll be happy. Wouldn't want to embarrass the big tycoon."

"Sound a little bitter, Valerie. Be careful. Don't let your anger get in the way."

"I won't. What's Ken's timeline? When is he looking for me to have all the information?"

"As soon as possible, but don't take chances with your safety. He'd like as much as you can get by Friday."

"Not long term, that's for sure. The sooner we can get back home and take care of this, the better."

Shinara and I finished in less than twenty minutes. When we returned to the party, I was surprised that Jay was nowhere to be seen. Shinara circulated among the few guests remaining as I looked from room to room for him with no luck. Deciding to wait on the porch for him to return from wherever, I noticed that the porch wrapped around the entire house. When I followed it to the west, I thought I heard his voice. Walking closer to the back of the house, I heard a woman's voice. I didn't recognize it—not that I would. I didn't know anyone in the Caymans'.

"I think we should slow down a little, wait until next week before the final purchases are made," the woman said. "The impact on the stock market is going to confirm what Ken and Val have been reporting to the country. There will be no turning back, and astounding repercussions."

"We're not waiting. Time's up. I've been working on this for too long. We're doing it Friday," Jay said.

Doing what? I thought, sliding back against the house so I couldn't be seen. I had to get this information back to Shinara and to Ken. Maybe one of them would know what it was all about. I quietly walked along the house and back into the entrance hall, where the guests were saying their good-byes to Shinara. My eyes implored her to look at me. I must have looked as anxious as I felt, because she turned toward me and excused herself from her other guests.

"We have to move the timeline up. I overheard Jay talking to a woman. Something big's going down Friday, something that will have a deleterious effect on the stock market. Let Ken know."

As she finished, Jay appeared at her elbow. "What's wrong?" he said. "You look upset."

"No, planning a girls' lunch out tomorrow. We don't have plans, do we?" I said, pandering to his controlling character.

"As a matter of fact, that works out perfect. I have to fly to one of the other islands for business. Maybe you can make a day of it."

Jay appeared distracted when we returned to his house. "I'm sorry, but I think I have to work tonight. Do you mind?" he said.

"Of course not," I said. I turned to kiss and hug him, feeling totally relieved that I didn't have to feign a headache. I'd worry about the coming nights when they arrived.

CHAPTER 34

I awoke alone in the king-sized bed, sun streaming through the windows, wondering if Jay had come to bed last night. After donning my robe, I walked through the open door onto the veranda. Looking out over the Caribbean, I could almost understand how Jay could get hooked on this way of life—but never enough to hurt others, all for the money to live this way. It wasn't worth it.

I planned my day. I'd go to the bank, photograph the records, and meet Shinara to pass on what I'd found. Feeling strange, I turned and saw that Jay was standing there, watching me.

"You're beautiful," he said.

My fake smile took over, and I put my arms around his neck and drew him to me. "What time do you have to go?" I asked. Maybe I would try to find some acting gigs when this was over.

"I'm afraid I have to leave soon. Going to Little Cayman," he said. "I'll be gone until late tomorrow night. I hope you won't mind staying here. I'd take you with me, but it'll be boring, just meetings on where to put our money. I've been studying the best options for a long time, but I have to finalize things in the next few days so everything I've done to this point is secure."

"No problem," I said. "Is there anything I can do to help from here?"

"No, everything's set except the final setup of the Special Purpose Entity. Nothing you have to worry about."

What a chauvinist, condescending pig. I'd always known his father dismissed women, but somehow I thought Jay didn't inherit that trait.

"I guess I'll go back to the Grand Bank and study the records. I'm afraid I didn't take much in while we were at the bank yesterday. It was all a bit of a shock."

"That's a great idea. I want you to know everything, and enjoy making new friends, but don't get any ideas about going to work. You're not going to have to work."

"What if I want to?" I said.

"We won't have time," he said. "I'd like you to be available to travel with me."

Oh, my God, I thought. It's all about him. How in the hell did I miss this side of him? He thought I was going to be a bauble dangling from his arm.

"Well then," I said. "What time do you leave?"

"Keith will drive me to the airport in about twenty minutes. Then he'll be available to you the rest of the day. He'll be happy to take you to the bank and anywhere else you'd like to explore. He can take you and Shinara to lunch, if you still have plans with her."

"As far as I know, we may go to dinner. She's busy today," I said. "This is such a different way to live. Hope I can get used to it," I laughed.

"I have time for coffee. Want to join me on the terrace?" Jay said.

"Sure," I said.

The next twenty minutes until Jay left seemed like hours. As soon as he was out of sight, I started my search. He'd given me the time to find his computer and photograph everything I needed, but it turned out not to be as easy as I'd thought. He didn't leave with a briefcase or computer bag, so I assumed his computer must be here somewhere, but I'd be damned if I could find it.

I thought he must have a secret room devoted to his scheme. I started in the office off the den on the first floor. Nothing that I could find.

I'd gone to the kitchen for a bottle of water when a buzz from the intercom made me jump. Pushing the button, I said, "Yes?"

"It's Keith Jackson."

"Yes?" I said again.

"Jay said you might want me to drive you somewhere today."

"Yes, would you be available to drive me to the Grand Bank in about an hour? Oh, by the way, can you recommend a restaurant where I can take Shinara Bennett for dinner?"

"The Foster House has good food and a rich atmosphere."

"Will it be difficult to obtain a reservation?"

"Not at all, Ms. Jacobs. I'll call for you. What time would you like to have dinner?"

"Please, Keith, call me Val. I'll call Ms. Bennett and get back to you with the time."

"Yes, Ms. Jacobs." He cut off communication.

I went to the bedroom to retrieve my phone and call Shinara. She answered right away.

"Would you like a ride to dinner? One of Jay's minions is making reservations at the Foster House. What time's good for you?"

"Seven will be good, but I can't talk now," Shinara said. "I'll talk to you at dinner. Must go. Very busy." The connection was broken.

I hung up. I didn't usually drink this early in the day, but I could use a glass of wine before going to the bank. I remembered the wine cellar from Jay's grand tour. Might as well take advantage of the good stuff. I opened the door in the kitchen and followed the winding staircase to the wine cellar. Ah! Temperature controlled. Nice and cool. There was a ten-foot-long rack with about ten bottles down on each of twenty vertical padded shelves. I was pulling out wine bottles to find one that looked good, not that I really knew. I never paid much attention, usually let whomever I was with choose the correct drink. I bent to the bottom and reached for a bottle, but fell forward before I had my hand around the neck. My hand inadvertently pushed the neck of the bottle to the floor. There was a creak. As I jumped back, the wine rack split and opened inward.

I looked behind me, but there was no one there. I crept into the room, trying to adjust my eyes to the darkness. As light from the wine cellar leaked into the room, I found a light switch. Wow. Guess I found his computer. There were Macs, PCs, and TV monitors around the outside of the room. A desk with only a lamp and a laptop sat in the middle of the space. There were no files, filing cabinets, or old-style office trappings. This was strictly a high-tech room.

I approached the laptop first, Jay's primary choice in computers. I knew it would be password protected, but I might be able to figure it out. Hopefully it didn't need a fingerprint. I was confident his conceit would hold true and he had thought no one would ever find this room. Of course, I had to admit I'd found the room only due to my clumsiness.

It was password protected, but what would the password be? Arrogant asshole? Probably not. I tried a few combinations—mother's name, father's name, usmarines, hoorah, iamthegreatest. Nothing worked. Then my thoughts reverted to our childhood—his first horse, Rusty, no, his first dog, Ranger, no, combination of RustyRanger.

That was it! I had his desktop. Now to find the financial information I needed. I went into the Finder and typed in "banks." Up popped a list of banks, organized by country. There must have been thirty of them. I started calling them up and copying the account information onto the thumb drive Shinara had given me. I was about midway when all of a sudden, the computer shut down and the lights went out. I grabbed the thumb drive out of the laptop and turned toward the way I'd come in.

The doors were closing. I ran, but I couldn't make it. What had happened? How would I get out of here? My heart pounded, and I started sweating. I walked around the outside of the room, feeling my way, trying to find another path out. I couldn't see a thing. I tripped over something and fell. I stayed down, breathing hard. The air was leaving the room. Was that possible? Would I suffocate?

I had to get myself under control and think this through if I was going to get out. Jay was gone until tomorrow. Was there a trip on the computer that shut it down? Or a trip on the door to the room? Couldn't be, or Jay wouldn't be able to work in here, unless there was an alarm he turned off when he used the room. I should have thought of that when I came in. Or was there an alarm that went to Keith Jackson in his quarters when Jay was away?

I breathed deeply a few times. Okay. Think. I had my phone. I reached into my pocket. I didn't have it. I'd left it on the counter in the kitchen when I came down for the wine. Too many mistakes. I'd try to turn on the computer again. I crawled my way to the center of the room to the desk and felt my way up to the laptop. I pressed the on button. Nothing. Don't give up. Think. If the alarm went to Keith, would he come rescue me? Or would he kill me? Or did the alarm go to a police station? That wouldn't be good.

I'd better come up with a plausible story. This was a large room, not a small, closed-in place. I could wait, but I wouldn't. I tried the laptop again. Nothing.

I stood, steadied myself, and worked my way to the door where I'd come in. There must be a way to open it. Knowing I entered from the bottom, I walked to the far side of door, got down on my knees, and started feeling along the floor and then up the surface. I felt a difference in the door near the hinge. Trying not to hope too much, I pushed on one side of an indentation—nothing. I pushed on the other side, and the doors separated. I was standing at the middle as they opened.

Keith Jackson stood on the other side of the doors with an assault weapon.

"Oh my God, what are you doing," I said, trying to make him seem like the one in the wrong place.

"What are you doing, Ms. Jacobs? You are not supposed to be here. No one is allowed in this room except Jay."

"I came down for some wine, tripped, grabbed a bottle, and suddenly the wine racks opened and I fell in. I showed him the lump already rising on my leg where I'd hit the desk."

"Why were you on the computer?" he said, still not lowering the gun.

"When I saw the computer on the desk, I figured I might as well check my email. All of a sudden, everything shut down and the doors closed. I didn't know what was going on."

I didn't think he believed me, but I wasn't sure he knew what else to do, so he said he'd be glad to come down to get me wine when I wanted it.

"Anything you recommend for an evening drink?" I said. "I want to ask Shinara back here after dinner. Oh, by the way, I talked with her and seven is good for the reservation. What time will we have to leave here? Would you mind taking us to the Foster House after I return from the bank?" I hoped I could distract him. I also hoped Jay didn't check in with him while he was gone. I was sure he wouldn't believe a word of my story.

I'd probably have to disappear from here before he got back tomorrow, especially if he talked to Keith. That gave me about twenty-four hours to get the information from the bank, return to his computer, and copy the information I needed.

Keith took me to the bank and waited in the lobby while I uneventfully copied the information from Jay's files. Almost too easy. We returned to the house, where I took a shower and dressed. Keith chauffeured Shinara and me to the restaurant.

I was counting on him not leaving me alone since my foray into the wine cellar. "I'm not feeling terribly well," I told him. "Would you mind waiting around in case I don't feel well enough to stay? You're welcome to come in and eat with us."

"I'd be more comfortable eating in the restaurant downstairs. Less formal."

"Of course," I said. "I might be more comfortable there, too," I whispered to him. Louder, I said, "I'll call you on your cell when we're ready."

Shinara and I walked into the restaurant. I told her what had happened, and we walked out the back door and hailed a cab. It was a long shot, but we had to get back to the house, get the information, and forward it to Ken.

I was pretty sure this would work. I'd left the alarm off in the house and walked down to the garage to meet Keith, knowing if he came to the house, he might check the alarm to ensure it was activated. I'd covered everything, I thought. We even had the cab drop us at Shinara's, making sure there was no record of a stop at Jay's. The beach was crowded by then, and we walked to Jay's, knowing we wouldn't stand out.

When we arrived and I opened the front door, the alarm started counting down. "Oh no," I said. "Keith must have a remote to check and set the alarm."

"Don't worry," Shinara said. "We've got about twenty seconds left to think of what code he'd use. Got any ideas?"

Think, think, think. What was the code to his safety deposit box? I tried it and pushed the button. Thank God. It stopped ticking.

"Reset the alarm," Shinara said, "in case Keith returns."

I did, and we headed for the stairs. We didn't have much time. Keith could go upstairs in the restaurant at any time and we'd be found out.

"Everything might shut down again. There must be a failsafe when the computer is on for a certain length of time," I said.

"You get into the computer. I'll make sure the doors don't close, and I'll look for the alarm. We don't want it to be tripped. Keith probably has an alert on his phone." She shoved a chair between the doors so we couldn't be locked in. It took less time than I'd taken before, probably because I didn't gawk around. I was able to go directly to the computer and get the information quickly.

We were out of the room and back to Shinara's house within forty-five minutes of leaving the restaurant. Shinara drove her car back to the restaurant and left it about three blocks from the Foster House. We walked to the delivery door. I'd ordered dinner for eight, placing the call after Keith made the original reservation. We were shown to our table by the host and took our seats just before the waiter delivered our dinner.

"Not sure I can eat," I said.

"I can," Shinara said, picking up her fork and steak knife and digging in.

I put a fork full of potatoes in my mouth, then glanced toward the entrance and saw Keith standing by the front door. Had he been there when we came in? "Don't look toward the front door, but Keith is standing there," I said. "Do you think he was there when we were seated?"

"No, I looked around when we sat down. He wasn't there," Shinara said. "Did he see you?"

"Don't know."

"Just keep eating," Shinara said, and laughed.

I responded with a laugh and continued eating.

"Nothing we can do now," Shinara said. "We'll enjoy our dinner and worry about it later."

"How can you be so cool? I'm thinking about what he could know and what's going to happen to us because of it."

"I'm going to order a bottle of wine," she said. "We're going to have to act a little drunk when we're done. We can always say we were in a booth at the bar before coming into the dining room. I doubt he checked every inch of the place."

When the waiter brought another bottle of wine, Keith disappeared, possibly back downstairs to the bar. We finished what we wanted of our dinner and called Keith for the car.

Tripping a little going down the front steps of the restaurant, Shinara grabbed my arm to help steady her. Keith approached and held her other arm, assuming we'd had a little too much. So far, so good.

"Would you like to come in for some more wine?" Shinara asked me when we arrived at her house.

"Sure," I said. "I'll walk down the beach later," I addressed Keith.

"That's not such a good idea," Keith said. "You might not be safe."

"I'll be fine," I said. "Maybe a couple of coffees would be better than a wine."

"Right, you could be correct," Shinara said.

"But I'm responsible for your safety," Keith said. "Jay would be upset if I let you go off on your own and you got hurt."

"I promise you I'll be fine. If it gets too late and Shinara doesn't think I should walk, I'll call you, okay?"

"Yes, Ms. Jacobs."

When we were safely in Shinara's house, she took the flash drive to her computer and called Ken on the phone. "We've got it," she said. "No, we haven't taken time to look at it. I'm going to put it on my computer and forward it to you. Please call me as soon as you download it to make sure we have everything you need. If you have everything, I think we should get Val out of here before morning by private plane. There were a few complications obtaining the information. I don't think we can be sure Jay doesn't know."

Shinara started uploading the information to Ken. I was still uploading the bank records I obtained when my phone rang. "It's Jay," I said. "I don't know if I can act like nothing's wrong. Maybe I shouldn't answer it. Keith has probably called him."

"I'll answer," Shinara said. "Hi, Jay? She just went into the ladies' room. We're at my house. Can I help you with anything, or would you like to wait for Val? By the way, we had a fantastic time tonight. Val and I have so much in common, and thanks for letting Keith drive us. It allowed us both to have a little too much wine."

CHAPTER 35

"**J**ay said he'd be coming in on the first flight tomorrow, arriving at 6:40 a.m. at Robert Owens via Jetcost Airlines," Shinara said.

"That doesn't give us much time. We'd better call Ken again."

"Use my phone," Shinara said. "Tell him we're in trouble. Jay asked that you come to the airport when Keith picks him up. I don't think you can trust he doesn't know you obtained his records. We need to get you out of here before morning. Let me talk to Ken when you're done."

"I have FBI financial experts standing by to evaluate the records you sent me," Ken said. "I understand you may be in danger if Jay knows what you did, but we need more. I need you to get Jay back to the United States. By the time he gets here, hopefully we'll have enough for the FBI to bring Jay in for questioning. They'll be waiting to make the arrest when you arrive in Miami."

"Of course," I said. "Whatever I have to do to get what we need to put Jay and his cronies away."

"Can you come up with a story to explain your entrance into his hidden room?"

"The truth. I tripped and fell, my hand hit a wine bottle on the bottom row, and the doors opened. He knows I wouldn't be able to keep my hands off the computer once I found it. I'll be okay."

"Run if you have to," Ken said. "If you feel your life is in danger at any time, get out. Go wherever you have to and call me. I'll make sure you get help."

"I want proof he was involved in Nate's death. The financials should give us that, right?"

"Maybe," Ken said. "We'll see where the money goes.

"Try connecting payments from Jay to Keith Jackson," I said. "And can you determine if Keith was at home when Nate was killed? I have a feeling he'd have no problem killing if he were compensated. Do you have any idea how I can persuade him back to the US?"

"I've talked to your sister-in-law. She's going to call Jay early tomorrow morning and tell him she wasn't able to reach you on your cell. She'll tell him Annie's been in an accident and she needs you home as soon as possible. I can't imagine Jay will stop you. Your job will be to talk him into coming back with you."

"I can do that. I've become quite an actress," I said. "Shinara wants to talk with you."

"Get some rest," Ken said. "Be careful. I think you should stay where you are tonight. Call Keith and ask him to pick you up on his way to the airport. Tell him the wine made you ill or something."

"Okay, here's Shinara."

CHAPTER 36

'd called and left a message for Keith to pick me up at Shinara's in the morning. He responded that he'd collect me. Unbelievable. Must have thought he was an English chauffeur or something. At 5:30, I groaned. It had been a short night.

After a couple hours of restless sleep, Shinara loaned me a sundress, and walked me down to the street side of the house to wait for Keith. He was already there with a frown on his face as he opened the door for me.

"Hi, Keith," I said. He didn't reply.

He started the short drive to the airport. "Is the wine on the Islands stronger than back home?" I said, holding my head.

"No."

Oh boy, this wasn't good. "Sorry if I woke you when I sent you the message last night," I tried again. "I didn't want you to worry when I didn't come home."

No answer.

I let it go and rode the rest of the way in silence. I rehearsed what I'd say to Jay when he undoubtedly questioned me, at the very least. Hopefully he wasn't going to take me for a ride to a deserted field on the island and do away with me. I wasn't really that nonchalant about it. It was my way of coping with what might happen. I was really scared but needed to approach this in a way that didn't get me killed.

His plane was on time. Keith pulled up in front of the exit doors for Jet-cost, got out of the car, and opened the back door toward the airport. When I saw Jay, I started to move to the open door. "Stay where you are," Keith said in a deeper voice than I thought possible.

"Okay," I said. Wait until we take you down, I wanted to say, but for once, I held my tongue.

Jay slithered into the car—at least that was the way I saw him now. He asked Keith to close the privacy partition. He reached for my neck and I instinctively jumped back. "What's wrong?" he said, and pulled me to him and gave me a tender kiss." Maybe Keith didn't tell him. He might have been afraid he'd be in trouble if Jay found out I'd been in the hidden room.

"Sorry," I said. "Shinara and I went to the Foster House last night. I'm afraid we drank too much wine at the bar before we ate. I got sick and stayed at her house for the night. Still not feeling great."

"Val, stop talking. Have you heard from Jess today?"

"No, I probably should have called her, but I wasn't sure how I'd tell her I wasn't coming home," I said as I'd rehearsed.

"Have you given her your new number?"

"No, not yet. What's going on? Why all the questions?"

"Jess called me this morning. Couldn't get in touch with you."

"Now you're scaring me."

"No easy way to tell you. Annie's been in a car accident. She's in the hospital. Jess needs you to come home immediately."

"Oh no! How badly is she hurt?"

"Badly enough that Jess's distraught. She said she needs you home."

"Of course. Let's go back to the airport and get the first flight out. Please, Jay, will you come with me? First Nate and now Annie. I don't think I can deal with this alone."

"I will, but we have some things to talk over on the way. Do you have your passport with you?"

"I always carry it in my bag," I said.

"Are you all right to go to the desk and get our tickets while I talk to Keith?"

"Yes," I said. "I'll meet you near the security gate."

It was easier than I'd thought to convince Jay to travel home with me, but it didn't take him long to start asking questions. It turned out Keith had told him he found me in his secret computer room.

"I hear you were in my computer room," he said.

"Fell right into it." I pointed to my swollen shin that had turned purplish. "I was looking for a bottle of wine but fell over something on the floor. My hand hit a bottle on the bottom shelf, and the wall opened. Practically scared the shit out of me."

"And you had to go in and play with the computer?"

"You do know me, right?" I tried to laugh. He didn't.

"I know you're nosy as hell, but I thought you'd respect my privacy. I would have let you have at it when I got home, but I would've expected you to at least ask me before you turned on my personal computer."

"I thought you wanted me to know everything," I said.

"I do," he said, seemingly not bothered by my actions. "And when Annie's recovered and we return to the island, I'll show you everything. It's probably just as well we're going home today. I'd like to be with Mom and Dad when the president makes the announcement tonight."

"What announcement?" I said.

"At midnight, the president will address the nation. He will tell the people that beginning at 12:01 a.m. tomorrow, the national farms will be in control of all the farms in the United States. They will slowly be turned over to national control to save the American people millions of dollars. Martial law will be declared for the smooth takeover. Farmers who currently own land are welcome to continue working those farms, but they will report to the secretary of agriculture, and all finances will be handled by the Department of Agriculture."

I was sitting on a plane, unable to contact Ken or anyone else. They had to know what was happening in a matter of hours. Our plane was due to land at noon in Miami. That wasn't much time to stop the president's address and reverse the conspirators' scheme.

"The three largest oil and gas companies will be in charge of the oil and gas resources in our country," Jay continued. "There will be no problem with pipelines or fracking bans from now on.

"So there's no confusion about the water supplies in the country, the federal government will take over the contracts from the counties in the West and set up similar contracts in the East and throughout the United States. The president will explain we must ensure future water supplies for the citizens of our country."

Jay sounded like he actually believed what he was saying. I found it physically painful to listen to and agree with him. It seemed forever until our plane landed in Miami. It was difficult to contain myself when we deplaned. My hands shook, but Jay suspected nothing as we walked past the security area, out the door, and onto the street.

I don't think Jay thought anything of it even when two black vans drove up and stopped next to the sidewalk. Eight FBI agents stepped out, approached, and stopped. "Mr. Jay Benson, you are under arrest for conspiracy against the government and people of the United States of America. You have the right to remain silent. Anything you say can and will be used against you in a court of law. You have the right to talk to a lawyer and have him present while you are being questioned. If you cannot afford to hire a lawyer, one will be appointed to represent you before any questioning, if you wish. You can decide at any time to exercise these rights and not answer any questions or make any statements," one of the agents read from a card.

"There must be a mistake," Jay said. "I am working with Ms. Jacobs and Ken Bentz to inform the American people of a conspiracy perpetrated by corrupt officials and businesspeople across our country."

The agent faced me. "Is this correct, Ms. Jacobs?"

"I'm afraid it is *not*," I said, turned from Jay, and walked to where Ken waited for me inside the terminal. I didn't look back, but I was sure Jay was speechless I hadn't stood by him. I hoped I'd never have to look at him again.

I told Ken about the planned announcement by the president. He notified the director of the FBI, who was standing by for immediate action.

"You can probably use some good news," Ken said.

"Sure could," I said.

"The assignment I gave Uncle Jeb was to find out what happened to Rosemary. He found her."

"I'm so sorry, Ken," I said.

"I'll be eternally grateful to your uncle," he said.

I looked at him, questioning.

"She's in the hospital, but she'll recover," he said.

"So I was wrong. She did have a pulse when I checked her. How could I make such a mistake?"

"She'd been given a drug temporarily paralyzing her and lowering her pulse to the point it couldn't be felt. The man who told you he was an EMT was actually working for a pharmaceutical company involved in the take-over. He kidnapped Rosemary and held her until Jeb found her. Their intention was to frighten us or use Rosemary's life as leverage to stop our investigation.

"You were right suspecting Keith Jackson. He received a hundred thousand dollars from Jay the day after your brother was killed. Jeb's gone back to the farm to investigate and confirm Keith Jackson killed your brother."

"But he's still in Grand Cayman. Can he be extradited?"

"It's in the works. The United States has an extradition treaty with the

Cayman Islands through the United Kingdom. As Jay was being detained in Miami, Jackson was being arrested on suspicion of murder in Grand Cayman. He'll be held awaiting extradition."

Tears filled my eyes, not only with happiness that Rosemary was alive, but releasing the tension I'd been under, and, of course, the sorrow that Nate was gone. I could finally grieve the loss of my brother.

We watched the news on Ken's laptop on our flight to DC. Across the country there were simultaneous arrests of people involved in the conspiracy. United States senators, representatives, the secretary of agriculture, the assistant secretary of the interior, plus two governors and dozens of state politicians. The heads of several businesses, including agricultural, energy, and equipment companies, were brought in for questioning, although the owners, CEOs, and CFOs would probably never spend time in prison. They'd use scapegoats, lower-level employees to do the time for their crimes.

I wasn't sure why no farmers other than Jay had been arrested, but I'd find out eventually. It would take some time to assess Jay's records, but I suspected the lists were not correct, that he'd included people not involved in the conspiracy to impress me. He probably thought I'd think so many people couldn't be wrong.

The FBI hadn't finished evaluating all the financials, but it was expected most of the money not spent would be recovered and returned to the government agencies from which it had been taken. The national farms would be closed and the equipment sold at auctions open only to farmers.

Although Jay had tried to convince me of the involvement of the other farmers in the conspiracy, the financial trail showed the money was in Jay's accounts. Politicians and businesses involved slinked silently away with few consequences except the knowledge they'd been defrauded by a single man who wanted to prove he was smarter.

Jay Benson would come to trial for conspiracy to commit murder in the death of Nathaniel Jacobs and the attempted murder of Rosemary Casper.

It was yet to be determined if fraud charges would be levied due to the resistance of government and business entities to admit their vulnerability and culpability.

CHAPTER 37

I walked up two steps and then the third into the back door I'd used so many times when I was growing up. My stomach flipped, much like it had when Annie and I'd asked Mom to drive faster over the hills on our road. We'd gasp, and Mom would laugh. "Oh, I didn't mean to go so fast," she'd say.

I wondered if she remembered any of those times. Having picnics in the fields and down by the creek, hunting for a calf after the cow had freshened and hidden its offspring in the tall grass, preparing meals for neighbors during harvest, watching me play high school basketball at both home and away games.

I hoped she remembered all the good things and none of the sleepless nights I'd put her through. I hesitated at the kitchen door, then turned the knob and walked in. Closing the door behind me, I didn't hear her breathing, coughing, laughing. Nothing. My feet were heavy. I was hardly able to put one after the other.

When I managed to turn the corner to where she lay in her bed, I was surprised to see a slight smile. That tiny little body in a fetal position, wasting away, her hands curled into claws, but a smile. I pulled a straight chair up beside the bed, trying with all my being to return the smile and not to cry.

"It's Valerie, Mom."

She'd progressed in her disease to the point of not speaking, instead grunting, weeping, or crying when she needed something. Sometimes Jess could tell what she needed, sometimes not.

My sister-in-law had done a wonderful job caring for Mom, but now it was my turn. With the courts in charge of deciding the disposition of the conspirators' futures, I'd returned home. Ken agreed to give me time off to help with Mom. He'd told me I could have the job back when I was ready.

Annie would stay in the apartment Ken found for me in DC and attend Georgetown. When I returned to work, we'd stay together. Jess was back to school—relieved, I think, that I'd be with Mom. No more hired help to take care of her.

I'd planned to tell her how sorry I was about Nate and my involvement in his death, but she was comfortable and smiling. It would wait. I decided to talk to her about the past, the happy times, maybe read to her.

"Do you remember when neighbors helped each other? When the Bensons, Hadleys, Smiths, and us, used to put crops in together and you fixed dinner for everyone? Do you remember the parties on the farm with the neighbors, the kids laughing, playing softball and badminton? When everyone got along with each other and was able to disagree and talk without yelling, when we all respected each other?"

Mom raised her left arm, her hand hanging limply in the air. It looked like she was trying to tell me something, but without language, it was difficult.

"Once," she said, as clearly as she'd ever spoken. "Once," she repeated, and her arm dropped.